I ESCAPED SERIES COLLECTION #3

3 Survival Adventures For Kids

I ESCAPED

ELLIE CROWE

SCOTT PETERS

I Escaped Series Collection #3

ISBN: 978-1-951019-51-8 (Paperback)

Cover design by Susan Wyshynski

Best Day Books For Young Readers

CONTENTS

I ESCAPED
THE WORLD'S DEADLIEST SHARK ATTACK

THE SINKING OF THE USS-INDIANAPOLIS, WWII

ELLIE CROWE + SCOTT PETERS

The Last Mission of
the USS Indianapolis

Departed
July 16, 1945

Ship's
Route

San
Francisco
USA

HAWAII, USA
(Pearl Harbor)

EQUATOR

PACIFIC
OCEAN

Dropped Crate
at Tinian
July 26

SANK
JULY 30

JAPAN
Hiroshima

Nagasaki

ASIA

PHILIPPINES

CHAPTER ONE

MONDAY JULY 30, 1945
THE PHILIPPINE SEA
00:30 HOURS

The USS Indianapolis—the invincible warship, the flagship of the United States Navy—was split in two, on fire, and sinking fast. Leaping from the deck, Josh hit the water with a stinging belly flop. Down he spiraled, down, down into the pitch-dark ocean. Swirling blackness surrounded him. Mind spinning, heart racing, he somersaulted, trying to work out which way was up.

Was that the moon shining through the sea? He kicked furiously, his legs struggling against the leaden weight of his boots. The kapok life vest, already waterlogged when he put it on, could barely do its job.

Come on, come on! Almost there!

Flaying wildly, he broke into the open air, gasping in long heaving breaths.

To his horror, a nasty sight waited—the sinking warship's propellers churning in huge, powerful strokes, ready to grind him to pieces. The massive metal blades could cut clean through an army of men. Frantic, he threw himself backward.

"She'll suck us under," a voice screamed. "Swim! Swim!"

Above, sailors still swarmed the tilting vessel, teeming like ants on a stick. How could this be happening? Moments ago, they'd all been high and dry. Now, he was swimming with no land in sight for hundreds of miles.

The pull of the dying ship sucked him closer. Terrified but refusing to give in, Josh clawed at the water. His dungarees hamstrung his legs and his boots felt like anvils. Every stroke was a fight.

He was out of his element in this surging sea. Totally out of it. He was sixteen, a baseball player from San Antonio, Texas. A good athlete. But the ocean wasn't his world. He was no Olympic swimmer—why on earth had he ever joined the Navy?

The USS Indianapolis groaned and shrieked. Then, in a terrible death plunge, the massive warship disappeared carrying the men still aboard into the dark depths.

Cascades of water crashed over Josh's head, pulling at his limbs.

I'm being sucked down.

His mind reeled, fear flooded his body as he again found himself flailing beneath the surface. His ears exploded. His eyeballs popped.

All he could hear was the ship, like a dying monster, moaning way down below. He could still see the lights from raging flames glowing through the portholes. They blazed in the lonely darkness as the mighty boat sank toward its watery grave. And he was going with it. Spiraling down. Down.

He couldn't hold his breath much longer. Any moment, his lungs would give up and he'd gulp in water. That, he knew, would be the end of him. He'd never see home, never see his mom and kid brother Sammy, never get to say goodbye.

He was so deep he could no longer see any light. He kicked, but which way was up? What if he was kicking down further?

His life vest still had some strength in it for it tugged at him, pulling his shoulders away from his legs. Suddenly, like a miracle, the boat lost its powerful drag. Released, Josh shot upward. For good measure, he kicked with all he had left. Like a cork, he exploded to the surface, vomiting fuel oil and saltwater.

He coughed and coughed, sucked in air until his lungs stopped aching and he could see straight again.

Thank God he'd pulled on a life vest. Without it, he'd probably still be down there.

The full moon appeared from behind the clouds. Bright

yellow light slashed across the rough swells. Ahead of him, something moved.

He stayed motionless as the shape disappeared behind a wave. The ocean heaved, and it reappeared.

It was a person. Another sailor. What a relief.

"Hey!" Josh shouted. "Wait for me!"

Kicking and splashing, he swam toward the man.

"Hey!" Josh called again. Then stopped swimming.

The man was staring at him.

With zombie eyes.

The top half of the man's body, still wearing a life vest, rose high into the air. Then crashed back down into the water. And disappeared. Like something had pulled him under. Blinking, treading furiously, Josh stared. What the heck? He wiped engine oil from his stinging eyes and tried to focus.

Then the man's life jacket popped up.

Empty.

Suddenly Josh saw them—the dark, white-tipped fins—slicing their way through the ocean. Slowly. Smoothly. Surely. Beginning to circle.

Deep in his gut, he knew what they were.

Sharks.

He swallowed hard. Pictured his feet dangling beneath him in the blackness. Drew his legs in tight. There was nothing to scramble on top of. No way to climb clear.

His fists were his only weapons.

And he was surrounded by hundreds of man-eating sharks.

CHAPTER TWO

Midnight. Joshua Layton, sixteen years old, had finished his watch on the USS Indianapolis. Whistling, he made his way along the winding corridors.

The mighty warship was heading from San Francisco to the port of Leyte in the Philippines, through choppy seas and long rolling swells. The ship shook with the violence of the spinning propellers, the roar of the powerful engines.

Must be pushing the engines to the max, Josh thought. Wherever we're going, someone in charge wants to get there fast. Well, that's fine with me.

He knew his way around the warship now. Mostly, anyway. The USS Indianapolis was huge, the length of two football fields. After two weeks at sea, he almost felt at home.

7

They'd only made one stop, a brief one at the United States Army Air Force Base on the island of Tinian in Guam. The crew had unloaded a mysterious canister and crate before heading back out to sea. As to what that cargo contained, no one had any clue. Airplane parts? A new, high tech weapon? Food supplies? He'd probably never find out.

The USS Indianapolis Underway

Whatever the case, it was good to be part of the action, to be one of the men fighting the Japanese, the enemy who'd killed his dad.

Although World War II raged in Europe and in the Pacific, on the Indy all was calm and under control. And Josh was hungry. He lifted his arm and sniffed his blue shirt. Phew, he stank. I should have a shower, he thought, but I'm starved. They work you hard in the Navy!

Luckily he knew just where to get something good to eat. Still whistling, he snuck into the officer's wardroom—the officers always had the best food. He checked out the leftovers. The egg and mayo sandwiches looked good. He grabbed two, wrapped them in waxed sandwich paper, and slipped them into the top pocket of his blue dungarees.

Quickly he looked around the table, checking for leftover dessert. Pete, also wearing his blue shirt and blue dungarees, was digging into a chocolate cake.

Pete grinned at Josh. "Cake's good."

Josh laughed. "The officers sure have great desserts!" He already knew the chocolate cake with the super-gooey chocolate icing was the best. And he knew they wouldn't mind if he took a thin slice or two. The officers on the USS Indianapolis were good guys. Pete's cousin was a lieutenant. He'd told them the leftovers in the officers' wardroom were up for grabs after midnight.

Josh had met Pete two weeks ago when they'd boarded the warship in San Francisco. Josh was fresh from boot camp. He'd been glad to see so many other sailors were young, too. Not as young as he was, for Josh had lied to the recruiting officer—the Navy didn't accept sixteen-year-olds. You had to be eighteen to enlist, or seventeen if you had your parents' permission. But a lot of the other guys looked barely older than him. And there were so many guys. More than a thousand!

Pete swallowed a mouthful of cake. Icing stuck to his chin. "I just heard something weird," he said. "My cousin Mike, he's a lieutenant, he says we're on a secret mission."

Josh looked up with interest. "Yeah?"

"Remember that big crate and canister the Marines loaded before we left San Francisco?" Pete said. "The ones we offloaded in Tinian Island?"

Josh nodded. Funny, he'd just been thinking about that. "Yeah. What's in them?"

"He doesn't know. Something important, though.

Remember all that top brass on the wharf and those planes flying protective formations overhead?"

"Yeah. And all those Marines with guns!"

"Exactly. Mike was one of those armed Marines. He says it's real important stuff," Pete said. "So important, no one's allowed to know what was inside, only maybe Captain McVay. And President Truman. It's all top secret."

"Okay!" Josh tried to look cool. Wow. A secret mission! That must be why they'd called up the crew so fast. He wished he was one of the Marines with the lethal-looking guns. Maybe in the Philippines, he'd be accepted for gunnery training. Then he could be one of the gun crew.

"You going to start gunnery training?" he asked Pete.

Pete laughed. The guy's red-hair and freckles reminded him of his kid brother, Sammy. "I wish. Joe says I won't be doing anything exciting soon. He says we're all too *green*, and the Navy's going to train us at Leyte. In the Philippines. Until we get there, he says I'll be scrubbing decks." He grimaced

"I hope we invade Japan soon!" Josh said. This was what he wanted to do. This was why he enlisted in the Navy. Why he lied and gave his age as seventeen. Why he'd forged his mom's signature on the Parental Consent Form.

The Japanese killed his dad when they bombed Pearl Harbor, Hawaii. That was over three years ago now: December 7th, 1941, two and a half weeks before the worst Christmas of his life. He, Mom, and Sammy were shattered, lost without him. The Japanese had broken his family. The sooner he could fight the enemy, the better. They had to be stopped. He owed it to his father, the best person in the world he'd ever known.

Josh swallowed hard, wiped the sweat from his forehead. Ran his fingers over his dark curly hair, spiky in his new Navy buzz-cut. July in the Pacific was hot. "I'm heading to the forward turret," he said. "Got permission to sleep up there tonight."

"Good for you," Pete said. "It's an oven down in the bunkroom."

Josh grabbed a slice of chocolate cake, wrapped it in sandwich paper, too, and filled his canteen with water. He was glad to be sleeping out on deck. He'd picnic. Write a letter to Mom and Sammy. Tell them how much he missed them. Tell them he was fine, that life on board was great.

First, though, he needed to pay a visit to the head. Sort of a weird name for the toilet, but that was the Navy for you. He'd had to learn a lot of odd names for all sorts of things.

Agile as a monkey, he climbed a steel ladder to the forecastle deck.

He hopped inside the head, shut the door, and unbuckled his dungarees.

The first torpedo struck.

CHAPTER THREE

MONDAY JULY 30, 1945
THE PHILIPPINE SEA
00:15 HOURS

The explosion flung Josh sideways in the tiny cubicle. His head slammed into the basin. He crashed to the floor, seeing stars. What the heck! What was that? Ears ringing, he struggled to his feet.

The second explosion knocked him to his knees.

He staggered and shoved open the door.

Someone screamed, "Look out!"

A wall of flames shot down the corridor, burning his face. He yelled and jumped back.

Then came the third explosion.

The massive warship lurched to starboard. Thick black smoke poured down the hall, making him choke and cough.

What the heck? I've got to get outta here!

Heart pounding, eyes wide in disbelief, he saw flames

blazing in both directions. If he ran through this, he'd be torched.

But if he stayed . . . Flipping out, he turned the seawater tap on full blast and splashed seawater all over his body, soaking his denim shirt and dungarees. Wrapping a wet towel around his head, he raced down the corridor, leaping through the heat and flickering flames.

He kept going, scrambling up a metal ladder. With relief, he saw the night sky above. He'd made it out. But the place was a madhouse.

Half-naked sailors, pulled from their beds, charged around deck. Who was in charge?

A man's high-pitched scream rang out, "Help! Help me!"

Josh raced to the railing and peered over. Stunned, he saw that the bow—the front end of the warship—was gone. Completely gone! Swallowed up by the waves. The Indy had been split in two. Yet somehow the massive warship's back end still plowed ahead through the ocean. Insane. This thing must be taking on thousands of gallons of water. Fast. Scooping it straight into the decks below.

With a wrenching snap, the steel-plated deck cracked open beneath his feet. Flames and smoke poured through as he jumped sideways. A pillar of fire shot from the ship's heart into the sky. The fuel tanks must have copped it, were pouring fuel on the blaze. It lit up the whole world in gruesome fiery reds and blacks. Waves of heat wobbled in the air. What remained of the Indy was burning fast.

Two sailors struggled to work a fire hose then flung it down.

"No water pressure," a red-faced man shouted.

Josh had no idea where to go, but the cracks underfoot were widening. He raced across the burning deck, slipped in what looked like blood, nearly lost his balance. Around him, injured sailors and officers yelled and screamed. Metallic, high-pitched sounds tore through the night—sounds you prayed you'd never hear on a ship: metal ripping, electrical cords sparking. Thick smoke mushroomed from the forward deck.

"What's going on?" someone roared "Do we abandon ship?"

Wildly, Josh wondered when someone would take control of this madness. Were they supposed to abandon ship? Captain McVay hadn't given the command.

He pictured the black ocean roiling below, and his stomach clenched. It was safer on the Indy. The warship had survived battles and even direct hits before. A ship this size wouldn't just sink. They'd seal bulkheads, find a way to keep the water out.

"We're goners," a young sailor screamed.

"Put on a life vest," an older man replied. "We ain't gone yet, are we?"

Life vests. Mine's in the bunkroom! I need another one. Fast.

Josh knew where the emergency buoyancy devices were kept. He raced to join two sailors cutting a net holding bundles of kapok life vest, pulling his jackknife from his calf holster as he ran.

With relief, he spotted the tall figure of Lieutenant Commander Moore.

"She's taking on too much water," Moore shouted. "We have to stop the flooding." He turned to an officer. "Where's the Captain?"

"I don't know. Communications are down, Sir," the officer replied.

"Why haven't they stopped the engines?" Moore demanded.

"We don't know, we can't reach them on the radio."

Lieutenant Commander Moore turned to Josh. "Sailor!" he barked. "Get down to that engine room. Tell Chief Engineer Redmayne his orders are to stop the engines and close the watertight doors. Immediately."

Who? Me?

No way did Josh want to go back down! The engine room was below the waterline, deep in the ship's bowels. The absolute worst place to be if the ship sank. He'd be trapped. There'd be no way out.

"Yes, Sir," he said, almost choking on the words.

CHAPTER FOUR

MONDAY JULY 30, 1945
THE PHILIPPINE SEA
00:17 HOURS

Hands sizzling on the metal ladder rungs, Josh descended into the billowing smoke. Rung by rung. It felt like suicide. It probably was. Adrenaline flooded his body. His mind urged him to flee. He wanted to flee. His legs shook. *Run! Get out of here. Fast!* He forced himself to keep climbing down.

Emergency lights cast eerie shadows everywhere. Panicked men pushed past, going the other way. The way he wanted to go. Shouting at him and cursing.

"Move over!"

"Get outta here!"

"Idiot! What are you doing? You're going the wrong way!"

Josh longed to join them. He'd deliver the message, then he'd get out.

Coughing, choking, he groped his way deeper until he

finally reached the engine room. As he stepped inside, an officer pushed past. Josh caught the officer's arm. "Sir, I've got a message for Chief Engineer Redmayne," he stammered. "Captain's orders are to stop the engines."

"The Chief isn't here," the officer said, his face dripping with sweat. "Communications are down. We've had no such orders. The Chief has gone to find the Captain."

"Sir, orders from the bridge are to stop the engines," Josh said. "Immediately."

The officer looked confused. "Sailor, I have no authority to do that. There's only one engine left anyway. If we stop moving, we'll be a better target for the Japs."

Sparks flew from the ventilator ducts, showering him and the men. The ship tilted and let out a sickening screech.

A sailor bellowed, "Clear out! Everyone. Go. GO!"

"Don your life vests!" someone shouted.

This was crazy. Why hadn't he grabbed a life vest when he had the chance? He'd have to sprint to his bunkroom, grab his life vest, and get back on deck.

The corridor teetered at an angle as he raced, slip-sliding. At his sleeping room door, he reeled back. The once quiet refuge was a disaster zone. Bunk racks had collapsed. Smashed bed frames littered the floor. Sailors, thrown from their bunks, writhed under the wreckage.

"Help me. Help!" a man screamed. "I'm stuck!"

"Men, give me a hand," came the deep voice of Marine Private First Class McCoy.

Josh raced to join McCoy. Furiously, they began digging victims out from under the fallen lockers and rubble.

An open hatch led to an upper corridor.

Under it, a chain of uninjured men pushed the wounded up the ladder. Everywhere, faces were tense with fear.

Everyone worked as fast as possible, all waiting for their chance to get up the ladder and out the hatch, the only way out.

The ship tilted sharply. Josh lost his footing and fell, landing hard on a trapped sailor. The guy, who looked no older than Josh, cried out in pain.

"I'm sorry. I'm sorry!" Josh stammered.

How could this even be happening? This was insane!

"Get me out," the sailor begged, his face scrunched in agony. "My arm, it's stuck."

Josh nodded, unsure if he could lift the metal cabinet trapping the guy against the floor. "Hold on." Gritting his teeth, Josh braced against it and pushed hard. A second later, he freed the sailor. Eyes unfocused in pain, the guy staggered to his feet.

From above, a voice rang out. "Sorry, men. We're dogging the hatch."

Dogging the hatch? Did that mean . . .

"No!" Josh screamed. "No, wait!"

He couldn't believe his ears. They were closing the hatch? With all of them still below? He and these men would be trapped! If the ship sank, they'd die.

"Hold on, wait," he shouted. "We'll be buried alive!"

With a sickening thud, the hatch slammed shut.

CHAPTER FIVE

MONDAY JULY 30, 1945
THE PHILIPPINE SEA
00:19 HOURS

In a remote, reasoning section of his brain, Josh understood what was happening. The hatches had to be closed to stop the ship from sinking. The USS Indianapolis had to be made watertight. He and these injured men would be sacrificed to save the others. They'd be sacrificed to save the ship.

That knowledge didn't make it any better.

Desperate voices rose around him, shouting, shoving, pushing.

"Let us out!" they shouted.

Men swarmed up the ladder and hammered on the hatch. Others kicked the walls.

Josh stood frozen next to the injured sailor, his mind racing.

"What happened?" the guy groaned, clutching his arm.

"Kamikaze attack, had to be," someone said, his eyes shadowed in the emergency lamplight.

An older man shook his head. "Nope. A sub. Fired a torpedo, I think. More than one. I bet there's a Jap sub down there right now. I bet the Jap captain is celebrating his glorious hit."

Josh thought of his dad, blown to pieces by Japanese bombs. He hated the Japanese. Hated them. If he could, he'd kill every single one of them.

In the bunk room, a doomed silence descended.

Josh looked at the injured sailor. He'd seen the guy before but they'd never spoken. Other guys claimed the kid was a Jap. Uneasily, Josh looked into the sailor's dark, almond-shaped eyes. Was it possible he'd come on board as a Japanese spy? Had this guy secretly broadcast their position to the enemy? Was he the reason they were sinking?

"Are you Japanese?" he blurted.

"No," the young sailor groaned, cradling his injured arm. "I'm not. I was born in Hawaii. My dad was Chinese, my mom's Hawaiian. My name is Lee Wong. It's a good Chinese name. I'm Chinese-American. Okay?"

"Okay," Josh said.

The kid nodded at his bleeding arm. "I gotta bandage this thing. I'm getting kinda lightheaded."

"All right." Nearby, a man lay unmoving. Josh knew he was dead, that he wouldn't need his shirt any longer, but that didn't make him feel any better. Trying not to look, he bent, tore away a section of fabric, and wrapped Lee's bleeding arm.

Blood seeped through the cotton. Lee stared at it ruefully. "If we have to abandon ship, I'm dead."

"What?"

"If the Indy goes down, we'll be in the Philippine Sea. It's full of sharks."

"Sharks?"

"Yeah. Lots of men are injured. The sharks will smell the blood."

Josh grimaced, tried not to picture gnashing jaws and foaming water.

Suddenly that loud voice, that bringer of life and death, came again. "All right, men. Last chance. Get outta here!"

Someone was opening the hatch!

Josh sprang forward, pulling Lee with him. He joined Officer McCoy and the line of uninjured men helping the wounded up the ladder. Josh pushed Lee forward. "Go!" he said. "Get out."

Taut with nerves, wanting to cut and run, he waited his turn, helping the injured first. Ahead of him, boys and men scrambled feverishly up the rungs, diving out the opening.

Then the dreaded warning came again. "Sorry men, that's it!"

"No!"

"We're still in here!"

"Don't close it!"

"You can't! Don't close it!"

The human chain burst apart as panicked men leaped up the ladder. Josh, already near the top rung, squeezed out the hatch. McCoy was the last one to hurl himself through.

Racing down the corridor, Josh heard the hatch slam shut.

CHAPTER SIX

MONDAY JULY 30, 1945
THE PHILIPPINE SEA
00:22 HOURS

The warship shuddered, thundering and twisting. Ahead, the corridor was a furnace of flames and smoke. How could Josh reach the main deck when fire blocked his path?

In the distance, wounded men screamed, "Help! Get me out of here!"

To his left, the officers' wardroom door sagged open. Hard to believe he'd been in there half an hour ago, merrily grabbing sandwiches and talking about chocolate cake.

He dove inside and looked around. Hazy smoke made it difficult to see.

A radio operator pushed past him, heading back down the corridor. Must be trying to get to Radio Central, Josh thought. He's trying to get off an SOS.

He choked, coughing and staying low. If he could find a

porthole, he could open it, get some air. He stumbled across the dim room, colliding with the buffet table. Sandwiches and cakes crashed to the floor.

"Stupid table!" he shouted, angry and scared.

"Josh?" a voice rang out. "Over here!"

To his relief, he spotted Lee at an open porthole and ran to join him. Together, they poked their heads out, gulping air. They eyed the dark, churning waves below.

"Sure looks deep," Lee said.

"Yeah."

"And full of sharks."

Josh stared down. He wished this guy would stop talking about sharks. Things were bad enough. Dark rolling swells surged and broke against the hull.

"Like you said, it's a deep ocean. How would sharks know

we're here?"

"My dad had a fishing boat. Believe me, they know. They smell blood. From long distances."

"Well, it doesn't matter. We're not abandoning ship. The Captain will keep us afloat until a rescue crew comes."

"Maybe, but unless we find a way up on deck, we're going to choke to death."

Coughing, Josh leaned out further. The guy was right, the smoke was growing thicker by the minute. The blazing corridor wasn't an option. They had only one choice: keep their heads out the window and hope for the best.

Something hit his face. A rope!

He looked up. The rope dangled from a life raft secured high above.

"Let's climb up," he said.

Lee nodded. His face looked strained. "Go for it."

"What's the matter?"

Lee raised his injured arm. "I'm not going anywhere with this."

"Yes, you are. Look, I'll climb up first. Then you tie the rope around your waist and I'll haul you up. Deal?"

Lee said nothing.

With a deep breath, Josh steeled himself and grabbed hold of the porthole's rim. He forced his eyes away from the ocean whirling far below. *Just do it,* he told himself.

He wriggled his shoulders through, then tested the rope with a hard tug. It held. He prayed it would carry his weight. He still didn't have a life vest. If he fell, the ocean would swallow him whole. *Idiot.* If he wanted to live through this, he'd better think harder.

There was a panicked moment as he first hung suspended. With a determined growl, he started climbing.

Hand over hand, inch by inch, swinging left and right, kicking his feet to try and keep from spinning. A final lunge upward took him to a gun mount. He leaped onto the main deck. He'd made it!

The chaos up here was insane.

"Catch!" he shouted, swinging the rope toward Lee.

After what felt like forever, Lee struggled out of the porthole with the rope knotted around him. Josh started hauling.

Nearby in a slick of bloody water, Chief Pharmacist John Schmeuck knelt amongst a sprawl of badly burned men. Grim-faced, Schmueck spotted Josh.

"Sailor!" he yelled to him. "Over here! We need life vests!"

The ship rolled, a sickening movement. Josh slid across the deck, still holding the rope. He staggered, then regained his balance. He looked back just in time to see Lee struggle up over the side.

"Sailor!" Schmueck yelled again. "Get over here. Now! That's an order."

Knife in hand, Josh raced over and hacked until the net holding a clump of life vests gave way. A pile tumbled to the deck. Men pounced on them. Pushing his way in, Josh grabbed an armful.

He began putting a kapok life vest over the head of a badly burned man.

"Get away from me!" the man screamed. "I'm burned! I'm not leaving this fricking ship. There's sharks down there."

Josh pulled the life vest over his own head. He turned to the next injured man. As he handed him a life vest, the ship flipped ninety degrees.

The deck turned into a steel slide.

Josh fell onto his butt and slid toward the railing. Reaching out, he grabbed the lifeline rope. He hung on with all his strength. Down below, the ocean roared by. Ocean spray whipped his face

"Release that lifeboat," a hysterical voice rang out.

Josh clung to his line, watched in disbelief as Lee, Schmeuck, and most of the injured men slid down the deck and smacked into the ocean.

The dark water whirled by, leaving him alone and hanging.

"Abandon ship!" a mighty voice rang out. "Abandon ship! Abandon ship!"

A huge wave crashed over the deck.

It swept Josh overboard and into the hungry sea.

CHAPTER SEVEN

MONDAY JULY 30, 1945
THE PHILIPPINE SEA
00:26 HOURS

Josh hit the water with a stinging belly flop. Down he spiraled, down, down, down into the pitch-dark ocean. Mind spinning, heart racing, he spun around trying to work out which way was up. Dark water surrounded him. He couldn't hold his breath much longer. Which way was up?

He needed air. Needed air. Suddenly, flaying wildly, he reached the surface, only to come face-to-face with the ship's massive, deadly propellers. Thrashing with everything he had, he threw himself backward.

"She'll suck us under," a voice screamed. "Swim! Swim!"

Josh could see sailors still on the vessel, swarming like ants on a stick.

How could this be happening?

The pull of the dying ship sucked him closer. Terrified but

refusing to give in, Josh clawed and kicked. His heavy dungarees hamstrung his legs and his boots felt like anvils. Every stroke was a fight. He was no Olympic swimmer—why on earth had he ever joined the Navy?

The USS Indianapolis groaned and shrieked. Then, in a terrible death plunge, the heavy cruiser disappeared into the dark depths.

Cascades of water crashed over Josh's head, pulling at his limbs, sucking him down all over again. His ears exploded. His eyeballs popped.

All he could hear was the ship, like a dying monster, moaning way down below. He could still see the lights from raging flames glowing through the portholes. They blazed in the lonely darkness as the mighty boat sank toward its watery grave. And he was going with it. Spiraling down. Down.

In a frantic fight, he broke free of its grip and surged to the surface.

A hundred yards away, a man bobbed in the sea.

A man with zombie eyes.

To Josh's confused horror, the man was pulled under. A second later, the sailor's life jacket popped up. Empty.

Suddenly, he saw the shark and he understood.

Its fin cut through the water, began to circle.

Where were the lifeboats? *Where were the lifeboats?*

"Help!" he shouted. "Hey! *Anyone!* Is anyone out there?"

Something bumped his arm and he lurched sideways, heart hammering straight out of his chest. He saw a small crate. Then more floating stuff. Chairs, powder cans, railings, chunks of wood, and poisonous fuel oil littered the ocean.

He began pulling it toward him, praying the junk would confuse the shark. Or at least make it harder for it to get him.

"Lee!" he shouted, wondering if sharks could hear, if calling out was stupid. "Officer Schmeuck! . . . Pete! . . . Is anybody there?"

A wave poured over his head. He shook water from his eyes.

Where was everyone?

With horror, the truth dawned. The whole time the warship was sinking, it had kept moving, plowing rapidly ahead. The survivors would be scattered for miles. He'd seen men jumping. He'd also seen men colliding with the churning, slashing propeller blades. They'd be in the ocean now, bleeding.

He'd been lucky. He hadn't been cut.

He spun slowly, searching for the shark's knife-like fin, but it was nowhere in sight. He breathed out, realizing that the floating junk had given him his first win.

But he'd need a lot more than bits of floating junk to stay alive out here. Hundreds of miles of water surrounded him. It's not like he could swim to safety.

How could the USS Indianapolis—the invincible battleship, the flagship of the US Navy—go down? A floating base, complete with airplane catapults, anti-aircraft guns and cannons, and nearly twelve hundred men on board—how could it be gone, just like that? It seemed impossible. But the Japs had blown her in half and sunk her in less than fifteen minutes.

He struggled to keep hold of his garbage fortress. Shivering in the surging ocean beneath an angry moon, he thought about home. About Mom and Sammy. About his best friends, Jack and Danny, who'd lied to enlist, too. They'd all been torn apart by this war. Would any of them make it back to San Antonio? Would any of them find peace?

He wondered if sharks preferred their food dead or alive. Wondered if it was better to keep still or try swimming, try searching for others, for a life raft. Wondered how long the floating junk would keep them at bay.

In the roaring ocean, he saw no one.

Hours went by. Had the radio operator sent out an SOS? Would anyone come looking for him? Was it possible he was the only survivor?

He longed to spot even one sailor.

Finally, a red sun stained the horizon. In the faint rays, he spied small lumps bobbing above the water. Eyes narrowed, he stared. Prayed.

Then, as the salty swells rose and fell, he made out hundreds of heads.

Men. There were men in the distance.

They were moving. They were alive.

CHAPTER EIGHT

TUESDAY JULY 31, 1945
THE PHILIPPINE SEA
DAY ONE | DAWN

Josh called out, but the men were too far away.

The thought of swimming through shark-infested swells freaked him out, but he had to go for it. The survivors would have rafts. He'd be safe, as long as he made it across the watery distance. It was now or never, for the men were drifting away.

He took a deep breath, then heart racing, moving slowly, he cupped his hands and pulled himself through the water. His water-logged boots made it near impossible. He hated the idea of going barefoot but knew he'd never make it like this. With difficulty, he untied the soggy laces and kicked them off. His sturdy, navy-issue boots sank quickly and were gone.

Freer, he began to move again. In the eerie dawn, every wave peak looked like a shark's fin. Swimming through the thick top layer of fuel oil was like crawling through mud. His eyes, throat, and nose burned. The more oil and salt-water he swallowed, the worse his stomach roiled. He ducked under countless foul waves until he could barely move his arms.

It seemed to take forever to reach the other survivors. A large group of men, eyes jumping with fear and dread, huddled in silence as he joined them. Josh slowly paddled amongst them, trying to spot Lee or Pete or someone he knew.

He passed a group holding an injured friend on their shoulders, struggling to keep the man's badly burned body out of the stinging salt and oil.

A man in a life vest had one arm around a friend without one. "I've got you, Mickey," he said. "You're okay. I've got you!"

So many didn't have life vests. How long could they tread water? Even wearing one, Josh felt half-drowned as waves splashed into his mouth.

A strong arm snaked around his neck. His face went under. He struggled to push free. "What are you doing?"

"I need a vest!" A burly man, his face black with oil shoved up against him. Lips drawn back, like a dog about to bite, he heaved his beefy body up onto Josh.

"Get off of me!" Josh sputtered, trying to keep his head above water. First sharks and now this guy? No way would he hand over his life vest. With all his strength, Josh aimed his knee at the man's crotch and lashed out. Hard. Those years of sports training paid off. Howling with rage, his assailant fell back. Josh swam away, fast.

Up and down the swells he floated. A panicked-looking sailor bobbing beside him stared out at the ocean.

"Swarms of sharks out there," he said, voice trembling. "Hear them? They're going after the dead."

A bolt of terror shot through Josh as he turned and saw the mass of dark fins and frothing water in the distance. He thought of the zombie-eyed man and shuddered. "I saw one. Right in front of me. It bit a guy in half. Ate him right out of his life vest."

"We've got to get the dead away from us," the man said. "The dead are attracting the monsters."

Others agreed. Soon, the call echoed through the survivors. "Move out the dead! Form a circle, men, stay inside. Move out the dead!"

Grim-faced men pushed the bodies of the dead out from the group. Out to sea. Into the Dead Zone.

Josh murmured a prayer for the men who'd died.

"The sharks are afraid of the rest of us," someone said. "They know we'll punch the daylights out of them."

"You hope!"

"We all hope."

"Wishful thinking, pal."

"They can smell blood," a gruff voice whispered nearby. "Stay away from the wounded if you know what's good for you."

Josh thought of Lee's injured, bloody arm. Was the bandage they'd made enough to stop the bleeding? Had Lee even survived sliding off the deck?

Out loud, he said, "How long do you think before help arrives?"

The gruff-voiced sailor said, "Soon, I reckon. A couple more hours." The man sounded confident, a good sign. "Navy will get the SOS. Or a plane will spot us first. There's a thousand guys floating in the ocean. They'll see us for sure."

Josh nodded. "You're right. No sweat, we'll be visible for miles."

CHAPTER NINE

TUESDAY JULY 31, 1945
THE PHILIPPINE SEA
DAY ONE | NOON

No one arrived.

By noon, massive thunder clouds blackened the sky.

The sounds of the sharks doing their dirty work sickened Josh. Where were his friends, Lee and Pete? The guys from his bunkroom? Were they out in the frenzy? Josh floated in the grim circle and tried to believe they were nearby.

People licked their salty lips, their mouths clearly aching with thirst. Josh's were cracked and sunbaked. No one spoke of water or food, though.

Not yet.

Every salt-reddened eye stayed glued to the horizon in hope. But no rescue team came.

Night fell. The blackness made it impossible to see the sharks. How could Josh defend himself if he couldn't see them coming? The sounds of splashing, corpse-shredding rose to a fury. He clapped his waterlogged hands to his ears, clenched his jaws tight.

"Feeding frenzy," the gruff-voiced sailor informed him. "Oceanic whitetips do that. Bet tiger sharks are out there too. They can hear heartbeats."

As lightning ripped the night sky and thunder boomed, Josh pictured the predators cruising the ocean. He pictured their massive grinning mouths and rows of serrated teeth. When the sky opened up and rain fell, he tipped his own head back and drank the falling drops. They rolled down his parched throat, wetting his tongue. Who knew how long they'd be out here?

Who knew if he'd get the chance to drink again?

Josh was dreaming. He was out on the baseball pitch, in the middle of the third inning. The game was tied. His friends that weren't on the field packed the stands. His family was up there too, his Mom and kid brother, his grandparents, even his cousins, aunts and uncles. All of them cheering him on.

Go, Josh! Go, Josh!

Gripping the bat, Josh spotted his dad. Somehow, he was still alive! Dad grinned and held up a huge, hand-drawn sign. *You can do it, son!*

Josh jerked awake at the sound of someone shouting nearby.

He tried to hold onto Dad's image as he blinked in the light.

A blood-red sun bulged along the horizon. A hundred feet away, a fin broke the water's surface. Josh's heartbeat revved to maximum. He could hear it, drumming in his ears. The shark would hear it, too. He started taking deep breaths, closed ranks with the other men, tried to force a calm he couldn't feel.

"He's hunting for more dead," someone said. "Don't worry. Only the dead."

"Yeah, but for how long?" the gruff-voiced man said darkly.

A calm, familiar voice said, "Push the wounded deeper into the center, men. That's what it's after. It can smell the blood. Tighten the circle around them." It was Dr. Haynes.

People started corralling the injured into the group's middle.

A second shark appeared, and then a third.

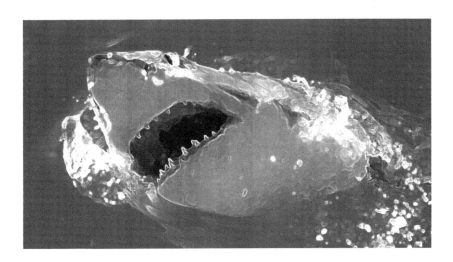

A sailor said, "Splash, men, kick and splash, it'll scare them off."

Josh doubted anything scared sharks. And the predators were growing bolder now, circling closer.

Where were the life rafts? They needed to get out of the water! Desperately, he scanned the swells. There had to be more than a hundred men in this group. And no sign of a raft. No food. Not a drop to drink.

An empty tin floated by and he grabbed it. With dark clouds still looming, it would surely rain again. He'd use it to catch water. He tucked the can into his life vest and stuck his hands in his armpits to try and keep warm. After the long night, he shook with cold. Guys would be suffering from hypothermia soon.

Something bumped his foot. "Aargh!" he shouted, curling his body up.

"Sorry!" the sailor next to him grunted. "Just my leg."

"Okay," Josh muttered. *I wish I hadn't taken off my shoes. I bet my white feet look like juicy fish. I have to find a life raft!* Eyes narrowed, he scanned for something big and solid bobbing on the cascading blue waves.

"Hey!" a red-haired sailor shouted. "Land! I see land!"

Josh rubbed his salt-encrusted eyes. Land? He saw nothing. The Philippines were hundreds of miles away. But maybe there was an island. Just a small one. Any island would be great.

"Follow me!" The red-haired sailor pointed to the horizon and began swimming hard.

He'd have to swim right through the sharks. Josh watched, picturing a small island. Shady palm trees swaying. Fresh coconuts. It would be wonderful to stand on dry land, to be safe. They could build shelters from palm fronds. Drink coconut milk. He squinted harder. The longed-for island was nowhere in sight.

Four men broke from the pack and followed. Should he join them? Wait, was that red-haired guy Pete? He wasn't sure, every face was covered with fuel oil. Still trying to make up his mind, Josh watched the group swim off, side by side. There was safety in numbers. He'd have to go now.

Then he saw the fins.

The sharks moved fast.

Within seconds, the air filled with blood-curdling screams. "Help! No!"

Red, bloody clouds colored the water.

"They're enormous!" a sailor screamed.

"They're twenty feet," another shouted as a shark veered toward the tightly packed circle.

"Stay together!" Dr. Haynes called out. "Splash! Kick!"

A huge gray shape whooshed under Josh's feet. "Get away," he shouted. "Get away from me!"

Others joined him, shouting, fighting. But more sharks started coming.

"They're after the injured," someone shouted. "Push them to the edge."

Suddenly, a voice said, "Josh! Is that you?"

He turned to see Lee, the whites of his almond-shaped eyes showing in a face covered with oil.

"Lee!" he shouted. Then, as his friend neared, his heart sank. Lee's bandaged arm was dark red. If someone spotted that bloody dressing, Lee would be pushed out. And he didn't even have a life vest.

"Lee!" He grabbed his friend's shoulder, so glad to see a familiar face, and hissed into his ear. "Hide your arm. We've got to get you a life vest."

"From where?"

From the only place one could be salvaged: the Dead Zone. But what choice did they have? "Follow me."

"Are you crazy?" Lee said when he saw where Josh was headed.

"Do you want a life vest or not?"

"When you put it like that," Lee said. "Fine. But I'll go myself."

"No."

Maybe it was crazy, but he didn't care. He'd found a friend and didn't plan to lose him. Swimming past the main group, Josh waited until a corpse bobbed within reach. Together, they tugged off the lifejacket and shirt. Josh helped Lee struggle into the life vest and wrapped the shirt around Lee's arm. But as they'd worked, the swells had carried them to the group's dangerous outer rim.

With a sharp cry, Lee pointed, and Josh geared himself for attack. Then he saw what Lee was staring at. Something big and floppy floated a ways off. A life raft! Men sat atop it, high and dry.

His hopes of survival soared.

They had to risk it. "We have to get onto that raft."

Lee nodded and spat out a mouthful of greasy water. "But listen to me. I know sharks. I'm from Hawaii, remember? If one grabs you, jab his eyes. Stick your fingers in hard as you can. Punch the nose. Punch the gills. Those are the weak spots."

"Okay."

"Swim slowly. No splashing. Don't draw their attention."

Josh nodded. "All right. Let's do it."

Side by side Josh and Lee half swam, half drifted, moving toward the raft.

CHAPTER TEN

TUESDAY AUGUST 1, 1945
THE PHILIPPINE SEA
DAY TWO | MORNING

Josh reached the raft first. It rode the wild swells, much smaller than he'd expected. Good thing he and Lee spotted it early, for it could barely hold the five men already seated there. The men, black with fuel oil, huddled on the balsam wood platform and watched the newcomers with resentful eyes.

Breathing hard, Josh caught hold of a dangling rope. A black-bearded man scowled but grabbed his life vest and hauled him on board.

"Thanks," Josh spluttered, struggling to keep hold of the slippery platform. The raft's center was empty, and he quickly saw why: the latticed wood floor had big gaps. It looked flimsy and water surged through. Not good, with sharks swimming below.

He felt sick and nauseous from swallowing so much gunk. Gagging, he spat out fuel oil and saltwater. Lee was struggling to climb on now. Great. It felt incredible to be out of the ocean.

A bullet-headed sailor heaved himself forward. Josh thought the man would give Lee a hand up.

Instead, he smashed his fist straight into Lee's face.

Horrified, Josh scrambled forward. "What? What are you doing?" he shouted. "What did you do that for?" He leaned out, grabbed his friend's life vest, and tried to haul Lee up.

"We don't want no Jap spies on this raft," Bullet Head snarled.

"He's not a Jap spy!" Josh hung onto Lee's life vest. His friend's nose streamed blood. He had to get him out of the water. He'd attract sharks!

"'Course he's a Jap spy. Look at his slanting eyes," the man sneered.

"He's from Hawaii!" Josh shouted. "He's Chinese-American. His name is Lee Wong. He's my friend."

"Well, go ahead," Bullet Head said. "Jump down and join him, then."

Josh turned to the others for help, but no one met his eyes. He couldn't believe what was happening. How could they act like this? They were all on the same team. All fighting for America.

He searched the five oil-black faces and was shocked to recognize Timmy, a farmer's son. Timmy, he noted, wore just briefs, his chicken-skin legs shaking with cold. The poor guy must have had no time to grab clothes. And he had no life vest.

"Timmy! Come on, help me out," he said. "You know me. I'm Josh. Don't you recognize me?" He swiped the muck from his cheeks. "Lee's not a Jap. And he's bleeding. We need to get him out of the ocean."

"Can't even help myself," Timmy muttered through chattering teeth.

A wave tried to yank Lee from Josh's grip.

"Tie onto this rope," Josh told him. "We'll have to wait until these guys calm down. But if a shark comes, I'm pulling you up, got it?"

Lee fastened the rope to his wrist. "I'm okay."

But Josh knew it was a lie. Lee was bleeding--he was in grave danger. Talk about unfair. Lee was fighting this war, too. He'd volunteered for the Navy. And now his shipmates—men who should have his back—were giving him the shaft because of the shape of his eyes.

The two friends fell silent, watching the ocean.

Like a rollercoaster operated by a maniac, the raft rose and fell in the ten-foot waves. Josh's stomach heaved up and down, up and down. *You're lucky to be on this thing*, he told himself. He could picture his mom saying the same thing. And then telling him to do something useful. Maybe he could find something to help them all. Maybe then they'd feel more friendly and help Lee.

It seemed strange no one had emergency blankets or water cans. Where were the signal mirrors and flares? The survival kits? Surely the raft held supplies? He ran his hands along the sides. Then he gasped as he saw the problem. The float was upside down!

He looked at the men. The bearded guy with his ropy arms and legs seemed most approachable.

"Sir," he said. "I think the raft is upside down."

The officer frowned.

A young, dark-skinned sailor jumped to his feet. "It is!" he shouted. "Look at the floor lattice! It's all twisted. That's why it's broken. The whole thing's flipped."

"I bet there're emergency kits down below," Josh said.

Bullet Head waved his gun. "You check. I'll watch for sharks."

The bearded officer said, "Come with me, son. We'll grab what we can. And the name's Patterson."

"Thanks, Officer Patterson. My friend will help," Josh said.

"Yeah," Lee called. "I'm a good swimmer."

"All right, boys," Patterson said. "Stay alert."

Wary of the deadly, dark-finned predators swarming in the distance, Josh slid into the water. It was strange under the raft. A shadowy world of swirling ocean and small, darting fish.

He soon spotted canvas sacks attached to the siding. He opened one, and a tin of meat fell free and plummeted out of reach. Cursing his mistake, he moved more carefully to fill his arms. The others did the same. When Josh spotted a small first-aid kit, he jammed it into his pocket. He felt guilty but didn't trust the bullet-headed sailor. Lee needed medicine.

He surfaced twice under the lattice for air. Finally, the three swam back out into the blazing afternoon and the dark-skinned sailor hauled Josh aboard. Lee handed up two sacks and started to climb on.

"Not you," Bullet Head growled. "No Jap in my raft."

"Oh, come on, sir," Josh said. "My friend's not a Jap. I told you."

"Shut up."

An engine droned in the distance. Josh was flooded with relief as he spotted a plane. Rescue at last! He couldn't wait to get lifted to safety. He couldn't wait to get away from this creepy guy.

"They've come for us," Timmy yelled, leaping to his feet in his underwear.

"Praise God. The SOS went out!" Patterson growled. "They'll all be here soon. Planes. Tugboats."

Josh sent a silent thanks to the radio operator who'd climbed deep inside the burning ship to send out the SOS.

He joined the others, waving and screaming. Bullet Head fired his gun and the sound boomed in Josh's ears. The pilot would be sure to hear it. The plane roared directly overhead. Josh jumped up and down with excitement, almost overbalancing on the raft's heaving floor. The pilot had seen them!

But then the plane buzzed away.

Flying into the blue sky, it grew smaller and smaller, a speck vanishing over the horizon.

Despair gripped Josh. "He must have seen us. He must have!"

"Blind idiots," a sailor with a thick mustache shouted. "Come back here, you blinking, blind pilots."

Patterson gave a wry laugh.

Josh didn't think it was funny. He glanced at Lee, still bobbing in the ocean. His friend had been lucky so far, the sharks had stayed away, thrashing and feeding in the distance. But how long before they smelled Lee's blood?

"Sir, can I bring my friend up?" he asked Patterson.

Patterson nodded at Bullet Head's gun. "Nope. You heard the boss."

I was right to keep the medical kit, Josh thought. Bullet Head is nuts. Lee and I may have to leave here. Pray we spot another raft soon.

CHAPTER ELEVEN

TUESDAY AUGUST 1, 1945

THE PHILIPPINE SEA

DAY TWO | AFTERNOON

Bullet Head stashed the canvas supply sacks under his legs. The men watched intently as he opened them one by one. Beakers of water. Boxes of malt tablets. Cans of Spam. And, best of all, signal mirrors and a flare rocket.

The dark-skinned sailor opened a beaker of water. Sipped it. And spat. "Full of seawater," he muttered.

Josh groaned and licked his cracked, peeling lips.

Bullet Head handed each man two malt tablets and two crackers. Eagerly, Josh took his and shared half with Lee. He nibbled the wafer. It tasted cheesy and delicious and took away the horrible taste of fuel oil.

As the long day passed, other survivors swam to the raft. Soon angry men filled the platform, all fighting for a spot. Josh had to keep moving out of the way, struggling to keep his space. When the raft was overflowing, other swimmers joined Lee, floating alongside, hanging onto the few dangling ropes.

No one spoke of the horrors they'd seen, but the air smelled of fear.

A massive, gray shadow appeared on the horizon.

"A ship!" a sailor shouted. "A ship!"

Josh's heart thumped fast. After two nights, the Navy was finally coming for them. Relief flooded him. Maybe the pilot had seen them after all. Maybe he'd called the Navy. He leaned over the side and yelled at Lee, "A ship! We'll be on land before you know it!"

Lee, his face sickly, gave a thumbs-up sign.

The ship approached slowly, a submarine-shaped silhouette with a tower on top.

Bullet Head fired his gun.

Josh sent up a flare, the shot's recoil sending him reeling backward. He shouted in triumph as the blazing signal zoomed over the ocean.

"What if it's a Jap ship?" Timmy muttered. "Looks like a sub. What if it's the same Japs who sank us?" The men muttered. Uneasily, everyone watched to see what it would do.

Like a gray ghost, the ship disappeared.

Choked with disappointment, Josh sat heavily amongst the crush of sunburned, thirsty sailors. His stomach rumbled. Suddenly he had a happy thought. He still had the egg and mayo sandwiches wrapped in waxed paper! And the chocolate cake. They'd be soaked but still edible. He'd forgotten all about them!

He dug into his dungaree pockets and hauled out a squashed package. Opening it, he scraped out a section of wet bread and mashed up egg and mayo, surprised it hadn't dissolved. Bullet Head watched with narrowed eyes. Josh knew he'd have to share, so he carefully dug out more bread and the crumbly chocolate cake. The slick icing looked so good. He licked his dry lips as he separated a small portion for himself, intending to hand some of this treasure over the side to Lee and offer the rest to the others.

Standing slowly, Bullet Head stretched. Then he reached out and grabbed the lot. He grinned at Josh. A shark-like grin that never reached his eyes.

CHAPTER TWELVE

TUESDAY AUGUST 1, 1945
THE PHILIPPINE SEA
DAY TWO | LATE AFTERNOON

By late afternoon, the sun broiled the raft, burning faces and bodies. Out here, it was easy to feel like the world no longer existed. That there was only this deadly ocean. So he forced himself to think of home. Crazy to think how he and his friends had played pirates when they were kids, making each other walk the plank into a fake sea with pretend sharks waiting below. If only he could pretend this was all some lousy game . . . If only he could call it quits and go in for dinner.

For the moment, at least, the sharks had disappeared. Not a fin in sight. Instead of relief, though, it unsettled him.

The raft had floated clear of the fuel spill. The ocean sparkled in every direction, cool and tempting. He was so thirsty. His tongue was swollen, his voice hoarse. How long could you go without water? Somewhere he'd read four days, maybe a week. The sea sure looked inviting. He saw the other men eyeing it, too.

"How bad can it be? Should be safe to have a few sips," Bullet Head grunted, leaning to dip his hand in the water.

"No!" warned a bowlegged, older man. "Don't do it. Saltwater makes you crazy."

"How would you know? You're crazy already." Bullet Head grinned as he scooped a handful of saltwater into his mouth. "Tastes better than a pint of beer."

A few others took a gulp.

"Tastes fine," someone shouted.

"Better than dying of thirst," someone else agreed.

"It'll make you even more thirsty," the bowlegged sailor muttered.

"I'm just having a sip," Timmy said. "It's not so bad."

Josh wondered if they were right. His cracked lips stung and his tongue stuck to the roof of his dry mouth. How bad could a few drops be? If they weren't saved soon, he'd risk it.

The day lasted forever. At sunset, the sharks returned. This time they came close, circling the raft.

"Monsters!" Patterson shouted, his voice cracking. He reached into his dungarees and produced a lethal-looking knife. "Wait 'till I get you. Slit your throats, I will."

A scrawny sailor with grizzled hair grabbed a can of Spam from under Bullet Head's legs and gave a shout of triumph. "Spam! Let's eat, boys."

With a roar of approval, the men crowded forward, reaching out. Bullet Head scowled but did nothing.

The scrawny sailor ripped off the Spam lid and scooped out pink meat. The closest men shuffled and pushed for a bite.

The Spam smelled wonderful. Josh felt his dry mouth watering.

"No. No!" Eyes flashing terror, Patterson grabbed the can and flung it far into the ocean.

Too late.

As Patterson shouted a warning, Josh saw it, a massive white dorsal fin slicing through the ocean toward them.

Beside him, the bowlegged sailor groaned. "A white tip! Smelled the Spam. God save us." He stood and shouted to the men in the ocean. "Prepare yourselves, boys! A monster's headed our way."

Josh stared in horror.

The massive shark torpedoed toward them.

CHAPTER THIRTEEN

TUESDAY AUGUST 1, 1945
THE PHILIPPINE SEA
DAY TWO | LATE AFTERNOON

"It smells the Spam," the grizzled sailor shouted. "Splash, men! Kick!"

"Move!" Lee warned the men in the ocean. "Get out of the way! It's coming fast."

The desperate swimmers paddled wildly to the raft's far side. A few managed to force their way on top, falling onto those already on board.

The shark reached the flimsy raft and began to circle. Then, like a gentle, curious giant, it began to nudge the corners, seeming almost friendly. A spooky gray shape, it dove under and carefully poked at the floor's broken lattice.

It's playing with us, Josh thought. Tormenting us. It knows what it's doing. It's the hunter. We're the prey. And we've nowhere to go.

Suddenly the shark disappeared.

Anxiously, the men scanned the water. There was no sign of the creature. Josh breathed a sigh of relief. Maybe it was going after the can of Spam down below.

Without warning, the shark's giant pointed snout shoved through the broken wood lattice.

"Pull your legs up!" someone yelled. "Lie flat on your backs."

The men on the raft bunched on the balsam wood platform. Panicked men in the ocean began to sob. With a warrior scream, the dark-skinned sailor kicked the snout. The shark retreated. But it returned immediately. Rising up again, thumping at the latticework.

Josh could see the creature. It looked at least fifteen feet long. Incredible. Magnificent. Deadly. Rippling muscles under armored skin. Cold eyes filled with determination. The shark was determined to get in. To sink them all for good.

The dark-skinned sailor pulled a knife out of his holster. Fast as a whip, he stabbed the creature in the eye. "Got you!" he yelled. "I'm going to drink your blood, you sucker!"

Wild with pain and fury, the shark lashed out, slamming the raft with its leathery tail.

Screaming hysterically, the men crashed to the other side, falling on top of one another.

Josh, lying with his legs curled on the edge, lost his grip. Arms flailing wildly, he tried to find something to cling to. Within seconds, he was over the side and in the ocean, right beside the shark.

The creature eyeballed him. Flat, cold eyes.

It was so big. So unbelievably enormous.

I'm going to be eaten alive, he thought.

Rough, scaly skin sandpapered his arm. His brain fired on all cylinders. He had to act. If he didn't, he'd die.

"Jab the eyes!" he heard Lee scream. "Jab the eyes!"

Josh stuck his hand out blindly, feeling the creature's tough, scaly head. Where were its eyes? And then he felt a soft patch. An eye? He jabbed two fingers in as hard as he could.

The shark whirled around and dove down. With a thrill of triumph, Josh watched him go. "How'd you like that, sucker?" he shouted. "Got you in your good ole juicy eye."

Thrilled with his success, he clawed his way back to the raft.

As he tried to climb up and over the rim, Bullet Head pushed him down. "Get! Get away from us! Look at your arm, boy! You're bleeding like a stuck pig. You're shark bait."

Stunned. Too exhausted to argue, Josh joined Lee, hanging on to a line in the ocean.

Lee ripped at the edge of his shirt with his teeth and managed to tear off a strip. He wrapped it tightly around Josh's arm. But the makeshift bandage was soon red. As red as the bandage around Lee's arm. Together, they were definitely shark bait.

The men floating alongside the raft eyed them nervously and moved as far from them as they could.

Josh didn't blame them. How long, he thought, before they tell us to go?

When night fell, he pulled out the emergency kit, glad to have ointment for Lee and himself. But when he opened the tin, he saw it wasn't medical supplies. Instead, it held fishing hooks and lines. He popped it back in his dungaree pocket. Not what he'd thought, but who knew when he might be glad to have it.

CHAPTER FOURTEEN

WEDNESDAY AUGUST 2, 1945
THE PHILIPPINE SEA
DAY THREE | NOON

The relentless setting sun burned down on Josh's head. Even with his eyes closed, he could see its glare. The ocean sparkled, fresh, inviting, still as a lagoon. With no sharks in sight, men slid from the raft into the cool water, first splashing it on their heads and then sipping it defiantly.

Again, Josh wondered if he should risk it. Did saltwater really drive a man mad? Well, he'd find out soon as more and more men gulped it down.

Alongside Josh, a grizzled sailor dove and resurfaced, eyes rolling. "I had a drink! It's down there, friends. The ship's just down below. With all the water you can drink."

Was it true? For a moment, Josh almost believed it. Maybe he should dive down, see for himself.

"That's not possible," said a skeptical voice.

"You're lying," shouted Patterson, leaning over the side of the raft.

"Do you remember the scuttlebutt?" the grizzled sailor roared. "The one with lots of cold water? I dove down and turned it on, guys. It works. The water is fresh. Fresh. I'll show you! Follow me!"

Sobbing, a lost look in his eyes, Timmy plunged in. Other hysterical men followed, diving down to find the ship. Some even pulled off their life jackets before diving.

Could it possibly be true? Josh looked over at Lee, who licked his salt-white lips and shook his head.

"We saw the ship go down," Lee croaked. "It's too deep by now. There's no way we could reach it."

A wide-eyed sailor popped up, shouting, "There's pretty girls down there! Lots of them!"

"It's the saltwater," Lee said. "They're going crazy."

"There's a Jap over there," a man cried. "He's trying to kill me."

"Get the Jap! Kill him!" Screaming men, foaming at the mouth, turned on each other.

Were they after Lee?

In a panic, Josh spun, ready to fight for his friend. But thankfully no one was looking at Lee. Some other poor man was being attacked. The saltwater really was turning the men crazy.

Head throbbing, Josh watched in mounting horror. The scene grew worse and worse. Most sailors had knives, and now the knives were drawn. This was turning into a blood-bath. And he and Lee would be right in the middle!

He felt his calf, checking his blade was still in its holster. It was. Not much of a weapon, he thought, but I'm glad I have it.

A burly man with red eyes shoved his face right up to his. "Give me some of your water," he shouted.

Josh paddled backward. "I don't have water."

"You do. You're hiding it."

"I don't! I swear!"

The man shouted right in his face, his breath rancid, his face red with sunburn and fury. "I want some of that water, boy! And you're going to give it to me!" Looking around, he yelled. "Hey! Hey guys. This sneaky fella's got the beaker."

Three men, bobbing in their life vests, scowled at Lee and Josh.

"I don't have water," Josh shouted. "The beaker was cracked. Empty."

The men swam nearer. This wasn't looking good.

A voice rang out, the voice of authority. "No one has water, men. Just stay strong. Help will be here soon."

Marine Captain Parke! Josh thought. At last, an officer was here! Maybe Parke could control the men.

"Don't drink the saltwater. It'll make you mad," Parke shouted. "Won't be long before the Navy finds us, men. Tie your life vests together. Stay together. You don't want to drift away."

Good idea, Josh thought. He and Lee tied their vests together, bobbing side by side. Parke's voice reminded him of his dad. He felt a pang of longing. Dad was a good person to have around in a bad situation.

He remembered how once he, Dad, and Sammy had gone for a hike down a country road. A furious Doberman, teeth bared, charged through an open farm gate and cornered them, mean and growling, ready to attack.

"Back!" Dad ordered, his voice loud and firm. "Back! Down, boy! Down!"

Then he'd spoken softly to Josh. "Hold Sammy's hand and move away slowly. Don't run. Don't look into its eyes."

That's what these men were like now. Mad dogs. "Stay away from them," he whispered to Lee. "Don't look at their eyes. Let's swim behind the raft, get out of their way."

Clutching the line, Josh eyed the knot of defiant sailors who kept drinking saltwater. Parke's warning was right. The water was affecting them. Aghast, he watched as two men, mouths foaming, held their struggling friend underwater. The air filled with screams. The terrible fight went on and on. Soon, the bodies of dead and injured sailors littered the sea.

"Sharks," Lee groaned, pointing. "Look!"

Josh stared out to sea. Hundreds of black fins knifed through the water toward the raging group. The sharks, attracted by their blood and urine, were coming in for the kill. They attacked in a fury.

With a sick feeling, Josh listened for Parke's voice. For a while he could hear it bellowing orders, shouting warnings, trying to get the hysterical men back to the safety of the raft. Josh's heart pounded. Why didn't Parke return to the raft and save himself? Then suddenly, Parke's voice went silent.

The sharks ate for hours. Every bump on Josh's leg felt like a shark. He longed to be sitting on the raft but didn't dare challenge Bullet Head and his gun. Hang in there, he told himself. Help will arrive. Soon. Surely soon.

High in the sky, another plane passed over. And then another. Josh and Lee and the men around him waved furiously.

But no one noticed.

CHAPTER FIFTEEN

WEDNESDAY AUGUST 2, 1945
THE PHILIPPINE SEA
DAY THREE | LATE AFTERNOON

A barrel bobbed past.

"Hey! We can ride that thing," Lee shouted.

Josh looked at the bloody ocean, at the screaming, fighting men. He nodded. "Yeah. Let's get away from this crazy bunch."

Moving slowly but surely, they swam after the barrel. The hissing wind and rising waves struck Josh's face, pushing him back. He thought he heard jabbering. Were the crazed sailors after him? Trying to kill him? Trying to take his life vest?

He spun, but no one was following. He went to swim after Lee but couldn't see him. The barrel had disappeared too. All he could see were the endless swells, the breaking waves.

His soggy life vest had lost most of its buoyancy. Now his nose was only a few inches above the water. He ran his swollen tongue over his cracked lips and groaned. Perhaps a little sip wouldn't hurt. He scooped a handful of water and brought it to his lips.

"Don't!" Lee's voice rang out. "How would your mom feel if you went crazy?"

He groaned. "Yeah . . . you're right." He pictured his mom. She'd ask why he'd done such a dumb thing. Tears filled his eyes. He longed to see her face. Even if it was an angry face.

Mom must be so mad that he'd forged her signature on the permission form. *If I hadn't done that, I wouldn't be here now. Dying here now.* He squeezed his eyes shut. He loved his mom and little brother so much. He missed them. What was he doing here at all? He must have been crazy. What good had he thought he could do?

He'd wanted to fight the Japs. What a joke. The Japs had sure ended that plan fast. They'd sunk his ship, the beautiful Indy, before he'd had a chance to fight at all. Now he was probably going to die. To drown. To end up as some shark's dinner. Part of the whole dead-sailor-buffet.

He should have stayed home, should have been there for Sammy. He pictured his kid brother. So skinny and full of energy. Just like himself at Sammy's age, all long, knobby legs and long, scrawny neck. *Bones*, they'd called Josh at school. In third grade, some joker named him that, and it stuck.

He'd filled out later. Playing baseball and running track had done that. He should be at home right now playing catch with Sammy.

"Where's the barrel?" he shouted to Lee. "Thought you'd be riding it off into the sunset."

"I wish," Lee said. "Damn thing's moving fast."

They'd lost the barrel? What were they going to do now?

"Wait here," Lee croaked. "I'll try and get it."

"No way. I'm not waiting here."

The swells were growing. Low black clouds hung in the sky. Darkness was coming fast. Both of them were injured. They hadn't eaten or drank for days. On the raft, Josh had thought things couldn't get much worse. But now they were lost.

Then, as he rose up on a swell, he spotted what looked like a makeshift raft. For a moment, he couldn't believe it. A thrill of pure relief ran through him.

"Lee! Raft!" he stammered. "Over there!"

Lee whooped and they struck out, swimming as hard as they could. The raft meant the difference between life and death. No way would they let it drift off.

Puffing hard, they reached the makeshift float. Someone had lashed together two ammunition cans and three potato crates. Swimming closer, Josh saw a pair of sailors. One young guy about his age, his face bright red with sunburn, and an older man, his face peeling and his eyes bloodshot. I must look like that too, Josh thought, touching his stinging nose.

Both men shouted a greeting and leaned down to pull them up. The top of the raft was soft and dry, lined with kapok life vests. As Josh sank into the kapok, he gave a big sigh.

"Thank you," he said.

Thank heavens these men were friendly and not throwing him and Lee overboard.

"I'm Chris." The older sailor shook their hands, his eyes warm and creased. "We saw you guys swimming for us. Glad you made it."

"Hi! I'm Paul," said the young sailor, a freckled guy with a tattoo of the Indy on his right arm.

Josh and Lee introduced themselves. They pulled off their

sodden kapok life vests, squeezed them and laid them out to dry. Josh winced as he touched the blisters on his shoulders. It felt great to be free of the vest for a while.

Paul dug into one of the barrels and handed them each a rotten potato. Gratefully, Josh picked off the skin and the stinking, rotten parts, and slowly ate what was left. His stomach rumbled, still empty. It had been days since his last meal. Blinking, he looked around the raft, saw a broken paddle and some tin cans.

Suddenly, he remembered the fishing kit. He took it out, flipped up the lid.

"Is that what I think it is?" Chris said.

"Yep."

"Good man," Chris said.

Josh threaded a nylon line on to a hook. He handed the kit to Chris, who began assembling a line, too. Maybe they'd have fish for lunch!

"When do you think they'll come for us?" Paul said.

"Soon," Josh replied, watching the fishing line dangling in the ocean.

"I don't know," Paul said. "Something's gone badly wrong. If Navy Command knew the USS Indianapolis had gone down, they'd be here by now."

Josh said nothing but Paul's words rang true. It was what he feared, what he'd tried not to think. How long could they last out here? They had to hang on. And hanging on was hard when you'd lost all hope.

He could hear Dad's voice. *If you give up hope, you're dead.*

"We're going to die," Paul groaned.

You could talk yourself into giving up and dying. It would almost be easier. But he didn't want to die. Maybe he could talk himself into living.

"We're going to live," he told Paul. "We're not going to die. We're going to make it. Don't quit. Hang on."

He could almost hear Dad's voice telling him to never quit.

Had it really been three years ago that Dad, a Navy mechanic, received his transfer notice? At dinner, he'd told the family he was being sent to the Pacific Fleet Naval base at Pearl Harbor, Hawaii.

Josh, his mom, and his little brother heard the news in dismay. Although World War II was raging in Britain and Europe, American troops were not part of the battle. Life was peaceful in Josh's home town of San Antonio.

"Why?" Mom said. "America isn't at war."

Dad looked solemn. "It's only a matter of time before America joins the fight. The warships I'll be maintaining will be a big part of the action. America has to fight the German aggression. We have to fight for freedom. Sometimes you have to fight for what you believe in."

Josh was filled with pride. It sounded so exciting.

But it wasn't. Dad died when the Japanese bombed Pearl Harbor. Thousands of Americans died.

Before leaving, his father had said, "If I die, take care of your mom. And your little brother. Okay, son? You'll be the man of the family."

He'd promised. Yes. He'd take care of Mom and Sammy.

Now, guilt filled him because if he died out here, he'd fail to keep that promise.

Of course, his mother could take care of herself. She could probably take care of the whole Navy. But she'd be alone with both her men gone. Dead and gone. What if Germany and Japan combined forces? What if they attacked the very heartland of America? Who would defend Mom and Sammy then?

Chris, his creased blue eyes watching the ocean, patiently dangled his fishing line over the side of the raft. Every now and again, he glanced at Josh. Eventually, he spoke. "Deep thoughts, lad?"

Josh nodded.

"Sometimes you just have to do the best you can," Chris said.

"I guess."

"I'll take care of you guys for as long as I can," Chris said.

Paul looked up. "What makes you think you can take care of us?"

"Because I'm a Marine, I'm tougher than hell."

Paul laughed. Josh was glad to see he looked better, less dejected, more hopeful. "Well, I'm a farmer from Minnesota," Paul said. "That makes me tougher than you."

"Could be," Chris said. "Right now, I'm trying to catch us a fish for dinner. And I have a few fish down here that might be interested in my bait."

Josh slid over with his line. He watched, stomach

rumbling, as hundreds of small fish circled his bait. Did fish even eat rotten potato? It looked like they might.

The fish were pretty, bright yellow with black stripes. Almost too pretty to eat. How great it would be if they could catch one! His last real meal had been so long ago that his stomach thought his throat was cut.

Lee slid over and joined them. "We have those fish in Hawaii too," he said. "They're good to eat. Small but tasty. They're called Tang. See the black spot near their tails? It's a fake eye. Makes the fish seem bigger than it is. Or that's what the fish like to think."

Josh laughed, feeling a small moment of delight. There were wonderful things in the world. He just needed to make sure he lived long enough to see them. Well, don't quit, he told himself. People have survived for months on rafts. We could live on fish and rainwater. We could hold on for a long time.

"So where are you two from?" Chris asked.

"I'm from San Antonio," Josh said.

"Ah, San Antonio. Love that river." Chris smiled. "And that great fort. The Alamo. Do you know about the battle of the Alamo, son? Do you know how Davy Crockett fought there? How he fought for Texas?"

Josh nodded. "I sure do." His heart gave a momentary twinge, but it was a happy memory. His family had gone when he was little to see the Alamo fort and hear the story of Davy Crockett. That was one brave man, Davy Crockett, king of the wild frontier.

At the fort gift shop, they'd bought him a Davy Crockett fur hat. He'd worn it for months, refusing to go anywhere without it. He even wore that hot, sweaty hat to bed. He smiled at the thought.

When he got home, he'd buy Sammy a Davy Crockett hat. He'd tell him about Davy and his small group of brave soldiers who fought to the end and never quit. He and Sammy could shout the rousing battle cry *Remember the Alamo!*

Chris turned to Lee. "And you, son?"

"I'm from Hawaii," Lee said.

"Born in Hawaii, huh?"

Oh no . . . Not again. Josh knew why Chris was asking. What if Chris decided Lee was Japanese? What if he decided he was a spy and ordered him off the raft?

"Lee's Chinese-American," Josh said, stepping quickly into the conversation. "His grandparents came from China."

For a long minute, Chris studied Lee. Then he nodded. "I've never been to Hawaii. Must be a nice place."

"It is," Lee replied.

"Too bad the Japanese bombed it," Chris said. "Too bad they bombed Pearl Harbor. Lots of my mates died."

"I know. It was awful," Lee replied.

Josh didn't like the way the conversation was going. He had no way to prove that Lee was Chinese-American. What if Chris didn't believe him?

"Those Japanese planes just came in out of the blue and bombed our men," Chris muttered. "Why would people do something like that?"

Lee shook his head. Josh saw that his face had grown red.

Chris turned back to his fishing line, carefully attaching a piece of potato to the fishing hook. He sat silently, watching the ocean swells.

Josh and Lee sat silent too. *What was Chris thinking?*

It was late afternoon, feeding time for the sharks. On the horizon, swarms gathered. Josh could see their fins. The wind and waves were carrying the raft across the ocean in what

Chris said was a northerly direction. Soon they'd be far from Dr. Haynes' large group of survivors. If Lee was kicked off the raft here, what would they do?

Miles in the distance, something glinted. Josh leaped to his feet as rays from the setting sun caught the metal of a plane.

Then signal flares, faint plumes of smoke, rose from the sea. There were other survivors out there. A third group. And they had emergency flares! Josh's hopes soared. Surely the pilot would see that!

He watched, tense his eyes burning as he peered into the distance.

The plane circled. His hopes rose.

Then they crashed as the plane, like all the planes, disappeared into the sky.

CHAPTER SIXTEEN

"Josh?" Lee said, talking softly. "I need to tell you something."

"What?" Josh turned reluctantly. He didn't want to hear bad news. He wanted to stay determined. Upbeat. Was Lee going to confirm what he already feared? That they had almost no chance of ever being spotted by a plane? That a man's head bobbing in the ocean was the size of a bobbing coconut? That a small raft was invisible to a pilot miles high in the clouds?

Lee motioned him away from Chris, who was dozing in the dawn light.

Josh looked uneasily at his friend. Lee looked weird.

"I lied to you," Lee whispered. "I'm sorry, Josh. My name isn't Lee Wong. My father wasn't Chinese."

Josh stared at him. "What's your real name? And if you're not Chinese, what are you?"

Had Bullet Head been right? Was Lee a Japanese spy? Josh's brain felt scrambled. *What if Lee had signaled the Indy's position to the Jap sub?*

"My name is Lee Tanaka." Lee's voice trembled. "I'm so sorry, I shouldn't have lied. But I thought you wouldn't help me."

"So, you're Japanese?"

"Not Japanese. I'm Japanese-American," Lee said. "My grandfather was Japanese. He came from Japan to Hawaii years ago to work in the sugarcane fields. My dad was born in Hawaii. He was Japanese-American. And he wasn't a spy. I'm not a spy, I swear it. My dad died in France, fighting in this war. He volunteered to fight." There were tears in Lee's eyes. He dashed them away with his hand and wiped his nose. His face was scrunched with emotion.

"Okay." Josh glanced at the two other men on the raft. No one was listening. Chris was snoring and Paul was softly singing the Navy hymn, beating time with the broken oar on a tin can.

Not knowing what to say, Josh sat silent.

Paul kept singing. He was fudging some of the words, and his tune was shaky, but the song was beautiful. "Oh hear us when we cry to thee," Paul sang, "for those in peril on the sea."

Somehow, hearing the song soothed Josh's soul. "It's okay," he told Lee. "Let's not talk about it now."

It would be bad if Chris and Paul heard that Lee was Japanese. Who knew how they'd react? Maybe they'd act like Bullet Head. Josh couldn't picture them like that, but he couldn't take the chance.

He felt strange about Lee being Japanese. Lots of Americans were suspicious of Japanese-Americans. They feared they were spies. That's why so many had been interned in isolation camps. Because they weren't trusted. Could he trust Lee? Lee had lied to him.

"I understand if you don't trust me," Lee stammered. "My father's fighting unit, the 442nd Infantry Regiment, fought hard for America. When he died, I joined the Navy to fight in his name."

"I do trust you," Josh said. He realized that even though Lee had lied, he understood why. And he did trust him. He nodded gravely at his friend. "Of course I trust you. How many times have you helped me and even saved my life?"

"You saved mine," Lee said.

"I also joined the Navy because my father died," Josh said. "Are you under seventeen, too? Did you forge your mom's signature on the Navy permission form?"

Lee nodded. "Yeah. I sort of wish I hadn't."

Josh gave a hollow laugh. "Me too."

"So you're also sixteen?" Lee asked.

"Yeah. It would be just as bad out here if we were eighteen though!"

"But we'd have lived a couple more years," Lee said, wistfully. "We might have had girlfriends. I've never even kissed a girl. Not properly, anyway."

"Maybe it would've been harder, then," Josh said. "All those sobbing girls."

Lee laughed. "Yeah. Wish I'd had a chance to own a car. That would have been good. I was looking forward to driving my first car. A little convertible. With the top down."

"Still time," Josh said.

He wondered if that was true.

CHAPTER SEVENTEEN

THURSDAY AUGUST 3, 1945
THE PHILIPPINE SEA
DAY FOUR | MORNING

Josh looked out at the empty ocean. He felt awkward. He wished Lee had never told him he was Japanese. He hated the Japanese.

Chris had woken and taken up his fishing line.

"Why has no one come to save us, do you think?" Lee said.

"They will. They must realize by now something's wrong. They'll come soon," Josh said.

"I wonder if the Navy has told our families that we're missing," Lee said.

Josh pictured his mother's worried face. Gosh, he hoped they hadn't told her. He imagined Mom getting the telegram. *We regret to inform you that your son is missing in action.* He felt so guilty. He loved his mom so much.

When they'd heard about the Pearl Harbor attack, Josh had been in the yard fixing the brakes on his bike. The radio had been blaring out *Oh Susanna*, a song he liked, when an announcer interrupted the broadcast.

The radio announcer's voice was grim. "There's been an air raid on Pearl Harbor. This is not a drill."

He raced into the kitchen. "Mom!" he shouted. "There's been an air raid. The Japanese bombed the Naval base at Pearl Harbor!"

The USS Arizona burning at Pearl Harbor

His mom came running from the bedroom. She clutched the kitchen table and stood for a long moment, simply staring out of the window. Then, all day, he and his mom waited together, sick with anxiety, hunched over the radio, desperate for news.

The following day, the United States declared war on Japan. Clinging together, he and his mom listened as President Roosevelt spoke to the nation.

"The attack yesterday on the Hawaiian Islands has caused severe damage to American naval and military forces," the President said. "I regret to tell you that very many American lives have been lost."

Day after day, they waited for news. They had no idea if Dad was alive or dead or lying somewhere injured. As news broadcasts grew more detailed, his hatred for the Japanese grew.

"Dive bombers, high-level bombers, and torpedo planes tore the harbor apart," the radio announcer reported. "More than twenty-four hundred Americans have been killed, more than a thousand injured. The US Pacific Fleet has been decimated, twenty-one Pacific Fleet ships have been sunk or damaged, seventy-five percent of planes were damaged or destroyed."

Josh pictured the men fighting back as planes roared over and bomb after bomb hit the battleships. He imagined his dad fighting and felt sick with dread. He knew his dad would fight to the max. Dad would defend others. What were the chances that he was alive and uninjured?

For weeks, still no news came. No word if Dad was alive or dead. For endless nights, he listened as Mom prayed. Every time someone knocked on the front door, he and his mom cringed, expecting the dreaded telegram announcing that Dad had been killed.

And then, their worst fears came true. The telegram arrived. Dad had indeed been killed. He'd died in the fiery waters of Pearl Harbor during the second wave of Japanese bombs.

He hated the Japanese. Hated them. He'd joined the Navy to fight them. To avenge his father. But he didn't hate Lee. How could he? Lee was his friend. It wasn't Lee's fault Japan had gone to war against the United States. Lee was American. And Lee's own father died in the war.

He stole a quick look at Lee. His friend looked depressed. Josh felt an unexpected pang of sympathy. He guessed that after the attack at Pearl Harbor, it would be hard to be Japanese-American.

A commotion rose on the other side of the raft. Chris beamed widely as he reeled in his line. "A bite!" he yelled. "Look! Caught one!"

Josh and Lee jumped up. A big silver-blue fish dangled from the hook. "That's an ono!" Lee shouted. "That's a good fish! The word *ono* means good in Hawaiian!" He laughed. "That's how good that fish is! I'll slice it real thin with my knife. I'll turn it into sashimi. It'll be real, real good!"

Josh heard his stomach rumble. He was starving. Imagine Chris catching a really tasty fish! A fish would be juicy, not hard to swallow. He licked his lips. His spirits lifted. They really could survive out here!

Eyes narrowed in concentration, Chris reeled in his flapping catch.

He yelled triumphantly and tossed it into the raft as a shark leaped up out of the ocean. With one snap, it swallowed the fish, seeming to hover in the air for a brief, shocking second.

Then, the massive beast thumped onto the flimsy raft.

Right at Josh's feet.

CHAPTER EIGHTEEN

THURSDAY AUGUST 3, 1945
THE PHILIPPINE SEA
DAY FOUR | NOON

Josh leaped back as the raft rocked and swayed. Chris fell, landing on his hands and knees. Lee and Paul reeled back, gasping in shock.

The shark, at least a ten-to-twelve-foot oceanic whitetip, thrashed furiously. Blood from the ono dripped from its knife-like teeth.

"Get it off!" Paul screamed.

Josh grabbed the broken oar and swung it at the shark's head.

The shark lifted its chinless face and heaved itself forward.

Paul shrieked and fell against Josh.

Again Josh struck.

"Grab its tail!" Chris yelled. With a blood-curdling yell, he jumped onto the thrashing body. "Stay away from the teeth!"

Josh followed with Lee. Together they grappled with the powerful creature. Strong muscles moved and rippled under Josh's arms, its sandpaper hide tearing at Josh's skin. He pulled as hard as he could. They had to get the enormous, thrashing creature off the raft. Already, they were sinking. They'd land in the ocean with the rest of the sharks.

"Pull!" Chris yelled. "On three. *One, two, three!*"

Josh pulled with all his might. But there was no way to control the shark. The mighty monster snapped its jaws. Lashed its powerful tail. With an incredible heave, it rocketed forward. Chased off the raft and into the ocean.

They'd done it! The shark was gone.

Chris let out a triumphant yell.

The raft tipped.

Screaming, the four men plummeted into the water.

Josh hit the water hard. Gasping, he kicked to the surface. In a blur of horror he saw the shark, its leering face beside him, its mouth wide open. The razor-like teeth latched on to his life vest.

Down, the shark dove, rolling and twisting. And down Josh went. He shoved hard. The creature refused to let go.

Frantic, he reached to pull his knife from the calf-holster. The eye! He had to get it in the eye. Furiously, he jabbed at the beast. The blade connected with shark-skin, gritty as sandpaper, solid as armor. With a viselike grip, the shark held on, jerking its head.

Then Lee was beside him, diving at his side, jabbing the creature's head, trying to get at the eyes too.

The shark was big. So big. A massive dark-gray body

pulling him down. To a watery grave. This was the shark's world. Here, the shark was king. Josh fought hard but could feel himself weakening. He needed air. His lungs were bursting.

The shark jerked its head from side to side. Then it let go of the life vest.

For a moment, a wonderful moment, Josh was free.

Then the shark latched on to his arm.

First, he felt nothing. Just the pressure of something hard wrapped around his forearm. Then he saw the blood, his blood, turning the swirling ocean red. All it would take was one good jerk for the monster to tear it off.

Well, it wasn't going to win. Josh became a raging fury. With his good arm, he swung his knife at it again and again.

Lee was still with him, heading straight for the shark from the front. The shark let go of Josh and opened its huge mouth wider. The shark and Lee were face to face.

Hot with fear and fury, Josh buried the blade deep in the shark's gills.

The spiraled away.

Lungs heaving, Josh kicked his way up to the surface. He swam hard for the raft, gulping air. Chris grabbed him and hauled him on board.

Time stood still as Josh stared at his arm. Blood streamed, covering the floor. Wow, he thought, my blood really is red. Very red.

Lee scrambled into the raft after him. He pressed his hand on the wound, holding it tight. "Make a tourniquet," he shouted.

Chris tore a strip from his shirt and wound it around and around, tying it tight. Still, blood covered the floor. The blood would attract more sharks. More hungry sharks, smelling the feast.

Lightheaded, Josh watched, as if somewhere above it all. "Hey, Lee," he said. "I went for the gills. I turned him into sashimi."

And then he passed out.

CHAPTER NINETEEN

THURSDAY AUGUST 3, 1945
THE PHILIPPINE SEA
DAY FOUR | LATE AFTERNOON

Half-conscious, Josh lay on the bobbing raft. He felt dizzy and weak. He'd lost a lot of blood. Was this what it felt like to die? If he died, maybe he'd see Dad. Did that happen? Was it like the pastor said? Did you meet your loved ones in heaven? He hoped so.

Sometimes you've got to fight for what you believe in. That's what Dad had said. Well, he believed in fighting to stay alive. To get home.

He sat up, confused. He'd been out of it. Really out of it. He shivered. His arm throbbed. It felt huge and hot.

"We'll never get out of here," Lee groaned.

"Yes, we will," Josh managed. "We've hung on for days. You're going to drive that sports car in Hawaii."

Hang in there, he told himself. Don't lose it now. Eyes

half-open, he saw a bright white light. For a moment, he thought he was looking at heaven.

A buzzing sound came from overhead.

"A plane," Chris shouted. "A plane!"

Then Josh saw it, a bomber, high above. But instead of leaving, this plane banked. It began to circle. Did that mean . . . Yes! The pilot had seen them. Finally. *Finally!*

Josh reached to high-five Lee, Paul, and Chris.

Breathless they watched the plane's hatch yawn open. First, life vests rained down. Then kegs of water crashed into the ocean, barely missing the raft. The kegs landed hard. And split.

An SB-29 drops a lifeboat

Chris groaned. "Could have used that water," he muttered.

Something else fell from the hatch. It turned the ocean around them bright pink. A dye bomb, Josh thought. The pilot was keeping track of them.

The plane rose into the air and flew off, growing smaller and smaller until it disappeared into the distance.

"They came," Josh said. "They'll be back." He heard other

planes, pictured them soaring through the skies. "Look. Spotlights out there!"

Miles away, a spotlight bounced off the clouds. Other beams scanned the ocean. His heart leaped. A search-and-rescue mission was going on over there. Men were being saved. But the raft was drifting. The pink dye began to disappear. Would the pilot find them again?

All night Josh watched distant searchlights scanning the ocean. His arm ached and throbbed. He and Lee pressed their foreheads together, praying.

"Raft's sinking," Chris said.

Josh looked uneasily into the water. The waterlogged life vests that formed a major part of the makeshift raft were sinking. One of the barrels had cracked. Soon, they'd be left swimming. He pictured rows of sharp, jagged teeth.

"Look, over there!" Lee pointed. "A ship!"

All Josh saw were endless rolling swells. Then he spotted it, the lights of a large vessel towering in the foggy night. They had to get its attention. But how? They had no flares. And every moment, the waves were carrying the raft further from the searchlights.

At least some guys were being saved. But the survivors were spread over miles of ocean. Please God, he prayed. Please don't let anyone be left behind. Please let them see us.

He eyed the others' sunburned, blistered faces, their split lips. Alongside him, Lee cradled his burned arm.

Josh gave him a thumbs-up sign.

Be strong, he told himself. Stay strong. It would be worse, much worse to die with rescue so close. But rescue wasn't guaranteed. He knew that now.

CHAPTER TWENTY

FRIDAY AUGUST 4, 1945
THE PHILIPPINE SEA
DAY FIVE | DAWN

As the dawn sky grew pink and gold, Josh jerked awake to the roar of an engine. Again lights flooded the ocean. A seaplane. This time it was coming down.

Wild with excitement, Josh spotted the pilot in the bubble cockpit. *Yes!*

The seaplane banked and circled. The swells were huge. Could it really land in this? Its pontoons hit hard, rose back up into the air, and plowed into the rough water nearby. What an amazing sight. It bobbed in the ocean, around half a mile away.

The men on the raft shouted and waved.

"We're drifting away!" Chris yelled.

Josh groaned, grabbed the broken paddle and began to stroke with the last of his strength.

The seaplane began to taxi slowly. In the other direction. What the heck? Maybe the pilot hadn't even seen them!

Chris let out a frustrated scream. "I'm swimming for it!"

"No way!" Lee caught his life vest.

"I can do it."

"No! Look at the sharks!"

"How do we know the pilot's even seen us?" Chris said. "And we're drifting fast. We can't blow this. It's our one chance."

Tense, eyes glued to their only hope, Josh paddled while Chris, Paul, and Lee screamed and waved life vests.

The seaplane turned. Taxied closer. The side hatch opened and an airman appeared. Josh could see him clearly, a hefty guy with big muscles. He looked like a professional wrestler.

As the seaplane taxied closer, the airman's gaze fastened onto Lee. Not *again*.

The airman's voice rang out. "Hey, sailor! What city do the Dodgers play in?"

What the heck! What was going on now?

"Brooklyn," Josh and Lee shouted in unison.

"Right answer. Sorry! We just had to make sure you guys are Americans!"

Josh closed his eyes. They were shipwrecked in shark territory and he had to answer questions about the Dodgers. Lucky he got it right. Lucky his mind hadn't gone totally whacko.

"I'm Morgan Hensley," the hefty guy shouted, "Hang on. We're going to get you outta here!"

A rope ladder dropped down and the airman climbed onto the rungs. They were safe. They really were safe. Josh breathed a prayer of thanks.

"Steady! Got a few injured ones here, sir," someone said.

"Get them onto the plane. That float looks ready to sink."

Strong hands pulled Josh out of the raft. With a burst of strength, he grabbed the rope ladder.

Suddenly, the hefty airman shouted in alarm. "Sharks! Look at the sharks! Layers of them!"

"They're everywhere!" another airman shouted. "Look at the size of them!"

"Yeah. I know." Josh didn't look. He didn't need to see sharks. He'd seen enough. He didn't want to see more. Ever.

Whipped by wind and spray, the ladder swung and swayed. Josh white-knuckled each rung as he hauled himself up with his good hand. Rifle shots rang out. The men on the plane were firing at the sharks. Way to go.

Almost leaping through the seaplane door, he flopped onto the floor and lay there, giving the pilot a big grin. He was safe.

Lee, Chris, and Paul were hauled on board, followed soon by other stunned-looking men. Survivors laughed, cried, shouted, and vomited.

"I can't believe you came!" a sailor shouted, tears streaming down his face.

"I can't believe you took so long!" someone growled.

Soon the fuselage of the plane was packed totally full of men. Still more survivors were tied to the plane wings with parachute cord.

The pilot, a young man with kind, fierce eyes, surveyed the survivors, frowning at the oil-covered bodies, festering wounds, and sunken cheeks.

"I'm Adrian Marks," he said. "You're safe now, sailors. Just take it easy. We're trying to get as many of you as we can, and the ships will get the rest."

Lieutenant Marks and the plane's crew bathed and

bandaged the survivors' wounds as they taxied up and down the towering waves, searching for more survivors.

Morgan, the hefty crewman, sat next to Josh and fed him spoonfuls of sugar water. "We saw your heads down there," Morgan said. "Couldn't see much though, because of all the oil. You guys are like pickled in oil, yeah?"

Josh said, "Why didn't you come days ago?"

Lieutenant Marks said, "No one even knew the USS Indianapolis was in trouble. Thank God we saw you."

"But the radio operator sent an SOS," Josh said. "I saw him go down there."

"Well, no one had a clue you were missing," Morgan said. "When we spotted you, we didn't even know if you guys were American or Japanese. And then we saw the sharks." He grimaced. "When the Lieutenant saw that, he decided to help no matter who you were. The Navy said the seas were too rough to land. But we did it anyway." He grinned. "The Navy refused Lieutenant Marks permission to touch down. But he disobeyed orders. Messed up the plane's pontoons, though."

"I'm sure glad you did," Josh said. "Real glad!"

Suddenly he noticed the floor was wet. And getting wetter. He slid his good hand over it. Pulled himself up fast. "Plane's sprung a leak, Sir."

Josh, Lee, Morgan and three other able-bodied survivors began bailing furiously. Josh's injured arm throbbed with pain but he had priorities. He was not going down into that ocean again. No way.

"That should do it! We're taking off," the pilot called.

"Well done, sailor," Morgan said.

Josh grinned. Wish I could tell Dad about all of this, he thought. Wish I could tell him about Lee and Morgan and the pilot. He'd have liked these guys. Wish I could tell him how I got away from those sharks.

He lay back and took a deep, deep breath of relief. "Home," he said. "We're really going home."

"You gonna visit me in Hawaii?" Lee said.

"You bet," Josh replied. "If you let me drive that sports car around the island."

"Sounds good."

Too exhausted to talk, they lay back as the seaplane flew low over the ocean toward the hospital ship.

I'm safe! Josh thought. No more sharks! I'm going home.

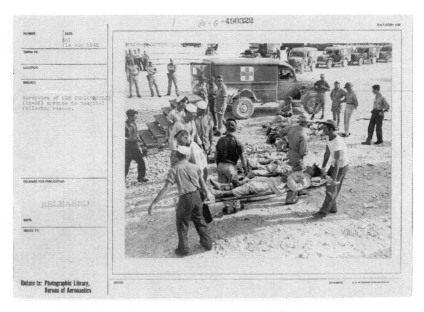

USS Indianapolis survivors enroute to hospital following their rescue.

CHAPTER TWENTY-ONE

DAYS LATER

GUAM, U.S. ISLAND TERRITORY

THE WESTERN PACIFIC OCEAN

Josh was going down, down. Into the pitch-black. The shark was after him. Coming at him. Right at him.

Josh shouted. Kicked. Hit out furiously. *Not now! Not again!*

"Hey! Hey, Josh, wake up! It's over, man. We're safe."

Josh lurched upright in the narrow hospital cot. In the next one over, Lee's sunburned face had finally stopped peeling and his infection was nearly gone. Pete, his red hair a sleep-wild frizz, was on his feet.

"Sorry," Josh groaned.

"No problem," Pete said. Josh noticed a tall, uniformed officer at his friend's side. "I want you to meet my cousin. Lieutenant Mike Bennet."

Josh jumped out of bed, trying to straighten his rumpled

T-shirt and shorts. His injured arm was still heavily bandaged. He stuck out his good one. "Pleased to meet you, sir."

Mike smiled warmly, shaking hands with Josh and Lee. He gave Pete a bear hug. "How are you all feeling?"

Josh rubbed his swollen limb. He could feel the punctures where the shark had sunk its teeth. He gave an embarrassed grin. "Guess I was yelling in my sleep. Just wrestling sharks."

"I had a mind-blowing nightmare last night," Pete said. "Dreamed I was swimming for that make-believe island, with the sharks coming after me. Guess we'll all have nightmares for a while."

"A heck of a lot's been happening since I waved goodbye to you at the harbor in San Francisco," Mike said.

The three boys listened warily. The scraps of news they'd received about the escalating war had grown worse day by day. Already, millions had died. And millions more were expected to die, fighting the Japanese in the Pacific in the coming months.

Mike's tense expression mirrored theirs. "I guess you heard the Japanese warlords refused to surrender."

"Yeah," Josh said. "We were hoping the Japanese emperor would convince them to back down."

"Nope," Mike said. "Not even the Soviet Union declaring war on their country has stopped them. President Truman has vowed to destroy Japan's power to attack the United States again. He won't let them strike Los Angeles or San Francisco the way they slaughtered our people at Pearl Harbor."

Mike was quiet for a moment. What he said next was more unbelievable than anything Josh had ever heard.

"Day before yesterday, we dropped a bomb on Japan's military base at Hiroshima. Another bomb was dropped on Nagasaki today." Mike's face was grim. "The president's about to make a news broadcast." He put his hand on Pete's shoulder. "I wanted to be with you guys."

Josh felt his body tense. Was the war growing even worse? He glanced at Lee. His friend had tears in his eyes.

"This is all terrible," Josh said. He didn't know what else to say.

Lee grimaced, "War is a terrible thing."

The quietness of the hospital ward was shattered as men gathered around the radio, talking animatedly to one another, trying to guess what the news broadcast would be about.

"As soon as they let me out of here," one said, "I'll be fighting again. We'll stop Japan. We have to."

"Yeah," someone said. "I don't want them coming after my family."

"They killed nine hundred of our mates on the Indy," someone else said.

Mike nodded. "And thousands upon thousands more across the globe. Our best and bravest."

"This has to stop."

The radio had been playing soft ragtime music. Now the music came to an abrupt halt. Someone turned it up. For a few moments, it hummed with loud static. Then a voice came over the airwaves.

Pete whirled around, silencing the survivors in the ward. "Listen! It's the press conference. It's President Truman!"

When Josh heard President Truman's deep voice, his heart sped up. He hoped some awful new thing hadn't happened.

"This is the day we have been waiting for since Pearl Harbor," President Truman said. "This is the day when Fascism finally dies, as we always knew it would."

What did that mean? Was the war over? How?

Around him, gaunt faces brightened and eyes widened

with shock and joy. The war was over!

The Indy sailors who'd been lucky enough to survive the gruesome torpedo attack listened in silence.

President Truman informed the nation that the Japanese Emperor Hirohito had surrendered to the Allied Forces. The United States had brought an end to the War in the Pacific. It had brought an end to World War II.

"Arrangements are now being made for the signing of the surrender terms at the earliest possible moment," President Truman said.

Wow! Just like that! After six long, terrible years, World War II was finally over. Josh couldn't believe his ears. *The war is over!*

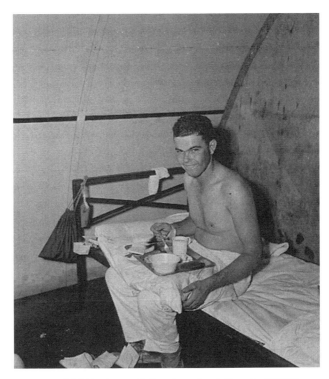

Actual USS Indianapolis Survivor Curtis Pace, S2c USNR

The hospital ward erupted in ear-shattering cheers and clapping. From the radio, Josh heard the sound of loud cheering, too. Survivors hugged one another.

Actual USS Indianapolis survivors: (L to R) Michael N. Kuryla, Jr., Cox. USNR; Robert M. McGwiggam, S1c USNR; and John H. Armistead, S2c, USNR

Some broke down and sobbed with relief. Even the badly injured raised their arms high in victory. Relief flooded Josh. Relief and joy. The Japanese had surrendered! World War II was finally over! It felt as if a huge weight had lifted from his chest.

Mike grinned and shouted for attention. "There's more. I came to tell you something," he said. "You men played a big part in bringing an end to this war. Remember the crate and canister the Marines loaded aboard in San Francisco?"

"Yeah," Josh nodded. He recalled the sinister, big steel canister in particular. And the heavily armed Marines that had guarded it.

"That crate contained the parts for the atomic bomb," Mike said. "The canister contained the radioactive plutonium."

Josh gaped. On that awful night when the torpedo struck, Pete had told him the USS Indianapolis was on a secret mission. So that was the mission. "The bomb was in the crates we had on the Indy? The crates we offloaded on Tinian Island?"

"Yeah. That bomb is what finally convinced Japan to surrender. The bomb ended the war."

"Wow."

The survivors of the USS Indianapolis shook their heads in amazement and began to talk loudly.

Josh was flooded with relief, but also something he couldn't quite understand. He was glad they'd won. Glad his dad's death had been avenged. But Lee's words stuck with him.

War is a terrible thing.

What Lee had said was true. So many lives had been lost. And how many soldiers were simply doing their duty to the country in which they'd been born? Why couldn't the world simply get along?

He sank back down on his bed and turned his thoughts toward home. He pictured Mom running to greet him, hugging him as hard as she could. Telling him she was furious with him for leaving, for joining the Navy. Then whispering she was proud of him for staying strong.

He pictured hugging his little brother. Showing Sammy his shark bite wounds. Teaching Sammy how to pitch a ball.

Thanksgiving's coming soon, he thought. *I can't wait to eat pumpkin pie!*

Thoughts whirled around in his head. World War II was over! It seemed it would never end. For what seemed an eternity, he thought he'd die in the ocean. Be eaten by sharks. Never come back at all.

But the war ended. He escaped the sharks. He was going home.

I'll do the best I can, he thought. I'll be there for Mom and Sammy, like Dad asked me to be. I'll try and fill in for him. He sighed. I wish Dad was here. I wish I could talk to him.

And then he realized that his dad was right there. In his head. In his heart. He'd heard his familiar, strong voice so many times as he'd struggled to stay alive. He could almost hear it now: *Hang in there, son. Don't quit.*

"I did it, Dad," he whispered. "*I did it. I hung in there. I didn't quit. I'm going home. I escaped.*"

THE END
Turn the page for survivor quotes, amazing facts about sharks, and more!

SURVIVOR QUOTES

"Every few minutes you'd see their fins - a dozen to two dozen fins in the water. They would come up and bump you. I was bumped a few times - you never know when they are going to attack you." - *Loel Dean Cox, Seaman Second Class*

"you could see the sharks eating your comrade." - *Granville Crane, Machinist's Mate Second Class*

"I didn't even have a life jacket, so I was swimming from midnight to 5:30 in the morning." - *Lyle Umenhoffer, Seaman First Class*

"It's much easier to die than it is to live. You've got to struggle to live." - *Edgar Harrell, Marine Corporal*

"When I was in the water and I wanted to give up, I saw my dad's face, and I wasn't going to give up for him. He brought me home." - *Dick Thelen, Seaman Second Class*

Eight hundred and seventy nine men lost their lives during those terrible five days.

Three hundred and sixteen men survived despite dire circumstances.

We salute and remember the brave sailors of the USS Indianapolis.

FAST FACTS ABOUT THE DISASTER

- The Indy sank on July 30, 1945, near the end of World War II
- It was struck by a Japanese torpedo
- It sank in only 12 minutes
- The survivors lacked the most basic survival gear. Many were without life jackets.
- They were rescued by chance when a PV-1 Ventura spotted them on routine patrol
- Total crewmen aboard: 1,195
- Total crewmen who went down with the ship: Approx. 300
- Initial survivor count in the ocean after sinking: Approx. 900
- Only 316 men survived

DID YOU KNOW?

The sinking of the USS Indianapolis resulted in the largest number of shark attacks on humans in history.

WHAT DREW SO MANY SHARKS?

Receptors on sharks' bodies pick up pressure changes and movement in the ocean. They can smell blood and urine from hundreds of yards away. With nine hundred men bobbing up and down in the waves—many injured and bleeding—sharks were naturally attracted to the area. Each day brought more sharks, all drawn by the survivors' blood and movements, as well as the scent of the dead.

WORLD'S DEADLIEST NAVAL DISASTER

The sinking of the USS Indianapolis also led to the greatest single loss of life at sea, from a single ship, in the history of the US Navy. The warship had just finished a trip to United States Army Air Force Base at Tinian to deliver parts of Little Boy, the first nuclear weapon ever used in combat, and was on her way to the Philippines to prepare for the invasion of Japan.

WHY DID NO ONE COME?

Questions remain today about why the rescue was delayed for so long. Originally, the Navy claimed no distress signal had been sent. However, the survivors knew SOS messages had gone out. In fact, *other ships reported receiving the distress signals!*

Here are two possible reasons:

1. The Navy might have thought the signals were fake because when Navy officials tried to contact the ship, they got no reply. Of course, the Indy couldn't reply. The warship had already gone down.

2. When Navy intelligence officials captured a Japanese submarine's signals claiming that it sank a warship along the Indy's route, they thought it was a hoax. Tragically, they believed the Japanese were trying to convince American rescue ships to come there so they could ambush and destroy them.

MORE COMMUNICATION PROBLEMS

At the time, only non-fighting ships (ones carrying

supplies and services) had to report their arrival to the Navy. Leyte Gulf had more than 1,500 ships reporting in preparation for the expected Japanese invasion.

The USS Indianapolis, however, was a fighting ship. A warship. So when it didn't show up on schedule, no one cared. It was none of their business. The ship was not required to check in.

TOP SECRET FAIL?

Some historians argue that communications between the USS Indianapolis and the Navy were minimized because the warship was on such a secret mission, carrying the atomic bomb.

MOVIES AND REPELLENTS

The horrific tales of shark attacks spurred new military research into shark repellents.

The tragic event inspired film makers and writers to tell the survivors' stories. There are numerous fiction and non-fiction accounts of the voyage, plus a 2007 television documentary film *Ocean of Fear: Worst Shark Attack Ever.* The movie, *USS Indianapolis, Men of Courage,* starring Nicolas Cage, premiered in 2016.

In a scene from the blockbuster movie *Jaws,* the character Quaint (Robert Shaw) recounts his experience surviving the sinking of the Indianapolis. Quint's harrowing story presents a true depiction of this strange and tragic event.

STRANGE AND FASCINATING SHARK FACTS

- Sharks are the apex predators of the ocean.
- Sharks have strong jaws, but they're not the strongest in the animal kingdom. Instead, they rely on slicing and head-shaking to rip off chunks of flesh
- Sharks have multiple rows of teeth. Some have two or three rows, some as many as fifteen.
- Sharks have excellent vision. Their night vision is better than that of cats or wolves.
- A shark's sense of smell is 10,000 times better than a human's. Sharks can smell a drop of blood in the water.
- Sharks have incredible hearing and can hear movement in the water from miles away.
- Sharks can detect electrical impulses, such as a human's beating heart.
- Unlike humans, whose jaws are fixed and can only open so wide, sharks can *unhinge* their jaws to grab and hang on to prey.
- Oceanic whitetip sharks are found in the deep open ocean. The species is known for feeding frenzies.
- Oceanic whitetip shark numbers are declining because they're the main ingredient in shark fin soup.
- The biggest shark is the whale shark. It can grow to over 66 in length.
- The fastest shark is the mako shark. It can reach speeds of 60 miles per hour when hunting.

- Sharks must keep moving or they'll drown.
- The odds of being attacked by a shark are low. More people are killed by cows and dogs. Most shark species generally do not attack humans.
- The most aggressive shark species are: the great white shark, the striped tiger shark and the bull shark.

LOWER YOUR CHANCES OF GETTING BIT

- Always swim in a group. Sharks usually attack lone individuals.
- Stay close to shore.
- Avoid the water at night, dawn, or dusk when sharks are more active, and better able to see you than you are to see them.
- Keep away from river mouths, particularly after it rains.
- Never enter the water if injured, bleeding, or menstruating. Sharks can smell and taste blood and track it from a long way away.
- Avoid wearing shiny jewelry. The reflected light looks like shining fish scales.
- Don't swim where sewage could be present. Sewage attracts bait fish and sharks.
- Stay away from fishing boats and anywhere people are fishing—particularly with bait.
- Leave immediately if a shark is seen.
- Avoid brightly colored clothes. Orange and yellow are said to attract sharks, as do contrasting colors.
- Avoid cloudy waters.
- Don't splash a lot or make seal noises.

- Keep pets out of the water.
- Avoid sandbars or steep drop-offs where sharks hang out.
- Remember that porpoises, seabirds, and turtles often eat the same foods as sharks. If turtles or fish behave erratically, leave the water.
- Don't touch a shark.
- If diving and approached by a shark, stay as still as possible. If you are carrying fish, release the fish.
- Report shark sightings to authorities

WHAT TO DO IF A SHARK ATTACKS

Do whatever you can to get away. Don't use your bare hands or feet if you can avoid it, as the shark's skin can scrape you.

If necessary, aim at the shark's delicate eyes, gills, or snout. Pound the shark in every way possible. Claw or jab at the eyes and gill openings. Shout for help.

Do not play dead.

If bitten, try to leave the water calmly and swiftly. While many sharks will not bite again, you cannot rule out a second attack.

Try to stop the bleeding. If surfing or bodyboarding, use the leash as a tourniquet.

Get immediate medical attention.

HOW TO HELP A SHARK BITE VICTIM

- Control the bleeding by applying firm pressure, by tightly wrapping the injury, or with a tourniquet.
- Remove the person from the water as soon as possible

- Protect victim from cold by wrapping in blanket or towels to minimize heat loss.
- Do not move victim unnecessarily.
- Call 911 for immediate medical help.

A FINAL NOTE

Sharks are dangerous but we must remember that the ocean is their home. They play an important role in keeping the oceans in balance. The United States is a leader in promoting the global conservation and management of sharks. To learn more, visit:

https://www.fisheries.noaa.gov/national/international-affairs/shark-conservation

USS INDIANAPOLIS • FURTHER READING
Left for Dead by Pete Nelson
In Harm's Way by Doug Stanton
Fatal Voyage by Dan Kurzman

STUDY GUIDE
Download this book's
reading comprehension guides at
http://bit.ly/sharkescape

How Hunter Scott, a 12-year-old boy cleared Captain McVay's Name

Charles Butler McVay was the USS Indianapolis's commanding officer when she was torpedoed and lost in action in 1945. He survived, only to be court-martialed by the US Navy and found guilty for the disaster!

This angered many survivors. They believed McVay was not at fault.

Instead, many believed the US Navy was using McVay as a scapegoat to cover up their own messy mistake. After all, the Navy *didn't even go searching* for the survivors! Over eleven-hundred men were left to die at sea. The last three hundred still alive were saved only because of a chance flyover. How could McVay be responsible for that?

Hunter Scott, a 12-year-old Pensacola, Florida student wrote about the USS Indianapolis for a National History Day project. During his research, Hunter formed the conclusion that the Navy had unjustly convicted Captain McVay. Although decades had passed and Captain McVay was no longer alive, Hunter wanted to act. He was horrified by the shameful court-martial of an innocent man who'd fought for this country. Hunter decided to raise awareness about this miscarriage of justice and try to overturn McVay's sentence.

Hunter's project won first prize at his school and first place at the county-finals. In the 1997 state finals, however, his project was disqualified. Why? His display of three-ring note-books was ruled an infraction!

Hunter felt bad. He'd failed to repair Captain McVay's legacy and had disappointed the survivors who were counting on him. *Never give up*, the sailors, now in their seventies, said. Hunter was sure they knew all about never giving up! He decided to keep fighting. But he was just a twelve-year-old kid trying to reverse a fifty-year-old injustice.

Luckily, Pensacola is a Navy city. Hunter's determined efforts attracted media attention. Pensacola newspapers ran articles about Hunter, then TV station NBC took up the story.

This is a middle school history project that seeks to correct history, said the newspapers and TV anchors.

At a USS Indianapolis reunion, the survivors welcomed Hunter. Adrian Marks, the pilot who'd risked his lift to land in twelve-foot waves and pluck out the wounded was there. When Hunter told them that he'd interviewed nearly one hundred and fifty Indy survivors and had reviewed eight hundred documents, the men were stunned.

Kimo McVay, Captain McVay's son, had been trying to clear his dad's name for over fifty years. He said Hunter had gotten further with his research than he and the survivors had in half a century!

Excited, Hunter, Kimo McVay, and a group of survivors banded together and headed for Washington DC to lobby Congress. They hoped somebody could overturn or reverse the guilty verdict. To do so, they'd have to move a bill through Congress, a difficult and time-consuming operation.

With the support of his Congressman, Hunter appeared before the US Congress, alongside the USS Indianapolis survivors. Hunter explained to the senators why McVay should be exonerated. The government was unaware of many facts he'd uncovered in his research.

Here's one example: the Navy received the Indy's desperate SOS signals—but Navy officials believed the SOS signals were a Japanese hoax. That's why they didn't respond! They didn't even bother to check to see if the ship was missing.

After years of efforts to clear Captain McVay's name, the survivors, Kimo McVay, and Hunter Scott finally succeeded. In October 2000, the United States Congress passed a resolution that McVay's record should reflect that "he is exonerated for the loss of the USS Indianapolis." President Clinton also signed the resolution.

In July 2001, Secretary of the Navy Gordon R. England ordered McVay's official Navy record purged of all wrongdoing.

Hunter went on to study economics and physics at the University of North Carolina at Chapel Hill on a Naval ROTC scholarship. In 2017, Lieutenant Hunter Scott, USN, became a Naval Aviator on the flight deck of USS Bonhomme Richard. He has shown what one determined child can do by never giving up.

I ESCAPED

THE

GRIZZLY MAZE

THE BESTSELLING KIDS SURVIVAL SERIES

ELLIE CROWE + SCOTT PETERS

CHAPTER ONE

THE GRIZZLY MAZE
KATMAI PENINSULA, ALASKA
OCTOBER 2003

Fifteen-year-old Cody shivered. Yikes, this place was cold. Out in the howling night, the wind shrieked and rain poured down. He wrapped his arms tighter around his chest and tried to catch some sleep.

Something rustled. Like a jack-in-the-box, Cody sat up. "What was that?"

A few feet away, his cousin Samantha tensed. "Don't know."

Then, like something out of a nightmare, the tent shuddered and a monster-sized head burst through the tent flap. Black eyes. Giant bear snout. Long teeth. Steaming breath reeking of fish and blood.

Terrified, Cody shouted. "Get away! Go! Get lost!"
Time stood still.

The grizzly watched him. Eyes cold. Focused. Strings of saliva dripped from its powerful jaws.

"Get out!" Samantha shrieked. "Get *out!*"

Her screams worked. The monster head disappeared.

"Whoa," Samantha breathed.

"Stay still," Cody hissed.

"I think it's gone," Samantha whispered. "I almost had a heart attack."

"Me too." Cody let out a nervous snort. "That was crazy. Too bad you didn't get a photo."

Without warning, a massive paw smashed through the flap.

CHAPTER TWO

CALIFORNIA
MAY 2003
FOUR MONTHS EARLIER

Cody studied the grizzly posters in the Waldorf School corridor. "That documentary was so cool. Check out the size of those bears!"

"Yeah." Fifteen-year-old Samantha's blond ponytail bobbed as she nodded. "Massive! Amazing how that guy, Timothy Treadwell, isn't scared of them. Did you see how they followed him like big, furry dogs?"

"Can you imagine?" Cody eyed the bears' sharp teeth and claws. "But like he said, if he showed any weakness, they'd tear him to pieces."

"Aw," Samantha said. "They didn't look dangerous. He was right up close to them."

"Ha, you wouldn't say that if you got lost in that place he

called the grizzly maze. What if a humongous bear came barreling down a tunnel right at you?

Samantha said, "First, I'd take a picture. Then, I'd scream."

Cody laughed. "Treadwell is living with the bears again this fall. It would be cool if we could visit Gramps' cabin in Kodiak. Maybe we could check out the grizzly maze. We might even be able to talk to Treadwell. Get him to show us around, maybe he'll even let us see his bears."

"We'd never be allowed to miss school. And who's going to pay for it?"

Cody thought for a minute. "I have that money that my grandma left me. I bet Mom and Dad would let me spend it."

"All of your savings? Are you sure?"

"It would be a once-in-a-lifetime trip. And the science fair is coming up. We could do a project on protecting grizzlies. Treadwell is right—we should protect animals like that from poachers. We could visit the maze, interview him while we're there, and take pictures and everything. That would be a great project."

"We'd have to set it up with Tim Treadwell first, though, don't you think?"

"No, I mean, we can see the maze for ourselves. We can document how the place works. And then we'll drop into his camp. It has to be a pretty established place. I bet he'll be excited to see two students interested in his work. It will be even better if it's a surprise. He'll be super impressed."

"My mom and dad *are* into eco-warriors," Samantha said. "Treadwell definitely counts. They might go for it."

Cody said, "So, should we? Go for it?"

"Yes! Plus, I'll get to photograph native birds for my portfolio. And I bet Gramps would be up for visitors."

Cody grinned. "Alaska, here we come."

CHAPTER THREE

KODIAK ISLAND,
ALASKA
OCTOBER 2003

The Alaska Airlines plane circled over Kodiak airport and landed smoothly. Weary from the long flight from Los Angeles, Cody and Samantha grabbed their backpacks from baggage control.

They walked out into the terminal. Cody spotted a tall guy with flyaway blond hair at the Alaska Airlines ticket counter. The man wore jeans, sunglasses, a camo-print bandana, and a black leather jacket and was talking to the ticket agent.

"Look," Cody said. "Over there! It's Tim Treadwell."

Samantha stared. "Wow! Is he just arriving, too? Talk about luck! Let's ask him for tips on the best places to see bears. Then we can casually mention we'd love to visit the grizzly maze—with him if possible."

"I like it. Stay cool, though," Cody said. "Not like a fangirl."

Samantha glared. "As if. You're the one fangirling."

"It's true," Cody said with a grin.

As they neared the ticket counter, the agent and Treadwell began arguing. Treadwell looked furious and the agent looked apologetic.

Treadwell's voice grew louder. "There's no way we're paying that. Highway robbery, that's what it is."

"I'm sorry, sir, if you want to leave Alaska today, that's the ticket price."

Treadwell was trying to leave? Cody was confused. He'd read that Treadwell was supposed to stay through the end of the month. What a bummer. They should have planned this better, not just assumed everything would work out. What had he been thinking?

Treadwell turned to the blond-haired woman at his side. Despite her high-heeled leather boots, she came to well below his shoulders.

"Come on, Amie," Treadwell said. "Let's get out of here. We'll go back to the maze and camp again. Ticket prices go down next week. We'll leave then." He grabbed his bags and headed for the exit.

The woman, Amie, grabbed her bags, tucked her long hair behind her ears, and hurried after him.

Cody was sorry for Treadwell having his plans ruined. Still, what a relief! They'd come all this way hoping to see him, and there he was. Cody shot Samantha an excited look and followed.

"In a way, it's good that we can't leave," Treadwell was saying. "Downy may be back at the maze. I'm worried about her. I haven't seen her all summer."

"I don't want to go back, Tim," Amie said. "It's too late in the season. There were a lot more bears, and those new alpha males were really aggressive."

"We'll be fine." Treadwell marched out of the terminal, looked up at the blue sky, and laughed. "The weather's glorious. No sign of winter. No need to worry. We'll grab our tents out of storage, pick up a week's supplies from Kodiak Sports, and get a floatplane out of here."

Cody was working up his courage to approach Treadwell when a mud-splattered jeep roared up, half-skidding out of control.

A familiar voice rang out. "Cody! Hey Cody! Come on. I can't park here, dude. Hurry up!"

Cody groaned. "What on earth is cousin Matt doing here?"

"No clue," Samantha muttered, sounding annoyed.

Their eighteen-year-old cousin had his usual wolverine look. Hairy. Greasy. Skinny arms covered in tattoos. At least instead of his usual scowl, Matt was grinning.

"Hey squirt, am I glad to see you," Matt called. "Gramps is on my case twenty-four-seven. It'll be good to have someone else he can pick on."

Cody winced. He hated being called squirt, and—cousin or not—he didn't like Matt. He had bad memories of Matt holding him upside down and shaking his lunch money and GI Joe out of his pockets. Cody hadn't enjoyed the head-in-the-toilet experience, either. Fortunately, he'd put on some muscle and grown a few inches. He'd be able to give as good as he got. But he still preferred to avoid Matt.

"I didn't know he'd be here," Samantha whispered as they headed toward the waiting jeep. "I guess Aunt Lucy is hoping Gramps can straighten him out. Did you hear he went joyriding in a neighbor's car and crashed into a streetlight?"

"Yep." Cody shot a frustrated glance toward Treadwell. The famous outdoorsman was hurrying toward a taxi. "Looks like we lost our chance to talk to him."

"We were so close!" Samantha said.

"Get a move on, dudes," Matt shouted.

Cody and Samantha climbed into the jeep.

Cody had an idea. "Hey Matt, you see that guy getting into the cab? That's Tim Treadwell."

"Okaaay?" Matt said. "Why should I care?"

"Just listen for a minute," Cody said. "He spent the last twelve summers living with grizzlies in Alaska. He's headed to Kodiak Sports to stock up so he can go back and camp there. Samantha and I want to ask if he'll take us."

Matt raised his eyebrows. "Huh! You know what? I saw that guy on the Discovery Channel. He's famous. I bet I could make some money if I got pictures of him with those massive bears. That'll be way better than being at Gramps. I'll come with you."

Cody grimaced. *Over my dead body.* "Do you know where Kodiak Sports is?"

"Sure. And I know a shortcut." Matt revved the engine and took off down a gravel road. "This thing can do seventy on dirt."

A wide-eyed pedestrian leaped out of the way as Matt sideswiped a garbage can.

"Watch where you're going, sucker!" Matt yelled.

With a screech of brakes, he skidded into a sports store parking lot. A stuffed grizzly stood in the window. Inside, bear skins hung on the walls. A bear skull lamp glowed. At the counter, three hunters discussed ammunition.

There was no sign of Tim Treadwell.

Matt wandered over to study the guns. Cody and Samantha approached the balding store owner.

"What's the best place to see grizzlies around here?" Cody said.

"Not many bears around Kodiak now. There's been a drought—hardly any berries, nothing for the bears to eat. Most grizzlies have headed north to feed on salmon."

In a tight voice, Samantha said, "Are those men going to hunt bears?"

"Sure," the store owner said. "They're off into the back-country."

"That's awful." Samantha wrinkled her upturned nose. "Grizzlies should be protected."

The store owner stiffened. "You want to put me out of business?"

Sensing an argument, Cody stepped in. "Have you heard of the grizzly maze?"

The man nodded. "Yep."

"Do you have a map of the area?" Cody asked.

"Maps are over there. The grizzly maze is on the Katmai Peninsula."

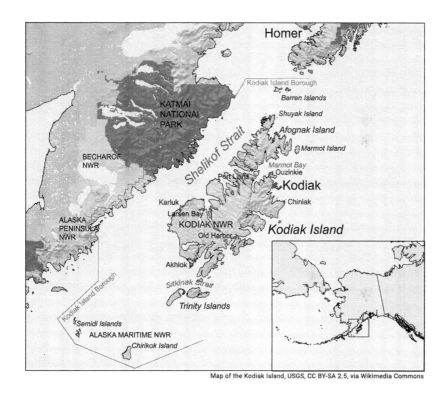

Map of the Kodiak Island, USGS, CC BY-SA 2.5, via Wikimedia Commons

The store owner turned to Samantha and, in a kinder voice, said, "Hunting's not allowed in Katmai National Park. Besides, there are over thirty-thousand grizzlies up there, miss, so you don't need to fret about them."

"Thirty-thousand," Samantha said. "That's incredible."

"Certainly is."

Cody said, "What's the best bush pilot company to fly us

up to the grizzly maze?" He'd researched a few but was curious to hear what the store owner had to say.

"They're all good. I don't recommend it, though, this late in the season. Place is dangerous right now. The bears are fattening up for their long winter hibernation and what with the drought, food is scarce."

"We know someone who goes there," Samantha said. "And he's going there now."

The store owner laughed. "Oh, I see. You met Tim Treadwell, did you?"

"Sort of," Cody said. "Do you know him?"

"Yep. But I doubt even Tim is going to the maze now." He chuckled, his rugged face crinkling. "Then again, I wouldn't put it past him. Tim is a great guy and he loves the grizzlies. But he believes they're his friends." His eyes darkened. "They're not."

A hunter who was listening in laughed. "Treadwell is just beggin' for trouble. Bears are wild animals, not friends. One wrong move and they'll tear you apart."

The store owner turned as the door opened. "Well, you're in luck, you can ask Treadwell all about it yourselves. Here he comes now."

CHAPTER FOUR

KODIAK ISLAND, ALASKA

Samantha's eyes widened as Tim Treadwell and his girlfriend breezed into the store. "They look like movie stars," she whispered.

The store owner rushed to greet the couple. "I thought you went home to Malibu for the winter, Tim."

Treadwell, tanned skin glowing from the cold, shook his head. "Didn't work out. We're flying up to the maze for another week."

"Bit late in the season, isn't it?"

"It's the toughest, most exciting month," Treadwell said. "Violent storms. Mobs of hungry bears."

The store owner looked worried. "Sounds dangerous."

"For some. Not me." Treadwell began filling a shopping basket with canned food. "The giant males are back at the maze. And lots of beautiful, sweet bears, too. I'm stopping poachers who shouldn't be hunting up there—my work is a success."

The store owner held up a spray can. "Need some bear spray?"

Cody noted the picture on the bear spray label—a ferocious grizzly poised to attack.

"Nah." Treadwell snorted. "Have you seen what that stuff does to bears? Why should they suffer for me?"

Amie touched Treadwell's arm. "We could get a few of those warning flares."

"Don't need them."

Amie said, "I'm scared of those big alphas that just arrived. We don't know them and they freak me out."

"Aw." Treadwell smiled down at her. "Those big males won't hurt you. They're just angry because they have no berries." He shook his fist at the roof. "God! Allah! We need more rain! Do you hear me? The bears are starving. Rain! We need it!"

Amie said, "This is the last time I'm going to the maze, Tim. I mean it."

Cody tried to think of something to say. This didn't seem the moment to talk to the eco-warrior.

Samantha nudged him.

Reluctantly, he stepped forward. "Um. Excuse me, sir, Mr. Treadwell. Could I talk to you for a moment?"

Treadwell turned. "Sure."

"My cousin and I saw the Discovery Channel documentary about you. It was great."

"Thanks," Treadwell said.

"We joined your group, the *Grizzly People*," Cody said. "We want to help protect grizzlies from illegal poachers."

"I appreciate it," Treadwell said. "Grizzlies are magnificent animals. Don't you think so, Amie?"

Amie gave a reluctant smile. "Tim says you haven't lived until you've bathed in a lake with grizzlies."

Cody grinned. "I sure haven't done that. But my cousin and I would love to go to the grizzly maze. Would that be possible, sir?"

"Sorry, guys. The grizzly maze is too dangerous for kids like you. Particularly now."

"Definitely too dangerous," Amie said. "Every bear in Katmai Peninsula is there."

"We'd stay out of your way," Cody said.

Matt chose that moment to show up. "We're not scared of grizzlies," he said. Then he laughed.

Treadwell eyed Matt up and down. "Not going to happen." He gathered up his purchases. As he and Amie went out the door, he waved at the store owner. "See you sometime in October if I don't perish."

Matt scowled and called out, "Poser!"

The door slammed.

Samantha rolled her eyes. "That helped."

"I don't care what that dude thinks," Matt said. "It's a free country. I'll go where I want. Hey, do either of you guys have credit cards?"

"Yeah, Dad authorized a credit card for me," Cody said. He didn't add that he'd be paying his dad back with his savings. "Why?"

"Duh! We need camping supplies."

"But Treadwell told us we can't go to the maze," Samantha said.

"He doesn't own the place," Matt said. "Now, start shopping. I'll get two pop-up tents; you grab sleeping bags and snacks and stuff. Enough for three days."

Samantha flashed Cody a worried look. "You're not seriously thinking of going up there, are you? After what Treadwell said?"

He sighed. "No. If he says it's a bad idea, I'm sure he's right. Bummer, though."

A hunter wandered over. "No need to go to the maze to see grizzlies. We got bears right here on Kodiak Island. Just head over to the Visitors Center—they'll give you directions where to camp."

"Great, thanks!" Cody said.

Camping would still be an adventure, even if they weren't with the world-famous bear expert. They'd make it work for the project.

If only Matt would lose interest now that they were staying in the area. Matt, though, got busy grabbing tents.

Cody filled his cart with a knife, matches, flashlight, cook pot, three sleeping bags, waterproof boots, fishing line, and a small ax. In the food aisle he added trail mix, granola bars, cans of Vienna sausages, sour-cream-and-onion Pringles, a water purifier, and a few bottles of water.

The bear spray was expensive. Cody studied the price, returned it to the shelf, then grabbed it again. Better safe than sorry.

He snuck a look at the stuffed grizzly in the store window. Wow, that was one huge bear. It stood nine feet high. Poor guy—doomed to stare out at a parking lot forever. In most places, grizzlies had been hunted to extinction. It was good to hear they were making a comeback in Katmai Park. But Treadwell said that illegal poachers were going after them. Cody's science project was worthwhile. He'd learn what he could in Kodiak and find a way to interview Treadwell by phone or email.

Nearby, Matt pulled the largest hunting rifle from the rack.

"We don't need that," Cody said. "I'm buying bear spray."

"You'll thank me later, kiddo," Matt said. "When I save your life."

Again, Cody hesitated. He was paying for all this stuff. Better safe than sorry.

The store owner rang up the supplies. "Remember, no one's allowed to camp near bears. In fact, even Katmai National Park has a new rule, a five-day limit at any camping spot. And tents must be kept at least a mile away from bears." He grinned. "Some rangers call it the Treadwell Rule."

"Why?" Samantha said.

"They reckon he bothers the bears."

"How could he bother the bears?" Cody said. "He's trying to protect them."

"You'd have to ask the rangers."

"I can't wait to see those grizzlies," Matt said. "The bigger, the better."

The store owner frowned. "Don't be like Treadwell. It's not a case of *if* something will happen to Tim. It's a case of *when*. He thinks they're his friends. Grizzlies aren't humans in bear costumes. Remember that."

CHAPTER FIVE

KODIAK ISLAND, ALASKA

Cody, Samantha, and Matt headed out of the store loaded down with gear. They jumped up into the jeep.

Samantha said, "How far is it to Gramps' cabin?"

"It's in the middle of nowhere," Matt said. "We'll call Gramps to say we're going camping, and we'll catch him in a couple of days."

"It's kind of late to find a campsite," Cody said, eyeing the darkening sky.

Matt snorted. "Who said we'd set up tonight? You've got a credit card. We'll check into the Best Western."

Cody made a quick calculation in his head. Now that he wasn't paying for flights up to the grizzly maze, he had money to spare. "Okay, we can do one night."

Samantha's eyes lit up. "Cool. Tomorrow, we'll go to the Visitors' Center and talk to a guide."

Hotel guests crammed the Kodiak Best Western's large

129

lobby. A huge bearskin covered the floor near the stone fire-place, and a bear skull hung on the wall. Hunters, anglers, and tourists, all bubbling and animated, filled the restaurant.

Excited to be in such an unusual place, Cody munched down fish and chips and watched boats bobbing on the dark blue marina. Samantha snapped photos of swooping seagulls. Matt was unusually quiet, staring out the large windows. Uneasy, Cody wondered what he was plotting.

Up in the hotel room, Matt claimed one of the two beds. Cody told Samantha to take the other one, and he called the front desk for a cot. Exhausted, he flopped onto it.

The sounds of screeching seagulls and grunting sea lions mingled with Matt's snores, and Cody fell asleep fast.

He woke to find Matt gone. Samantha ordered pancakes

from room service. Cody felt antsy. He wanted to get over to the Visitor's Center.

As he licked the last drop of maple syrup off his fork, Matt stomped in, grinning.

"Get dressed, hurry, we leave in an hour." Matt waved tickets at them. "We're going to the grizzly maze."

Cody stared. "You talked to Tim Treadwell? He's taking us?"

"Nope. We have our own ride. A floatplane. The flight to Katmai Peninsula leaves in thirty minutes."

Samantha pushed her bangs out of her eyes. "Wow! How are we doing that?"

"Easy. I got the front desk to book the flights." Matt handed a credit card to Cody. "Here's your card. I borrowed it."

Cody stared. "I never said you could use my credit card. That's more than my savings, and Dad said I could only go over it for emergencies."

Matt laughed. "Seemed like an emergency to me. Get a move on. I've got this whole thing under control!"

Cody grabbed the tickets. Matt had gotten the worst deal possible. "I can't do that. These cost a fortune. I have to check with my dad."

"No point," Matt said. "No refunds on the tickets. Get a move on. This is going to be a blast."

Samantha said, "But it's not safe."

"Don't be a baby," Matt said. "We're only going for one night. And if it gets sketchy, I'll call the pilot to pick us up. Now let's go!"

CHAPTER SIX

KATMAI NATIONAL PARK

The floatplane's engine built from a low grumble to a steady thud. Cody zipped up his windbreaker and fastened his seatbelt.

He tried to swallow his guilt and resentment and focused on being excited instead. They were actually going to Katmai National Park! He'd work as a lifeguard next summer to repay Mom and Dad.

The plane roared into the cloudy sky and the marina dropped away. Below, the ocean glittered like rippled steel. Wind whipped at the surface and a pod of whales emerged from the white caps.

"Storm's moving in," the pilot shouted over the engine noise. "Hang on, it's going to be a bumpy ride."

The small plane shuddered, and Cody held tight to the armrests. A violent gust tossed the seaplane upward. His stomach lurched.

"That's Katmai Peninsula," the pilot shouted.

Below lay boggy tidal flats and dark forests. Snow blanketed the jagged mountain peaks, and Cody spotted two blue lakes enclosed by high mountains. A river connected them, and the nearest lake emptied into the ocean through a narrow gap.

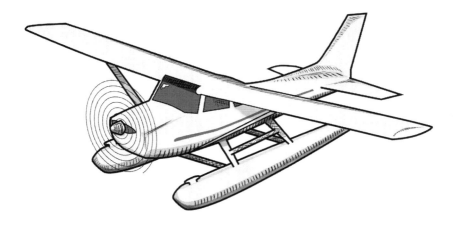

The pilot circled and descended. "Kaflia Lake," she said. "There are two lakes, an upper and a lower. I'll set us down in the ocean near the mouth of the lower lake."

Cody turned to Matt. "We don't know which lake Treadwell camps at."

Matt shrugged. "Who cares? We don't need Treadwell."

As the plane descended, Cody grabbed his binoculars and searched for Treadwell's camp without luck.

Below, dark slivers of spawning salmon leaped through the waves. He gaped when he saw a massive grizzly grabbing for fish with its claws. Then he saw another and another. Whoa. This place was unreal.

With a hissing thrum, the floatplane landed well clear of the bears. They taxied through the shallow water to the shore.

The pilot stood up and took off her headphones. "Everybody okay?"

"Yes!" Samantha beamed. "That was amazing!"

"No." Matt hurled all over Samantha's new boots.

The smell was horrible.

With a stoic expression, Samantha cleaned up with a bottle of water and some napkins.

"Not my fault," Matt said and glared at the pilot.

"So, you're camping with Tim Treadwell for a few days?" the pilot asked.

"Yeah," Matt said.

The pilot squinted at the creek around a mile away. "There're a lot of grizzlies over there. I don't like leaving you kids. What time is Treadwell meeting you?"

"Well, he's not—" Cody began.

"He's on his way," Matt interrupted. "We'll be fine. We've been here before. Lots of times."

Cody gaped at Matt. *Liar!*

"Okay." The pilot gave Matt a satellite phone. "This is included in our flight package—call us if there's an emergency. Just a heads up, though, sat phones are expensive. You break it, you pay for it. And stay away from that grizzly-packed creek."

"We will, thanks," Cody said. He focused his binoculars on the massive animals. His heart beat faster. Those guys were as big as Buicks. "What do you guess those grizzlies weigh?"

"More than a thousand pounds," the pilot said. "You'll only spot enormous ones like that out here in Katmai. Like I said, steer clear. There are some new aggressive alpha males in the pack. They're all fattening up for winter. Don't draw their attention."

Wide-eyed, Samantha swallowed hard.

"Thanks for the warning," Cody said. "Where are the park rangers?"

"There're no rangers here now," the pilot said. "The park advises tourists not to come when the bears are fattening up. I'm not sure why Treadwell invited you. If he doesn't turn up by four, call me and I'll come back for you."

"Thanks. We'll contact you if we don't find Treadwell," Cody said, and he meant it.

"Right," the pilot said. "I'll be listening for your call." She climbed into the cockpit and slammed the door.

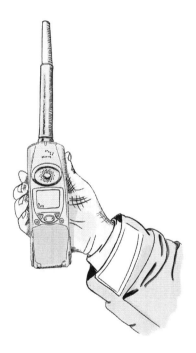

Matt muttered, "We know what we're doing and I have a rifle."

They waded to shore through the icy water. Cody was glad he'd bought rain boots, though they felt a size too big. He kept a wary eye on the grizzlies, even though they were a mile away.

Over there, tangled brambles and alder trees with skeletal, spiky branches stretched away from the lakeshore. That must be the gnarled woods known as the grizzly maze. How had Treadwell described it? As a labyrinth of tunnels made by bears.

Now that Cody saw it for real, it wasn't like some nature movie. It was scary and he couldn't believe Treadwell wandered around in there.

"Let's pitch the tents," Matt said.

"Not till Treadwell's plane lands," Cody replied. "Otherwise, we're leaving at four. I'm surprised he's not here yet."

"Coward," Matt muttered.

"Let's eat something. Then I want to take notes and make some sketches for the project," Cody said.

"Sound good," Samantha agreed. "I'll unpack my zoom lens. I should be able to get some great photos."

Sitting on his bag, Cody crunched Pringles. He could smell the sour cream and onion on his fingers. Would it attract bears? He rubbed his smelly hands with wet sand.

He studied the grizzlies through his binoculars. They hadn't come closer and weren't looking this way. Still, they were fast—with a powerful sense of smell.

He shoved the empty Pringles can into his backpack. "No food lying around, okay?"

Matt laughed. "Chill out, will you?"

Cody said, "Hey, grizzlies killed two girls in Glacier National Park because tourists left garbage around, and the bears smelled it."

Matt laughed. "You worry too much."

"It's not worry, it's common sense. They're wild animals,

and this is their habitat. We're just visitors, and we have to respect that."

"Blah blah blah," Matt said.

"Really? What would you do if a grizzly came right at us?" Cody said.

"I'd run," Samantha said.

"Running is the worst thing to do," Cody said. "A grizzly can run forty miles an hour. That's like a car."

Samantha shot him a mischievous smile. "Yeah. But I'd only have to run faster than you."

Cody rolled his eyes, laughing. "Great, I'll keep that in mind."

Then he took out his notebook, she set up her camera, and they both got to work.

CHAPTER SEVEN

KATMAI NATIONAL PARK

An hour later, the grizzlies were still foraging in the creek.

"The tide's going out," Cody said. "I want to check out the sea floor. Anyone coming?"

"In a minute." Samantha had her eyes glued to the white trumpeter swans cruising the lake. "Ooh, look! That swan's taking off. Check out the wings. Those must be five feet across."

"Later." Matt yawned.

"If you're going down to the ocean, take the rifle," Samantha said.

Matt got to his feet. "No way. It's my rifle." He lunged, putting Cody in a fake-friendly headlock.

Cody stepped hard on Matt's foot. He'd grown six inches since he'd last seen his cousin. *Not so easy to headlock me now, huh?*

"I don't want the rifle," Cody said.

Notebook in one hand and ax in the other, Cody hiked down the sloping dunes. The low tide had exposed miles of rippling sea floor. Tiny pools of water glistened, caught between the rocks. They brimmed with sea creatures. He stomped through a patch of seagrass, rounded a massive wet boulder, and gasped.

A cream-colored mother bear with two cubs rummaged in the sand, scooping up clams.

Cody backed away and ducked behind the boulder, heart pounding, then took a careful peek.

Incredible!

He knew mother bears were dangerous and that he should leave. But the bear was beautiful, and the roly-poly cubs were so cute—balls of wiggly fur, tumbling, wrestling, and munching on clams. He crouched lower and did a rough sketch, making notes in the margin.

- *mother bear has good coat but thin overall*
- *both cubs stay close, one copies mother bear's digging*
- *mother sniffs sand to locate more clams, she clearly smells them through the dirt*
- *she crushes whole clam in her mouth and spits out the shell, like eating sunflower seeds!*

A red fox darted between the mother bear's legs and grabbed a clam. Cody muffled a surprised laugh at the gutsy fox.

Wait till everyone at school hears about this.

Matt might have acted like a jerk, but Cody was suddenly glad they'd come. No wonder Treadwell loved this place. The grizzlies were unreal; no wonder he wanted to protect them.

A thrumming sound broke the silence. A floatplane leveled and descended, coming to a halt in the ocean shallows.

Awesome! Treadwell was here, everything was going to work out. Cody stowed his notebook and prepared to wave his arms.

But it wasn't Treadwell. Instead, two bearded men in canvas jackets and waterproof pants climbed out onto the floats. Both men held shotguns.

Poachers!

The mother grizzly reared up. Muscles rippling, eyes narrowed, it focused on the poachers.

Horrified, Cody watched as a poacher aimed and fired.

The grizzly reeled sideways. Then the mother and cubs loped away. If only he'd taken the rifle, he could fire it into the air and scare off the men.

Instead, all he could do was wave his ax wildly. "That's illegal! Get away from here!"

The poacher whirled around. "What the heck? Mind your own business, kid!"

"I just contacted the rangers," Cody yelled. "They're on their way."

The poachers scowled.

Meanwhile, the bears had disappeared.

The poachers shook their heads and climbed back into the floatplane. Cody sighed in relief as it rose into the sky.

A hundred feet away, the cubs darted out of the seagrass, shaking like frightened puppies. Eyes confused, they wandered toward Cody, wailing. Where was the mother bear? Had she been injured? He crouched and dug up a clam, stomped on it, and heard the satisfying crack of a shell.

He tossed the clam to the cubs. "Here you are, little guys."

Too late, he remembered you weren't supposed to feed wild animals.

A dark shape rose from the seagrass. Oops. The mother bear was right there. Cody dropped down fast. He didn't dare move. Shivering, he lay flat for what seemed ages. Finally, the mother bear went back to sniffing and digging for clams.

Something prodded his boot. Muscles spring-loaded, he turned.

The fox was trying to get its teeth into the sole that had smashed the clam. Smiling, Cody moved his foot and the fox darted away.

A faint, cracking sound echoed from the distant surf. A massive bear was feasting on the beached carcass of a killer whale. Yikes. Paws holding the skull, the grizzly gnawed into it fast and hard.

If that bear got hold of me, it could bite through my leg bone like a toothpick. Good thing it's far away.

Still, he was spooked and crept away fast. He was nearing dry sand when he heard a scream.

"Bear!" Matt's voice was shrill.

Before Cody could work out what was happening, Matt charged down the dunes right at him. A brown grizzly with a powerfully muscled body followed at a gallop.

Face frantic, breathing hard, Matt raced right by Cody, heading toward the sea.

The grizzly slowed.

Keen, dark eyes focused on Cody.

Cody stepped back. One of his too-large boots caught on a rock and he stumbled. Down he went, on to his knee. His mind seized up.

I'm going to die.

"Help!" Matt screamed. "Help!"

The grizzly pivoted and zoned in on Matt.

This is my chance. Blind with fear, Cody ran in the opposite direction.

Matt shrieked. "Help me! Cody, help me!"

Cody slowed. All he wanted to do was keep running. Why should he risk his life to save that jerk?

"Help, Cody! Help!" Matt slipped and landed on his butt with a splash.

Cody gritted his teeth and forced himself to shout and wave the ax. The bear turned halfway between the cousins.

We're going to be ripped to shreds.

The grizzly held its ground.

Cody stomped hard. "Get! You get!"

It was two against one. But the odds were still in favor of the grizzly.

"Get! Now!" Cody shouted, spinning the ax. Treadwell's words in the documentary pounded in his brain. *Make the bear believe you are more powerful than he is.*

They faced off—Cody wielding the ax round and round, yelling in a deep voice, the bear moving forward with fake charges and then retreating.

Just don't trip on another rock, whatever you do. Remember your flipping boots are too big. Do not trip!

Cody shouted again, his throat hoarse. To his utter amazement, the bear turned and loped off.

"I guess that one was a vegetarian." Cody's voice shook so hard he could barely speak. "What were you doing? You almost got us killed."

"Relax, dude. Don't be a drama queen." Matt talked big, but he was pale with shock.

"I'm calling that pilot for a ride out. Right now," Cody said.

"Whatever." Matt got to his feet, his pants dripping wet.

Cody held out his hand. "Where's the sat phone?"

"I have it." Hands shaking, Matt fiddled with the thing. He scowled. "Piece of junk. There's no reception."

"It worked at the tent," Cody said.

Trembling, Matt stumbled through the waves toward shore, holding the sat phone high. "Hello, hello, come in, come in," he yelled, hands shaking. "Hello. Hello. Anyone there?"

Matt collided with a rock and lost his footing.

Cody grabbed Matt's jacket.

Matt reached for Cody to steady himself.

And dropped the sat phone into the sea.

CHAPTER EIGHT

Katmai National Park

Cody dove for the sat phone. He dried it on his shirt and shook it. "Dead."

"No problem," Matt said. "It'll work again if we bury it in sand."

"Sand! Give me a break."

"Sure, it will. I dropped my phone in the toilet and I put it in rice, and it worked."

"Sand won't work."

"This is all your fault," Matt said. "If you hadn't tripped and grabbed my jacket, I never would have dropped the sat phone."

"I didn't grab your jacket because I tripped. I was trying to save you."

"Dude, you know you totally made me fall," Matt yelled. "You can't even run in those dumb rain boots."

"Cody!" Samantha shouted, running across the sand.

"Matt!" She hugged them both. "That was close. Call the pilot. I don't want to stay here another minute."

"The sat phone's fried," Cody said.

"Fried? It can't be. Let me see." Samantha shook the sat phone and rubbed it with her sweater. "Oh no. How are we going to get back? The pilot will think we're with Tim Treadwell. We're stuck."

Cody said, "We have to find Treadwell. He must have landed before we got here."

"We would have seen him," Samantha said.

"Maybe he's at the upper lake. He must be."

"Maybe."

Cody said, "We'll go there and get help."

Eager, Samantha nodded. "We'll be safe with him. He knows what he's doing."

Matt snorted. "Give me a break. You have to hike through those grizzly tunnels to get there. No way am I doing that."

"Well, Cody and I are going." Samantha's voice had turned to steel. Once she put her mind to something, she stuck to it.

"Good luck!" Matt said with a sneer.

"Thanks," she said. "Because unless we get a ride back to Kodiak, we're spending the winter here. In case you forgot, we didn't tell Gramps or anyone else where we were going."

Matt paled as the weight of her words sank in. To Cody's shock, he seemed about to cry.

"We never should have come," Matt said. "It's all your kids' fault."

Samantha's face turned red with indignation. "You bought the tickets!"

"I'm not walking through that maze. I'm staying here," Matt said. "Come get me when you find help."

Cody nodded. "Okay. When we find Treadwell, we'll use his sat phone to call our pilot to come get us. He must have one, don't you think? Just stay near the beach and keep an eye out."

"Whatever," Matt said. "Just hurry it up."

Samantha let out a yelp and took off toward their stuff. Cody's stomach dropped. What now?

Samantha charged across the dunes. "You little brat!"

Too late. The red fox had found their supplies. In dismay, Cody took in the mess. The trail mix packets were torn, raisins and nuts scattered. The energy bars were half-chewed. The only things left intact were cans and bottles. A strange smell covered everything.

Samantha looked close to tears. "Now we've hardly anything to eat. What if we don't find Treadwell?"

"You can't leave me here with no food," Matt said. "We'll have to catch a fish first."

"Catch one yourself." Cody was furious. "We have to get

through the grizzly maze before dark." He walked around, trying to salvage some food. Everything smelled like fox pee.

He opened the sports store map. "Good thing the fox didn't pee on this." A thin blue line showed a creek leading from the lower to the upper lake. Using the scale and his fingers, he tried to estimate the distance. "It's about a mile. We should go."

Matt grabbed the rifle and the energy bars. "I'll keep these."

The three glared at one another.

Cody backed down first. What was the point? Matt wasn't going to change. He picked up the ax and Samantha took half the fishing line and hooks. Hopefully, this wouldn't take long.

"Take care, Matt," Cody said. "You sure you want to stay by yourself?"

Matt nodded. "Yep."

"Then we'll see you soon," Cody said, picturing the dark, ominous tunnels that awaited them.

Samantha grimaced, uncertain. "Hopefully."

CHAPTER NINE

KATMAI NATIONAL PARK
THE GRIZZLY MAZE

Cody led the way around the lower lake, wading in knee-deep water. Small birds and dragonflies fluttered in the reeds.

"Awesome!" Samantha whipped out her camera. "Wait a sec."

"Hurry up, Ansel Adams," Cody said. "This water's cold."

He slipped a few times and barely managed to keep his balance. Tonight would be freezing, worse if he got soaked. Hypothermia was a real danger.

Samantha said, "It would be easier if we walked on the shore."

"Where? The brambles reach the water."

They moved as fast as possible, keeping an eye out for danger until they'd reached the rambling mess of brush and spiky alders. Here and there, narrow tunnels burrowed away into the gloom.

Puffing, Cody said, "The grizzly maze. This must be it."

"There sure are a lot of tunnels." Samantha glanced left and right, her shoulders up around her ears. "I wonder where the bears went?"

"I don't know," Cody said, lowering his voice. "Let's just count our luck and get going."

"I wonder which tunnel goes to the upper lake?"

"This one's wider." Cody edged into a snaking tunnel. "This place would be seriously cool if I wasn't so freaked out. Check out these bear prints," he whispered and put his foot into one of them. He wore size eleven shoes, but the print dwarfed his foot.

"Shh," Samantha warned. "Just walk."

The maze was creepy. A dark labyrinth, low and claustrophobic. In sections, Cody ducked to keep his baseball cap from catching in the brambles. Samantha kept stepping on his heels.

"It stinks like poop," she whispered.

"I know."

"What if a grizzly shows up?"

"Fall down and play dead. Don't think about it."

Samantha said nothing.

The tangled branches grew thicker until he had to squint to see. All around was stifling, clingy darkness.

A thought came to him. "In Glacier, Gramps had a hiking stick with a bell to warn bears."

"And?"

"Maybe we should warn the bears we're coming," he whispered. "Sing or something."

"Sing?" Samantha hissed. "I think we should be quiet."

"Gramps says bears don't want to meet humans any more than we want to meet them."

Samantha groaned. "I guess Gramps knows. Either that or you're going to get us killed." Quietly, she sang, "*If you go down to the woods today, you're sure of a big surprise. If you go down to the woods today, you better go in disguise. For every bear that ever there was, is gathered there for certain. Because . . .*"

"Don't sing that! That's an awful choice," Cody interrupted.

"Seemed appropriate to me."

He stifled a grin. "Fine."

They sang and they walked and maybe it worked, or maybe they got lucky. Either way, they puffed up a rugged series of humpback hills and burst out of the tunnel into the grey afternoon light.

"We made it," Samantha said.

"Awesome. We must be close."

"Which way?"

Ahead, a narrow track led through dry, waist-high grass. Bits of fur clung here and there. Beyond that, dark marshland, and further away, the upper lake. It gleamed silver, nestled between brush-covered knolls and high mountains.

"No sign of Treadwell, but I bet he's camped near the lake," Cody said. "He probably hides his tent."

"Let's leave our stuff here. I'm sick of carrying it."

They pushed their backpacks, tent, and sleeping bags into the brush and covered it all with leaves. Cody tagged the nearest tree with a strip from a plastic bag to mark the spot.

As they reached a knoll overlooking the lake, he spotted two green tents along the water.

"Those must be Treadwell's. Yay!" Cody said. "He's here."

"What a relief!" Samantha said. "But that's a crazy place to camp. Bears must walk right past the tents to get to the lake."

"I guess he isn't scared," Cody said. "Let's go."

They scrambled downward. Another few minutes and they'd be safe. They just had to reach Treadwell.

Something roared.

More roars. Grunts. Sharp, low woofs.

Cody's heart felt like it might burst out of his chest.

"Uh oh!" Samantha gasped.

Cody held his finger to his lips. "Shh."

The sound of running water gurgled and splashed nearby. Cody inched through the thick brush and came to a dead halt.

Treadwell's camp was in shouting distance, but between them lay a fast-flowing creek. And it was crammed with bears. Very big bears. Dozens of them. All were focused on catching salmon. Some grizzlies hunted in pools on the creek's rocky banks and some were in the water.

"What now?" Samantha whispered.

A massive bear casually lifted a boulder and tossed it.

Splash!

Salmon scattered and the victorious bear grabbed a fish. Biting off the salmon's head, he tore into it, sliding the flesh off the bones like a kid downing a popsicle. Incredible.

From here, he could smell the musky bear's fishy breath. He and Samantha dropped low in the brush.

He couldn't believe it when Samantha pulled out her camera and grabbed a few snaps.

Then again, if they needed material for their project, this was it. They were seeing these amazing predators in a way few people did. They were in grizzly central.

Heart thumping with terror and excitement, Cody watched, fascinated, taking it all in. This was why they'd come —to see it for themselves.

They were too close, part of him knew that, but another part understood Treadwell one hundred percent. It was a rush, a dangerous rush.

A smaller grizzly roared and attacked another bear its size. They clashed and rolled to the ground, biting and wrestling. Were they fighting or playing? Competing for dominance? Muscles rippled and claws swiped. Water splashed and gravel scattered. Other bears growled and galloped back a few feet.

Samantha dug her fingers into his arm. "There's Tim," she whispered. "Over there."

Cody glanced at the far bank. Tim Treadwell, dressed in sunglasses, black jeans, black bandana, and a black waterproof jacket, was crawling around on all fours.

What the heck was he doing?

"Weird," she said. "I think he's trying to look like a bear."

CHAPTER TEN

KATMAI NATIONAL PARK
UPPER KATMAI LAKE

Cody and Samantha watched from their hiding place.

Tim lumbered up on all fours to a cream-colored grizzly. Although it was a smaller bear, it was still enormous and powerful.

Tim leaned forward. Did he just kiss the grizzly's nose? Talk about taking a chance! That guy was out of control. Wait, was he singing? Cody strained to listen.

"Downy, Downy, you're such a beautiful bear," Tim sang in a high sing-song voice. *"Beautiful, beautiful Downy, you're my favorite bear. I'm so glad, Downy, that you are back at the maze."*

It was incredible. Downy seemed to accept Treadwell, for the bear plopped down right next to him!

This place, these beautiful, deadly-powerful animals, it was magical. And Treadwell was living right here with them. How?

How did he get them to be his friends? To think Tim had survived thirteen summers!

Crunch.

Grunt.

The warning sounds came from a hundred yards up the bank. Cody and Samantha shrank lower.

From out of the alders, a massive dark-brown grizzly emerged from a tunnel and ambled down to the creek.

Tim spotted him, too. He waved. "Hey! Mr. Chocolate! Great to see you. Come on over. Your friend, Downy, is here."

Mr. Chocolate—the largest, most powerfully muscled bear Cody had ever imagined—studied Tim for a moment and then waded into the water. It began grabbing at the leaping salmon.

Mr. Chocolate was fierce but clumsy. While some bears caught fish after fish, Mr. Chocolate kept missing.

"Hey, Mr. Chocolate," Tim shouted. "You should do what Downy's doing. She's catching more than you." It was like he was talking to a pet dog!

Mr. Chocolate ignored him. Instead, the bear lowered his huge body into the water and sat. As the current rushed over him, he grabbed the salmon that were leaping right into his big, hairy chest. Now that was clever.

Cody stifled a chuckle. He loved these bears.

Without warning, two battle-scarred alpha bears galloped out of a bear tunnel.

Instantly, the Eden-like atmosphere changed.

"Get down," Cody whispered.

The massive grizzlies lumbered along the bank. The females and smaller bears moved out of the newcomers' way.

Tim obviously feared them, too, because his face changed. Still on all fours like a bear, he watched warily.

"Hi Machine! Hi Demon!" he called, his voice calm and low. "Everything okay with you, Demon? Do you come in peace, Demon?"

Machine? Demon?

As if to live up to his name, Demon rose on his haunches and charged at Tim.

Instead of running or playing dead, Tim held his ground, still on all fours in his bear costume. Was he crazy?

Demon lurched to a halt.

Whew!

The charge was fake.

Still, Demon and Tim faced off, staring at one another.

Suddenly, Tim leaped up, standing tall, arms stretched

overhead. He took a firm step forward. "Back, Demon," he warned. "Back now."

Clearly Tim was trying to show that he was more powerful. But he wasn't. Demon was monstrous—standing on his hind legs, he was tall enough to look through a second-floor window. With a head four times the size of a human skull, forty-two deadly teeth, paws the size of frying pans, and twenty razor-sharp claws.

An apex predator that could finish Tim with one swipe.

Did Demon know Tim was bluffing?

Demon opened his jaws and roared.

If only Cody had the rifle, he could fire into the air to create a distraction!

Face strained, Tim changed strategy. He sidestepped, slid down the bank into the creek, and swam, smooth but quick, to Mr. Chocolate.

Samantha whispered, "He's going to Mr. Chocolate for help!"

Cody held his breath. What a move! This was a real-life game of chess. And the strategy worked. With Mr. Chocolate at Tim's side, Demon lost interest in the battle.

The rest of the bears went back to fishing. It reminded him of the dog park. Some animals were peaceful, some were aggressive. Mr. Chocolate was the largest predator in the creek, yet he didn't need to prove himself. What a bear!

It seemed like a good moment to get Tim's attention.

Cody raised an arm and waved.

Tim didn't notice.

"We have to find a way to signal Tim," Cody whispered. "If we shout, Demon will hear, and who knows what'll happen."

Shivering, Samantha nodded.

They tried waving over and over, but they were too far,

and he was too absorbed in his work. The excitement factor was wearing off, and the sweat from their walk had turned icy. More worrisome, though, the longer they sat here, the more danger they'd be in.

Samantha said, "There's no way. He doesn't see us, and Demon and Machine have control of the creek. We should go—wait for the bears to clear out. At least we know he's here."

"You're right."

They started back to where they'd left their camping stuff.

"How long do you think those bears will hang around the creek?" Samantha whispered, scanning for danger.

"I don't know. We better find a safe place to hang out for a few hours."

"How will we know it's a safe place?" she asked.

"Your guess is as good as mine."

"Those bears eat like they're starving," she murmured. "They didn't show that in the documentary."

"I guess they have to fatten up. Can you imagine sleeping for six or seven months without food? The clock is ticking. They're eating everything in sight before hibernation hits."

"Okay, I'm scared," she said.

"Who wouldn't be?"

This was nature in the raw.

Deep in the grass, something rustled.

CHAPTER ELEVEN

Katmai National Park

Samantha froze. She wheeled around. "What was that?"

Cody tensed to listen. Was something stalking them? The cold air bit at his exposed cheeks. "I don't hear anything."

"Well, I did."

"You probably imagined it," he said.

"Oh sure, a mysterious noise. No point in worrying!" Samantha whispered.

"Probably a rabbit. Or a squirrel."

Grunt. Thud. Snort.

Bear.

Samantha practically climbed onto Cody's shoulders in terror.

It was too late to run; the predator was nearly there! Cody lunged sideways into the long grass, dragging his cousin with him.

"It'll smell us," she gasped.

Cody's fingers squished into something warm. An awful stench assaulted his nostrils. Bear poop.

"Quick," he whispered. "Rub this on your arms. It'll hide our smell."

Trembling and stinking, they waited.

A large grizzly rumbled out of a nearby tunnel. It neared their hiding spot and ground to a halt. The bear sniffed.

Cody closed his eyes and held his breath. His wet boots stank. Did the bear recognize the smell of human feet?

Time stopped.

The grizzly scratched the dirt, popped a wiggling worm into its mouth, and rumbled off.

When the coast was clear, they wiped themselves clean as best they could with leaves and grass and hurried on. At a creek, they washed their hands and kept going.

The tent and sleeping bags lay in the bushes where they'd left them. But it looked like a tornado had hit. All their stuff was shredded.

Cody stared. "Oh, for Pete's sake! That's the last of our food."

Samantha groaned. "It stinks! Everything's been peed on. Again! It had to be that fox. I can't believe it! What are we going to eat?"

Cody spotted the culprit—a red fox watching from the brush. Cody charged, and the thief streaked off, one of their socks between its teeth.

"The red fox strikes again," he muttered.

"Just grab what we can," Samantha said, peering skyward. "Uh oh, storm clouds."

With their smelly belongings rolled into two bundles, they trekked until they reached an area protected by a massive boulder and an overhanging tree.

"This looks like our best bet." Cody dropped his pack.

"You think it's safe?"

His stomach growled. "I don't know, but I'm starving."

Samantha laughed. "I guess you should have had a bigger breakfast."

"Hey, it's way past lunch already. I'll backtrack to that creek and catch us a fish. Wait here."

"Not a chance," Samantha said. "I'm a better fisher."

It was safer to stick together anyway. Cody rummaged for the fishing lines.

"Bring the bear spray," Samantha said.

"Okay, and I'll bring the ax, too."

The creek gurgled and flashed. A rabbit hopped by. A squirrel chittered. Cody took it as a good sign—no bears on the hunt.

He formed a fishing rod from a branch and nylon line. Warily, he kept glancing over his shoulder and chanted. "I'm here, bear. Don't worry, bear, it's just me."

A salmon leaped out of the water and flew at him like an NFL player with the ball. Cody dropped his rod and made a grab. The slippery fish jumped clear.

Cody landed on his knees with a splash. Lucky Matt wasn't here to laugh at him being a klutz. Thinking of Matt, hopefully he was okay.

A bird swooped and made off with a fish. Great, even birds were better at fishing.

Fists on her hips, Samantha assessed the creek. After a moment, she waded into the water, hands cupped, and herded a salmon beneath an overhanging bank. Triumphant, she grasped the fish to her chest and grinned.

"Yes!" Cody cried, running to help. "Don't lose it, well done!"

They scrambled ashore.

"I'll clean it," he offered.

"Do it quick before a bear smells it and comes running."

Cody scaled and cleaned the salmon like Gramps had taught him. He was finishing in record time when the alders shook, and a massive form lumbered into view. A grizzly. Hunched. Ears back.

Cody's blood ran cold.

The grizzly closed in, picking up speed.

It was happening fast, but Cody's terror turned everything into slow motion. Like a close-up in a horror movie, the immense furry face with long scars came into focus.

"Back!" Cody yelled, stomping and sending pebbles scattering. "Get back! Don't even think about it!"

The grizzly roared. Slobber dripped from its jaws.

Samantha moved to his side. "Aaaargh!" she yelled. "Get away! Go!"

Cody pitched the salmon like a fastball, straight at the bear's head.

Smack!

It hit the grizzly right in the snout.

As one, Cody and Samantha yelled and waved and stomped. "Get away! Back! Back! Now!"

The grizzly lunged.

"The spray!" Samantha screamed.

Thankful he'd stuck it in his jacket pocket, Cody grabbed the can. He blasted the bear with an orange cloud. The grizzly reeled, spinning sideways. It coughed, ran, and rolled its head in the grass.

Enraged, the grizzly pulled itself up. The animal was going to charge again.

"Blast it!" Samantha screamed. "Blast it!"

Cody sprayed again.

The bear roared with rage and pain. Then it pivoted and disappeared into the dark.

Cody's teeth chattered. "Holy moly, that thing was massive. Even on all fours, it was taller than my head. One swipe of those paws could knock down a moose."

Still gripping the spray, he squinted into the dark trees.

Samantha looked ruefully at the salmon lying in the mud. "Guess that's the end of the salmon."

"No way." Cody brushed off the mud and rinsed it in the creek. "Let's go before he returns."

Samantha grabbed his elbow. "Uh, Cody?"

To his horror, another monster male rose out of the brush. The cousins backpedaled. This bear locked eyes with him. Cody dropped his glance and kept retreating. To his relief, maybe this was one of those bears Gramps mentioned, the kind that didn't like meeting humans, for it crashed away into the brush.

Samantha shivered. "I'm not going anywhere with that fish." Her voice had that stubborn tone that he knew so well.

But she was talking about his lunch and probably even his dinner.

"The fish won't be around long because I'm going to eat it," he said. "We can't hike miles and escape from bears if we don't eat."

Samantha glared. "Then hand over the spray. I'm keeping it in *my* jacket pocket."

"Suit yourself."

They hurried back to the tent. Samantha stood guard while he made a fire. The flames blazed bright and hot, sizzling as the first raindrops began to fall.

"That should help. Bears don't like fire." Cody speared pieces of salmon and blackened them. He handed some to Samantha, and they both tore into it like starving animals.

Samantha said, "Sort of raw."

"Sashimi," Cody said. "It would cost a fortune in Malibu."

She licked her lips. "I must be hungry because it's the best thing I ever tasted." She jumped as a gust of wind rattled the grass. "Whoa, that spooked me. How can Tim live here?"

That's when the downpour hit. They dove into the tent and zipped up the door.

"What if he decides to fly out early? Because of the storm? We need to get to him," Cody said.

"The minute the rain lets up, we'll head to his camp."

In the dim light, they eyed one another, suddenly serious. Then he said what they both were clearly thinking.

"If we get stuck here, we're doomed."

CHAPTER TWELVE

KATMAI NATIONAL PARK

As night fell, the storm only grew more violent. Temperatures dropped fast. At least the tent felt snug and dry. No one was going anywhere in this weather.

Cody had just curled up in his sleeping bag when Samantha shook his shoulder.

"I need to pee."

"Do it far from the tent," Cody muttered.

Samantha shook his shoulder again. "You have to come with me."

"No way I'm going out there again."

"Please," Samantha begged.

Cody groaned. "Just go by yourself and do it quickly."

"No!" Samantha wailed.

"You have to. And bury it. Or the bears will smell it. Cover it with dirt."

"Don't be mean. I'm not going out there alone."

Cody groaned. Flashlight in hand, he crawled out of the tent. Samantha followed. The wind whipped rain into his face.

"Hurry," Cody said. "I'll keep watch."

As she peed, Cody turned his back and shone the flashlight into the flurry of raindrops.

Two eyes shone back.

"Bear!" Samantha gasped and scrambled up.

"Stay still," Cody murmured. "Whatever you do, don't run."

The bear, his fur drenched, melted away into the trees.

Inside the tent, Cody lay shivering. He could hear Samantha's teeth chattering. Yikes, this place was cold. He wrapped his arms around his chest and listened to the downpour. Cody had never been so cold. His feet were frozen. He opened his sturdy Kevlar backpack and stuffed his feet—still in the sleeping bag—into it for extra protection. The backpack helped.

Outside, a twig snapped.

Like a jack-in-the-box, he sat up. Numbskull! They should have pitched the tent further from the maze.

"What was that?" Samantha whispered.

"Something's out there."

Something out of his worst nightmares. The tent shuddered and a monster head, haloed by a flash of lightning, burst through the flap. Giant snout. Shiny nose. Bulging jaws. Long teeth. Steaming breath, reeking of fish.

"Get away!" Cody shouted. "Get lost! Get out!"

Time stood still.

Lightning flashed again. The grizzly stared, eyes cold. Focused. Saliva drooling from its powerful jaws.

"Get out!" Samantha shrieked in the sudden darkness. "Get *out!*"

Her screams worked. When lightning flashed again, the monster head had disappeared.

"Whoa," Samantha breathed.

"Stay still," Cody hissed.

"I think it's gone," Samantha whispered. "I almost had a heart attack."

"Me too." Cody let out a nervous snort. "That was crazy. Too bad you didn't get a photo."

Samantha switched on her flashlight. "Did we scare it away?"

"Must have."

Without warning, a paw the size of a giant's baseball mitt ripped through the nylon. Dagger-like, three-inch-long claws swiped just inches from his nose.

"The spray," Cody yelled. Frantic, he rolled around, trying to find it while Samantha fumbled in her bag.

The grizzly clawed at the tent again, tearing another hole in the nylon.

"Get!" he screamed. "Get away, bear!"

One side of the tent caved inward. The grizzly's muzzle was outlined by the fabric. It lunged and bit downward. The massive jaws, weirdly hidden by the collapsing tent wall, closed around Cody's Kevlar backpack—with Cody's feet trapped inside!

"My legs!" Cody shouted.

The jaws squeezed tighter and tighter until his legs went numb.

"Get away!" he screamed, punching the fabric-clad head. "Get away!"

The grizzly squeezed harder. Pushing, pushing down. Did it think it had him by the neck? Did it think it was killing him? He could hear the grizzly's heavy, huffing breath.

"Get out of the sleeping bag!" Samantha shrieked.

"I can't! The zipper's stuck." Frantic now, Cody pulled at the zipper.

"Hit it!" she shouted, whacking it with the flashlight.

Wildly, Cody felt around for a weapon. His fingers closed over the iron pot. He beat at the bear's head. Hard. Over and over until he was sure the bear's skull would break.

The bear pulled back.

Rain spattered through the tent's gaping holes. Cody waited, every muscle tensed for survival.

The only sounds came from the cold downpour and the wailing wind.

The bear had gone.

"Are you okay?" Samantha whispered.

The flashlight illuminated the Kevlar bag. He wiggled his toes. "A bit numb, that's all. No wonder they use Kevlar for attack dog training. It worked for grizzly teeth, too. It saved my legs."

Samantha's face shone pale. "I wish we had full body armor right now. Do you think it's going to come back?"

"I don't know." Cody shone the light on the rips. The moisture along the edges was already turning to ice. The wind howled like a banshee, drenching everything inside. "We better fix this tent, though. Otherwise, we'll freeze to death."

He dug out some fishing line and a hook. Together, the cousins patched the tears as best they could. Then they huddled into the one corner that was still dry.

"Let's take turns keeping watch," he said.

"Good idea."

"I'll take the first shift."

Samantha nodded. But even after thirty minutes, he could tell from her breathing that she wasn't asleep.

So far, they'd been lucky. Incredibly lucky. With a sinking feeling, Cody knew their luck couldn't hold much longer.

And what about Matt? Was he all right?

They had to survive the night. They had to make their way to Treadwell's camp. They had to get a hold of his sat phone and call that pilot.

They'd been warned it was too dangerous to come. Multiple times by multiple people. Cody had ignored them and every instinct because of money—because Matt had bought those tickets.

If he could go back in time, knowing what he knew now, he'd gladly throw them away to be safely at Gramps.

CHAPTER THIRTEEN

KATMAI NATIONAL PARK

A feral shriek broke the silence. A gut-wrenching shriek.

Cody woke with a start, cursing himself for drifting off, and blinked in the weak pre-dawn light.

Samantha popped up. "What was that?"

"I don't know. A rabbit? A fox?"

"Poor thing," Samantha said. "I wonder what's happening to it."

The shrieks abruptly died out. Somewhere, an owl hooted, and other noises joined in. A pre-dawn chorus of tweets, chirps, whistles, and calls.

"Last night was a nightmare," Samantha said. "I thought we were finished."

Cody grimaced. "Me too."

"At least there's some good news."

"Really?" Cody said, surprised.

She triumphantly produced a chocolate peanut butter

protein bar. "Look what I found at the bottom of my bag. Your fave."

"You're kidding!"

She unwrapped the bar and handed him half.

"Yum!" Cody ate his share, savoring every bite. He was still hungry, but at least his stomach wasn't gnawing. "We better get moving."

The cousins rolled up their sleeping bags and crawled out of their ripped tent.

Cody inhaled sharply. "Check out those bear prints! They're huge. And not just one bear. Lots of bears. All prowling round our tent."

"I can't believe we survived." Samantha shuddered.

Cody picked up the ax, and Samantha pocketed the bear spray.

"Let's head back to Treadwell's camp. Hopefully, this time we can reach him."

"Fingers crossed," Samantha said.

Cody grinned. "Maybe he has some breakfast to share."

"Dream on," Samantha said.

"Eggs, pancakes, and double bacon work for me." Cody led the way, ax ready for action.

After an hour, Cody stopped. "We're lost."

"We should have found the river ages ago," she said.

They kept walking. The ground grew steeper, and after another hour, they'd climbed to a high point above the river. Cody pulled out his binoculars and searched the terrain below.

"I see it, there's Treadwell's camp."

It had to be at least a mile away. The river looked totally different this morning—no bears fishing, no bears fighting, just rushing water beneath a red-dawn sky.

Tim's two tents were still in the same spot.

"They're probably still asleep," he whispered.

"They wouldn't hear us even if we shouted." Samantha took a turn with the binoculars.

"Whoa. What the heck?" Cody said, watching Treadwell's camp for signs of movement. "There's a grizzly down there, right behind his tent."

"You're right! Uh oh. Something's wrong with it."

An emaciated grizzly lay by the larger tent. It shook its head as if to ward off a fly and rose to its haunches with difficulty. Moving slowly, it inched toward the water, dragging one of its back legs.

"It's injured," Cody said.

The grizzly made it a few more feet, then dropped to its belly and lay there.

"And I see more bears," Cody added, "In the grass. I just noticed them. A mother grizzly with two cubs. I bet Treadwell's feeding them and that injured one."

"Pretty risky, but I guess he knows what he's doing."

"I guess so. Let's climb down this way and see if we can head in his direction."

"Okay. Maybe we'll find some berries, too," Samantha said.

"I'm starving."

Ax in hand, Cody hacked a trail through the brush and grass. Things felt better this morning, easier. He was sure they could get Treadwell's attention today now that the river was mostly empty.

Once they used his sat phone to contact their pilot, the plane would be here in no time. They'd be on that flight and back to civilization early afternoon. And tonight, they'd be at Gramps' cabin. All of this would be an incredible survival story to tell their friends.

He walked with a spring in his step and cheered when they found a small patch of blueberries.

The ground started to rise again.

He slowed.

It shouldn't be going up.

Samantha said, "We should be there by now."

All around them, trees, boulders, and brush offered no clue which way to go.

"Let's keep walking."

It was hard to judge how much time had passed. Every path they chose took them closer to the jagged, snow-topped mountains. Big, dark clouds rolled down the sheer cliffs, surrounding them in a thick gray blur.

They broke free from the shelter of the alders and the wind blew hard, almost gale force.

"Snow!" Cody pulled up his hood as snowflakes whirled.

"I'm freezing." Samantha shuddered.

The trail led gradually uphill. The mountains loomed above them.

"Maybe if we get higher, we can figure out where we are," Cody said.

Climbing steadily, soon they were huffing. They needed a break. They'd been hiking for hours in the cold on half a protein bar and a handful of berries. And if they didn't warm up soon, they'd be in trouble.

"Is that dark spot in the cliff a cave?" Samantha said.

Cody squinted. "Yeah. That could work. As long as no bears live there. Hold on, I'll climb up and check."

As he scrambled up the rocks, the half-frozen mud under his feet gave way.

Samantha grabbed him.

And they both went sliding.

CHAPTER FOURTEEN

KATMAI NATIONAL PARK

Cody slid fast, hurtling between two sheer rock walls. Jagged rocks reared up in front of him. Grunting, he threw his body right and left, moving like a snowboarder to try and avoid them.

A huge boulder loomed. He wrapped his arms around his head, and his body spun. Suddenly he was somersaulting in a terrifying blur, like some mad stuntman.

Bang!

Thump!

His shoulder smashed into a rock, his butt into another. Bone-jarring hits that left him gasping. He lay, winded, in a mess of mud, rocks, and rubble.

Shrieking, Samantha landed on top of him.

They untangled their limbs and lay there puffing.

"Are you okay?" Cody said.

"Sort of. Ow! My ribs kill." Samantha grimaced. "Uh oh. Look how far we fell."

"I know. We're going to have to hike back up. This gorge is just some kind of rock crevice."

"Seriously?"

Cody nodded. At least Samantha wasn't blaming him.

As they stared upward, fresh gusts of snow, hurled by the wind, blinded them.

"We're stuck in the snow like the Donner Party," Samantha said.

"You mean the dudes who ate each other?"

Samantha tried to laugh through her chattering teeth. She wiped the mud from her face, which only made it worse. "I'm freezing. We better wait until the snow stops. The first rule of survival is shelter."

"Right." The gorge ended abruptly in a cliff about sixty feet wide. Cody scanned the cliff face. Yes! A dark slot. "A cave!"

Samantha's brows arched in worry. "That one looks big enough for a grizzly den."

"I'll check it out," Cody said. "Carefully, this time." He rubbed his throbbing shoulder and stood. "Wait here."

"No way," Samantha said.

"I'll be right back."

Samantha scoffed. "Famous last words heard in every horror movie. I'm coming with you."

After a difficult scramble, they reached the cave mouth and peered inside. He paused, trying to adjust his eyes to the dark. The blackness was eerily quiet. All he could hear was his heart beating in his ears.

He took a step inside, and something hard cracked under

his boot. Keeling, he picked up a half-gnawed bone. There were more bones. The whole entrance was littered with them.

A violent gust of wind nearly sent him toppling. Gusts hurled snow and grit into his eyes.

Bones or not, he'd heard no animal sounds. Whatever lived here wasn't home. Hopefully, they wouldn't come home for a while, at least not until the storm died down.

He almost had to shout to be heard over the gale. "Let's go inside."

"I'm right behind you," Samantha shouted back. "Yell if you see a bear!"

"You got it."

Heart in his throat, he led the way back into the cave.

Faraway, something howled, long and clear. Followed by a chorus of deep barks and short high-pitched howls. The hair on the back of Cody's neck stood on end. "Wolves."

"Is this their den?" Samantha's voice shook.

"I don't know," Cody said.

Samantha grabbed his arm. "Something's coming in!"

Frantic, Cody felt for the ax. Wasn't there.

A big head poked into the cave. It wasn't a grizzly; he could see from the shape. A horse? Wow, a horse would be great. For one glorious moment, he pictured himself riding out of the wilderness like Wyatt Earp.

No. The head was bigger than a horse.

Through the gale, he made out the shape of antlers. "A moose!" He grinned. "They're vegetarian. Won't eat us. Hey, big guy!"

The moose couldn't quite fit inside. It sniffed around, let out a disgusted snort, pulled its head back, and left.

"He didn't like your smell," Samantha said.

"Ha!" Cody sank down onto his backpack. "The ground

seems clean enough and there's piles of dry grass. Burrow into it. It'll keep us warmer."

"A grizzly probably brought that grass in here." Samantha said. "These are some grizzly family's beds."

Cody pictured a bear family in here with their cubs. That must be quite a sight. Adult bears were terrifying, but the cubs must look pretty cute all curled into balls.

After a moment, he said, "Well, the bears aren't home now and I don't see that we have any other choice. I'm lying in one."

Samantha took a deep breath. "Okay. You have a good point there. I kind of feel like Goldilocks, though. Too bad there's no porridge in this place."

"Ha ha, that would be good." Cody burrowed into the grass. "Grizzlies sure know how to hibernate. This is pretty comfy. Did you know that when they're hibernating, not only do they not eat, they don't pee or poo either."

"Really? Wow!" Samantha said. "Too bad I'm not a grizzly."

Samantha burrowed into her own pile. "This grass is dry enough to light a fire."

"You're right. That's a really good idea. Come on, help me make a fire."

They gathered a small pile near the entrance, and Cody flicked the lighter. A flame rose. Shivering, they huddled close to the crackling warmth. In the yellow light, Cody spotted branches further back that must have blown in here with the wind. He gathered an armful and fed a few to the flames.

"That's better," Samantha said. "Safer too. Though I wish we were at Gramp's cabin."

"Yeah," Cody agreed. "Cozy and chilling on the sofa. When we planned this, I sure didn't think we would end up this way."

"Don't say *end*." Samantha groaned. "I'm too tired to be scared anymore."

"Okay," Cody agreed. "Let's think about the great story we'll have for our school projects. Or we can plan our project for next year. I vote we do one at Disney World."

Samantha laughed. "Yeah. We'll watch the Bear Jamboree. Much safer!"

"And better food."

They grinned at one another.

"What would you eat right now if you could have anything?" Samantha asked.

"A burger—a huge, juicy burger on a soft bun. With melted cheese. Mustard. Ketchup. Pickles. A massive pile of crispy fries. And lemonade. Mom's homemade lemonade—sweet, with a dash of sour."

"Stop!" Samantha laughed. "I can't take it."

Too hungry to think, Cody climbed back into his straw bed, and Samantha did the same.

CHAPTER FIFTEEN

KATMAI NATIONAL PARK

Pink light was streaming into the cave when Cody blinked awake. He couldn't feel his feet. He thought of the Everest explorers who'd lost their limbs to hyperthermia. Quickly, he flexed his hands and toes.

"You woke me!" Samantha muttered. "What's all that noise?"

Cody blew on his throbbing fingers. "I'm freezing."

"What time is it?"

"Must be morning, we slept all night."

The air smelled smoky, and their fire was a mess of black coals. The stench must have kept predators away. At least they'd stayed alive two whole nights alone. That had to be worth something.

"Do you think Matt's okay?" Samantha asked.

"I hope so. Let's go. We can't afford to get lost again. We'll find Treadwell this time," he said, trying to sound sure.

Samantha didn't reply.

Again, he remembered they'd told no one they were up here. They'd ignored one of the most important rules of survival: Make sure people know where you are.

Cody felt woozy from hunger and thirst but tried to ignore it. Samantha didn't mention food; she had to be starving, too.

They stumbled out of the cave and landed in a snowbank. Fluffy snowdrifts covered everything.

A horrible thought ripped through his brain. "The storm's over. What if Tim calls his pilot to pick him up today? Instead of waiting until the end of the week? More bad weather might be coming."

Samantha blanched. "Let's go. Fast."

Cody studied the cliff. "No way we can climb back up that way now. There's a frozen overhang. We'll start an avalanche. We'll have to try that other section and hope it leads out."

"It's almost as steep as the cliff," Samantha protested.

"Only way to go," Cody said. "Come on."

Samantha groaned and tightened her backpack.

With his boots sinking into knee-high snowdrifts, Cody grabbed one snowy branch after another and hauled himself along. Climbing. Crawling. Sliding. Behind him, he heard Samantha puffing.

"Cody, look at those tracks! Big hoofs—must be from the moose."

"Yeah, and did you see those over there? Paw prints in single file. Wolves."

"Can you believe they walk in single file like that? I'm glad we weren't stuck outside last night." She licked her dry lips. "I'm so thirsty. Do you think it's okay to eat snow?"

"I guess. As long as it's not yellow."

"Funny, aren't you!" She nibbled at a handful of snow. "It's making me even colder."

Nervous tension filled him. He pictured the floatplane arriving early and carrying Tim and Amie back to Kodiak. He pictured it flying overhead, off to the safety of civilization. To dry hotel rooms and noisy restaurants and hot showers.

He pictured himself, Samantha, and Matt stuck alone, trying to find food and escape bears for seven long months.

They'd never make it.

"We have to get out of these snowdrifts," he called, heading over to a flat section of snow.

Too late, he realized his mistake. What he'd thought was a shallow ditch was a snow hole. The snow gave way beneath him, and he was falling all over again. Except that this time, it was worse. He was falling through thin air, plunging into darkness. Down he went.

Oof!

He landed hard against a snowy slope. Digging in, his heels hit something solid, and he jolted to a stop. The impact forced the air from his lungs. Yikes! The snow hole was deep, and he was only halfway down. All that supported him was a wedge of hard ice. If the wedge collapsed, he'd fall further and never get out.

Looking up, he saw daylight and Samantha's worry-scrunched face peering down.

"Are you hurt?" she shouted.

"Don't stand there!" Cody yelled. "The whole thing could collapse."

"Okay. I'll lie flat. Can you climb out?"

"I don't know. I'm afraid to move."

"I can't reach you. I wish we had a rope."

He felt weak, not his usual self. Worse, time was ticking—what if Tim's plane came?

For a minute, there was silence. Cody took a deep breath and winced as the frigid air hit his dry throat.

"Samantha, you should keep going," he called. "You can come back for me."

Maybe he'd never get out. The snow hole was an icy tomb.

"Try and climb out!" she called. "You can do it. Baby steps. One foot after another. Start! Now!"

"It's too steep and slippery." Still, he began to climb, cramming his cold, aching hands and feet into the icy walls. Every time he moved a few feet, he'd slip several inches. He was making progress but barely.

If he fell, he'd be history. His heart jack-hammered.

"Here!" Samantha pulled the strap off her backpack and extended it to its full length. With both arms outstretched, she dangled it down. "Can you reach this? I'll pull you out."

"It's too far."

"Keep climbing."

Cody struggled upward. Finally, the strap was within reach. He grabbed it with fingers that were weak from exertion. "Don't fall in, too."

"I won't." Samantha's voice trembled.

"I'm too heavy for you," Cody whispered through dry lips.

"Hang on to the strap with one hand and keep climbing."

Inch by inch, Cody climbed.

With a final grunt, Samantha took one hand off the strap and grabbed his arm. As she leaned back, tugging, Cody braced his knees and pushed. He threw one hand over the ledge, then the other. He was out.

They lay in the snow, gasping.

Samantha said, "Hey, no more falling, okay?"

"Deal. I thought I was gone. Thanks, cousin. I owe you." He rubbed his twisted knee. "Let's move. Faster the better."

Limping, he headed off. Coming out of the trees, he got a bird's-eye-view of the lake. It rippled below, like a shining plate of steel.

The day was way past noon when they reached the top of the gorge.

They paused to take in the sight. The air felt so much warmer down here, and it felt good to be on level ground. Even better, Cody was sure he recognized this place.

"I think we're close to Treadwell's camp. That's where we stored our camping gear the other day when we first came looking for him."

"You're right!"

"And I haven't heard any airplanes. We would have heard if one had come for him. So he has to still be here."

They both blew out relieved sighs.

Samantha pulled the brambles aside, searching for berries. "No wonder the bears are fighting for salmon. There's nothing else to eat."

"I'm so thirsty. I wonder how Matt is doing."

"He had those cans of beer," Samantha said. "He's probably drunk."

"I read a survival quiz," Cody puffed. "If your plane crashes and you only have beer, do you drink it?"

"I guess." Samantha started walking.

"The correct answer is no. Alcohol dehydrates you."

"Huh! What other questions were there?"

Cody cleared the painful dryness from his throat and croaked. "Your plane runs out of fuel over the desert. As the plane descends, you spot a hut. Do you hike to the hut?"

Samantha thought for a minute. "Yes."

"Nope," Cody replied. "The answer is to stay with the plane or vehicle so rescuers can find you."

"Well, going by that advice, we should have stayed at the lower lake where our pilot left us."

"Maybe," Cody admitted. "Except no one knows we need rescuing."

Faces grim, they kept moving.

A scream shattered the silence. "Get! Get away! You heard me—get away!"

Cody spun round. "What was that?

Samantha grabbed his arm. "It sounded like Matt."

"Did it?"

Wide-eyed, they stared at each other.

"Help! Help me!" the voice screamed. "I'm being killed out here. Help me!"

CHAPTER SIXTEEN

KATMAI NATIONAL PARK

"W-what's happening?" Samantha stuttered. "Where is he?"

"I don't know. He's being attacked! Sounds like he's somewhere in the maze."

"Oh no, Cody! He must have come looking for us."

The screaming changed from words to incoherent screeches. Wild yells, mixed with the wail of the wind.

Samantha's face screwed up with fear. "Sounds like a bear has him."

Shrill, agonized shrieks made Cody's stomach lurch. He had to help his cousin, but he'd lost the ax and Matt had the rifle.

Why didn't Matt shoot?

With Samantha on his heels, Cody thrust through the thick grass stalks. They followed the high, horrible, keening sound, running toward trouble, desperate to try and help.

As suddenly as it started, the screaming stopped.

The silence was deafening. With awful pictures racing through his mind, Cody flashed a look at Samantha.

Her face was ashen. "Oh Cody, what's happened?"

"We have to find him." As he ran, Cody thought of Matt.

His cousin hadn't always been a jerk. When they were little, they'd been friends. Their moms took them to the local park on weekends. Matt had been fun to play with.

What had made Matt change? Why had he become a bully?

He flashed back to a day in the park when Uncle John reluctantly came along for the ride. Matt fell off a swing. He hit the ground hard and started crying. His dad shouted that he was acting like a baby and he'd give him something to cry about.

Uncle John was a heavy drinker. He got mean when he drank, and that day he'd been putting away can after can of beer.

Now, as Cody ran, the thwack-thwack of his boots reminded him of Uncle John's angry smacks. Poor Matt. Even as a little kid, Cody had been shocked. His own dad would never have done that. His dad would have picked him up and made him feel safe. A year later, Uncle John left. Aunt Lucy said she didn't care, but Cody knew that Matt did. That must have been awful.

Cody kept running. They flew out of the maze and came to a halt. It felt like weeks since the pilot had dropped them off in this lost place.

In the distance, he spotted Matt's blue tent down the beach. So alone and small in the wild.

He forced his injured leg to move faster—he had to help his cousin, even though his brain warned that it didn't make sense. Matt wouldn't be in the tent. They'd heard him way back, somewhere in the maze.

"Wait!" Samantha puffed. "Check for bears."

"I don't see any."

Together, they ran, scanning left and right.

As Cody neared the tent, he heard muffled sobs. Hysterical but soft, as if someone was sobbing but trying not to be heard.

Matt, he was alive! How?

Terrified of what he'd see, expecting to witness a bloody mess, Cody lifted the tent flap.

Inside, Matt cowered, his sleeping bag pressed to his face.

No sign of blood; the bear must have gotten his legs or something. As Matt sobbed, his body shook. Cody scrambled inside and touched his cousin's shoulder.

Matt spun around, rifle in hand.

"Whoa!" Cody leaped back. "Put that rifle down. It's me. Are you hurt?"

"No." Matt still waved the rifle.

"Put that away!" Cody said, thrusting the barrel to the side.

Samantha looked Matt over in confusion. "We heard you screaming. It sounded like—"

"I wasn't screaming," Matt said. "I heard *you* screaming. I thought a grizzly was attacking you."

Samantha shoved her fingers through her hair, her eyes baffled. "We thought it was you."

"Well, it wasn't," Matt said. "But it could have been." He wiped his swollen eyes. "I went through that stupid maze looking for you. When I got to the other side, I thought a grizzly had you both. I thought it would come for me next. So, I ran all the way back here. Worst experience I ever had."

"Tell us what you heard," Cody said.

"Like I told you, I got to the other side of the maze, near this river—"

"I meant, what did you hear?"

"First, a guy shouted for help," Matt said. "Then he screamed, *Hit it! Hit it with the pan!* Then he shouted, *Run! Run! Save yourself.*"

A nauseous feeling rose in Cody's throat. It seemed impossible. "That must have been Tim and Amie. A grizzly must have attacked them."

"But Tim has lived with bears for years," Samantha said. "He knows how to handle them."

"Some of those big bears didn't seem like his friends," Cody said. "That Demon looked downright deadly."

Matt shook his head. "It wasn't Treadwell. I saw the guy just before. He was down at the lake."

"You saw him?" Cody said.

"Sure did."

Samantha said, "Maybe it was one of those poachers. You saw Tim? Did you tell him we need help?"

"Nope. Couldn't get near him. Crazy dude was standing in the middle of some huge bears. Flipping out, saying how he much loved them and how he hated the hunters and poachers."

"Well, someone was attacked. You have the rifle, Matt. Why didn't you at least fire it?" Cody said. "That might have scared it off."

Matt's face turned red. "Yeah. I thought of firing the rifle. But I didn't want the grizzlies to know I was here. Anyway, it ended fast. After about five minutes, the screams stopped."

Five minutes? Cody stared at him. Five minutes was tons of time to fire a rifle.

Matt said, "Don't look at me like that. I want to get out of here alive. If you're smart, you do, too."

CHAPTER SEVENTEEN

Katmai National Park

"Do you have any food left?" Cody asked.

"Ate it all. I was hoping you had some."

"We left it all with you, remember?" Cody said. "Listen, I'm going to get going. Give me the rifle."

"What for?" Matt said. "Where are you going?"

Seriously?

"To Treadwell's camp. So I can call for a plane."

Matt said, "Good luck with that, some maniac grizzly is on the prowl. You want to get killed?"

"No, but I don't want to get stuck here for the winter."

Samantha swallowed hard. "Matt's right. There's a dangerous animal out there."

"I have to go," Cody said, trying to sound confident. It didn't work. "Don't worry. I'll stay out of sight. I won't be long. You have the bear spray."

"I'm coming with you," Samantha said. "We've stuck together this long. I'm not letting you go alone."

Cody shook his head. "No, really. You don't have to."

"Wanna bet?" Samantha scrambled out of the tent after him. "Two heroes are safer than one."

Wide-eyed, she stared at the sky. Dark against the gray clouds, vultures circled. "Oh Cody, look—vultures! That's scary. Vultures circle when something is dead."

"Or badly injured," Cody said. "Stay here, please? Your parents will kill me if something happens to you."

"Don't play all macho. I'm going with you, dork."

Cody rolled his eyes.

From inside the tent, Matt shouted, "Hurry up and get back here. I don't want that bear to come after me."

Samantha said, "You've got the bear spray. Just remember to use it."

They headed off as fresh rain began to fall.

Soon it fell in a steady stream, pouring down their necks as they crept through the maze. What a miserable place!

Cody wiped rain out of his eyes and came to a grinding halt. Fifty yards away, a massive grizzly crouched over a pile of clothes. A leather jacket, jeans. Head down, it chewed.

Paralyzed with fear, Cody backed away.

Slowly. One foot behind the other. Quiet as a mouse . . .

His right heel caught on a rock.

With a gulp, he flung out his arms. Staggered.

Stones skittered, rattling across the wet ground.

The grizzly looked up. Eyes gleaming and far apart, locked on Cody. The massive animal reared up, each forearm bigger than Cody's whole body.

The bear roared.

Was the grizzly defending its meal? Were those more than just clothes?

Don't look into its eyes. Don't challenge it. It isn't after you. It thinks you're after its prey.

Cody inched away. Right into Samantha.

"Cody?" she whispered in a trembling voice.

He spoke softly. "Keep backing up."

Together, they crept out of view.

Once they were deep in the brush, he whispered. "I think that grizzly might have killed someone."

"Now what?" She sounded close to tears. "Oh Cody, we're dead, aren't we?"

"No." He had to focus, he couldn't give in to fear. "Come on. We'll take a different tunnel. Quietly."

Heart thumping, Cody led them on a circuitous route toward Treadwell's campsite. At the knoll, the silence was eerie—as if even animals were avoiding the place. He stared, appalled.

"What happened over there?" Samantha gasped.

Both tents were mashed flat.

There was no sign of Tim or Amie.

"I don't know." Stomach churning, Cody found a shallow spot in the river. They waded across, the water rising over their ankles.

A dark wet patch shone in front of the squashed big tent.

It was either mud or something awful, something he didn't want to think about.

Holding his breath, he lifted the tent canvas. Inside lay scattered clothes, water bottles, video camera equipment, sleeping bags, and a teddy bear. The fearless Tim Treadwell slept with a teddy bear.

Cody blinked hard as tears filled his eyes. "They're not here."

Samantha's face was ashen. "They might have gotten away."

"I don't think so," Cody said. "That leather jacket I saw on the trail, it looked like his. But Amie could still be alive. She may be hurt and hiding."

"If I was her, I'd stay hidden," Samantha said.

"I wonder if he called for help?" Cody said.

"Oh no," she said.

"What?"

"I hope he called for help before this happened," she said, striding toward a smashed object on the ground. She picked it up and showed him the broken remains.

"Is that his satellite phone? Oh no."

In the grass, a shadow moved. Something was watching.

Cody's skin prickled.

Then, the injured bear, the one he'd seen through the binoculars, limped into the campsite. It probably wanted Tim's help. This might be when Tim usually fed the bear.

Despite everything, Cody felt for the poor creature. It would have to fend for itself now.

"Let's go. We better regroup with Matt and come up with a new plan."

CHAPTER EIGHTEEN

"What took you so long?" Matt asked when they arrived back at the beach.

"I think Treadwell is dead."

Matt stared at Cody. "You can't be serious."

"I think Treadwell is dead and there's no way to call anyone."

"Now what?" Matt wailed.

"You're asking me? You're the one who bought the tickets. You're the one who dropped the sat phone—"

Samantha cut in. "Quit it, you guys. I'd like to get out of here alive, if possible? So someone better come up with a plan."

Cody and Matt glared at one another. After a long moment, Cody backed down.

"You're right," he said, his shoulders dropping. "All I know is that his ride back is flying here soon. We're just going to have to wait it out."

"How long's that gonna take?" Matt said.

Cody squinted at the sky. Clouds towered like mountains, moving ominously overhead. "I don't know."

As he spoke, he focused on a black dot moving along the horizon. Had to be a bird. The dot headed steadily toward them. A low droning noise blended with the wind.

Samantha grabbed Cody's arm. "That's a plane!"

Cody whooped. "We're saved!"

Even Matt cheered.

Then, an awful thought struck. "It'll go to the upper lake," Cody said. "Treadwell's pilot doesn't know we're here."

Samantha's eyes went wide in panic. "Run," she gasped. "Let's go."

All three started toward the maze when Cody stopped.

"No," he said, sick with a fresh realization that they were about to make a deadly mistake. "We don't know what the pickup spot is. What if Treadwell told the pilot to meet him here?"

"Oh, wow, you're right," Samantha said. "Matt, stay here."

"No way."

Cody said, "There's no time! Look, Samantha, you stay here with Matt and I'll run. Okay?"

"Forget it, I'll go," she said.

"Just give me the rifle and make sure Matt doesn't do anything stupid. You know he won't stay here alone."

"I'm keeping the gun!" Matt shouted.

Cody ignored him and grabbed the rifle. He left a stunned and furious Samantha holding her bear mace and staring after him as he darted alone into the maze.

One last run. One last time.

This was the sprint that counted.

He only hoped he could make it.

CHAPTER NINETEEN

KATMAI NATIONAL PARK

Cody knew his way by now. He took the long route, knowing it was the safest, even if his knee ached.

Overhead, the plane roared ever closer, circling for a landing.

Cody picked up speed, his too-large boot caught on a rock, and he went flying. He'd always been cursed with clumsiness. He landed hard on his injured leg just as a huge grizzly ambled down the tunnel.

Cody felt for the rifle and realized it had gone flying.

The bear paused and stared, tilting its head to one side as if trying to recognize him. It reminded Cody of a friendly dog.

Wait. He'd seen this chocolate-colored bear before . . . relief ripped through his veins. This mellow alpha was Tim's friend.

"Mr. Chocolate," he whispered.

Did the bear recognize its name? Mr. Chocolate blinked at

Cody, then turned and ambled back the way he'd come. Back toward the upper lake.

Cody retrieved the rifle and followed. The massive alpha didn't seem to mind. Filled with gratitude for this friendly escort, he stayed close to the broad back as it led the way through the gloomy tunnel.

Mr. Chocolate was saving him.

Mr. Chocolate was helping him.

No!

Mr. Chocolate was veering off the trail.

"Hey, Mr. Chocolate. Just a little further," he begged in a sing-song voice. "Just get me through the maze. Only a half mile more. Please!"

The grizzly looked back at him. Calm. Unfazed. Mr. Chocolate had other things to do. With a big paw, the bear uprooted a clump of soil and began scooping up bugs.

Feeling terribly alone, Cody kept moving.

In the sky, the buzzing floatplane began its descent.

A new fear spurred him forward. What if the pilot saw the damaged tents and decided it was too dangerous to get out of the plane? What if he took off after a few seconds of landing?

Cody threw all caution to the wind.

He sprinted like a linebacker, knowing every predator around would hear his footsteps but also knowing the end zone was in sight.

Almost there.

Fifty feet away, the arch ended. Long grass waved in the stormy breeze beyond. He leaped out into the open. It was a short dash, and then he was there, right on the upper lake's shore.

In the distance, the floatplane bobbed in the shallows. It was toy-sized from here.

Where was the pilot?

He wished he'd brought his binoculars.

He squinted at the knoll and Tim's campsite. A man with buzz-cut hair and broad shoulders stepped out of the trees. He strolled curiously toward the mashed tents. The pilot. He had no idea what danger he was in.

The man stopped and stared at the ruined tents, arms crossed. After a moment, he knelt and lifted the canvas. Then he reeled back and began hiking fast down the trail back to the lake. The pilot raised one hand to shield his eyes and nervously scanned the brush.

Cody was about to shout, to try and scream for the pilot

not to leave, that he was here with his cousins, that they desperately needed a ride out, when he saw the bear.

Demon.

The killer grizzly. Moving on silent paws, the predator stalked the pilot. Twenty feet away and closing in fast. It would be on the pilot in seconds.

"Grizzly!" Cody screamed. "Behind you! Watch out!"

The pilot stopped in his tracks. "What's that?" he called. "What did you say? Treadwell, is that you?"

The pilot was completely oblivious.

Demon was just three body lengths behind him.

Cody gritted his teeth, raised the rifle, and fired into the air.

The pilot whirled around in shock. Seeing the grizzly, he took off fast, sprinting into the water. He scrambled onto the floats and into the cockpit and slammed the door. The grizzly skidded to a stop. Eyes fixed on the pilot, it paced the water's edge, huffing and snorting.

Ice cold sweat covered Cody. The bear looked like it was planning how to add the pilot to its food buffet.

"Hey kid!" the pilot yelled, finally catching sight of Cody. "Get away from here. That grizzly's dangerous. I'm calling the rangers for backup."

Did he think it was the only dangerous grizzly around?

Where did he want Cody to go?

"We're stranded. We need a ride back!"

The pilot stuck his head out the window. "What? Hold on!" He turned away and spoke into what looked like a radio or sat phone.

Cody had to get closer. He scrambled along the shore toward the river shouting, "We're stranded. Do you hear me? My cousins, they're down at the lower lake!"

He could see the pilot clearly through the windshield now, talking frantically and gesturing with his free hand.

Wait, where had Demon gone?

A massive splashing sound made every hair on Cody's neck stand on end. The grizzly was behind him. He'd forgotten bears can run thirty-five miles an hour.

Cody turned as Demon reared up to its full height and roared.

The pilot leaned out the window and screamed, "Run!"

There was no way he could outrun it—grizzlies ran faster than Olympic sprinters.

Still, he could try.

Feet thudding, arms pumping, he ran for the alders. He was smaller. He could weave faster through the twisting trees. Mud sucked his boots. Brambles snagged his windbreaker and jeans. If only he could get a chance, a moment's breather, he'd fire the rifle.

But Demon was too close. He could almost feel its hot breath on his neck.

Suddenly, the alders thinned. Oh yikes, he was finished. Panic rose, sick in his throat. He pictured the claws sinking into his neck. His heart banged like a heavy metal drum.

Ahead lay a rocky outcrop. He'd climb up and make a stand. Just one good shot with the rifle could do it.

Boots sliding on the shale, he scrambled halfway up. The grizzly launched after him, its claws sending stones flying.

Trembling, Cody raised the rifle. Ready. Aim. Fire.

Bang!

Birds fluttered out of the brush. A creature screeched.

But he'd missed.

The grizzly roared. A bloodcurdling roar. Now the animal wasn't just after a meal. It was mad. It came leaping up the rocks. Demon would tear him to pieces.

Cody bounded the last few yards, moving like a mountain goat, his knee screaming in protest. Heaving for breath, he reached the top of the ridge. Below, white water cascaded into a pool. Was the creek deep enough to jump, or would he hit a rock?

The killer grizzly was mere feet away.

A wave of panic engulfed him.

Do something or die.

Cody flung his baseball cap at the bear. The grizzly lunged for it. That worked! Time to bolt.

Cody whirled around. Teetered at the edge of the ridge.

No! Not again. He struggled to keep his balance. With a sickening feeling, he realized he couldn't.

Down he went.

Down. Down. Down . . .

CHAPTER TWENTY

KATMAI NATIONAL PARK

Instinctively, Cody forced his limbs into place—legs straight, arms across his chest—just like he'd in an action movie.

He hit the water hard. Ice cold enveloped him. The shock made his whole body go stiff. He couldn't move, couldn't swim. The current shot him to the surface, and he gasped for air.

"Move," he shouted at his body through chattering teeth.

Painfully, his limbs struggling like dead weights, he managed to kick his head higher out of the surging stream.

The creek was moving fast. His boots weighed down his feet, and his jeans and waterproof jacket flapped awkwardly. His blood was turning to ice. He kicked again, harder this time.

Keep moving toward shore, keep moving and you'll stay warmer, have to get out!

The current dragged him tumbling down the creek, past rocks and fallen branches. He tried to aim for the bank.

To his horror, Demon was still tracking him.

Holy moly! No!

The grizzly loped along, jaws open like it was grinning. Like it knew where to nab its prey. It wasn't climbing into the river, though. The water must be too rough.

Cody looked around wildly. The current was depositing silt and branches on the opposite bank. That's where he needed to go. It was clear the grizzly couldn't cross over.

Pure adrenaline took over. He swam as he'd never swum in his life.

Almost there . . . shallow now . . .

Grunting, he grabbed a branch and pulled himself out. On his hands and knees, he crawled onto the muddy shore.

He lay, half-stunned and frozen.

"I win," he muttered through numb lips. "I win, Demon! Hear that? This win's for Treadwell."

He flopped back, breathing hard.

From the far bank, Cody heard a loud roar. When he finally found the energy to sit up again, the bear was gone.

Overhead, a second plane appeared. It circled, descending. He glimpsed the Alaska State Troopers insignia. Thank goodness. It would all be over soon.

He opened and closed his empty hands. Where was his rifle? He'd lost it when he fell.

Shaking with cold, he stumbled to his feet. Following the creek should lead him to the lower lake, to Samantha and Matt.

He staggered along, feeling like he was in the twilight zone. In a daze, he wandered until the river poured into the larger body of water.

His heart leaped when he spotted Matt's small blue tent.

"Samantha! Matt!" he shouted.

No answer.

"Samantha!"

Panting, he reached the tent. Empty.

A seagull screeched and wheeled.

What now?

And then he let out a deep breath of relief when he saw them running through the seagrass.

"Samantha!" he yelled.

She raced up and threw her arms around him. "I was worried. You were gone for ages. What happened with the plane? We saw it land. And another just flew over."

Matt scowled. "Yeah, you took long enough. What the heck! What's happened to our ride out? You should've got the pilot to fly here!"

Samantha held Cody by the shoulder as if only now realizing he was drenched and half frozen to death.

"Are you alright?" she demanded. "What happened?"

"Demon's on the hunt."

Matt wrinkled his nose. "Demon? What, is that some kind of joke?"

"It's a grizzly," Samantha said.

Cody cut in. "Quick. We need to start a fire. The biggest fire we can make. It might not just be Demon on the hunt. Something set the grizzlies off. Hurry!"

Matt started moaning but Samantha screamed, "Be quiet and do what Cody says. Right now, Matt!"

Startled, he scowled at her. Then he actually stomped around gathering wood.

Cody said, "We need to keep the bears away. And we need

to make the biggest signal fire we can. I want to make sure those rangers find us."

"Does the pilot know we're here?" Samantha said, arranging kindling on the beach.

"He knows Demon went after me. They'll be looking for us, I guarantee it."

She nodded. "So, you made it to the upper lake. Great job. You can tell me what happened later. Let's get this fire going."

CHAPTER TWENTY-ONE

KATMAI NATIONAL PARK

Cody, Samantha, and Matt built the blaze until it roared ten feet high. The heat felt fantastic. That and a sleeping bag around Cody's shoulders stripped the cold from his quaking limbs.

He sighed in relief as the Coast Guard plane came in for a perfect landing and taxied to the shore.

A wiry, red-haired trooper opened the door and leaned out. "Great job with the signal fire. Made our job finding you a whole lot easier."

The cousins hauled their stuff toward the plane. Even though much of their gear was ruined, they knew to respect the land. This was grizzly territory—and fox, wolf, moose, rabbit, and all the other animals that called this place home.

Leave nothing behind except your footprints.

Well, the axe was somewhere in the woods and the gun, too, but Cody and Samantha had done what they could.

While the trooper stowed their gear, the pilot gave them a hand up. "What are you kids doing here?"

"It's a long story," Cody said.

"I'm sure it is."

Cody squashed into a seat beside Samantha. Matt fell into the aisle seat. A second trooper, this one older and bearded, handed Samantha a blanket and a thermos.

She filled cups with hot coffee and passed them around. Cody gulped his share. It was sweet with lots of milk, and he decided it was the most delicious thing he'd ever tasted.

When the cup was empty, he wiped his mouth on his sleeve and asked the question he'd been dreading. But he had to know.

"Sir?" he said,

The red-haired trooper met his eyes.

"Did you find Tim Treadwell and Amie?"

The trooper watched him for a long moment and then turned to the window, gazing out. "I'm sorry, son. We did. They didn't make it."

The pilot pulled back the yoke, and the floatplane rose into the air.

Hot tears filled Cody's eyes. He pressed his face to the window and watched the dark grizzly maze spread out below. In the creeks, a few bears were still catching salmon as if nothing had happened.

Tim Treadwell, the incredible bear expert. And Amie, his friend and companion in this wild place. They were gone.

The troopers talked in low voices. Cody strained to hear.

"I thought I'd have a heart attack when that grizzly charged," the older man said. "That animal had no fear. Even against four of us."

"Yeah. And that second grizzly?" the red-haired trooper said. "I thought he'd get me for sure. He was just as aggressive."

Cody flashed a glance at Samantha. Quietly, he said, "Demon and Machine?"

"Sounds like it," she whispered. "Or some other starving bears."

The older trooper shook his head. "Terrible scene. But Treadwell shouldn't have been in the park, what with the drought and all. At this time of year? No one should be up here." He gave Cody, Samantha, and Matt a sharp look.

Cody stared at his feet. The trooper was right.

The plane's engine rumbled like a flying lawnmower as they soared over the dark ocean.

With an electronic squawk, the radio stuttered to life. The pilot turned up the volume:

Bodies presumed to be Timothy Treadwell and his companion. Park rangers will be returning to the site tomorrow.

The news had already caught wind of the story. Word traveled fast.

Cody's heart ached. There'd been something beautiful about Tim's love for the bears. He thought about Mr. Chocolate, the gentle bear who'd escorted him through the maze. Of the injured bear and the mother grizzly with her cubs. Miraculous as it seemed, Tim and many of the bears had formed a bond, anyone could see that.

Grizzlies were incredible animals, born to live in this wilderness.

If only Tim and Amie had taken the earlier flight home to California. Then the last few days would never have happened.

Samantha spoke up. "What I don't understand is why—after all this time Tim was up here—why would a grizzly suddenly attack him like that?"

"Who knows. Hunger? Aggression?"

Matt sneered. "Because they're killers, that's why."

"Truth is, most bears wouldn't kill a man," the older trooper said. "They're more interested in fish and other prey. But sometimes you get what they call the twenty-fifth grizzly —the bear that mauls and kills."

Cody nodded. He understood completely. For where there had been gentleness in Mr. Chocolate's eyes, in Demon's, there had been only rage. Just like people, bears came in all sorts.

Matt said, "Can't you fly this thing any faster? I thought you guys were the Coast Guard. How much longer? I need a beer."

Samantha planted her face in her hands and sighed with embarrassment. Cody groaned.

Some people never changed.

CHAPTER TWENTY-TWO

KODIAK ISLAND, ALASKA

At Kodiak Airport, Gramps met the plane. He hugged Cody, Matt, and Samantha, pulling them one-by-one into his bomber-jacket-clad chest.

Cody inhaled the familiar smell. Gramps smelled like a pipe and soap and felt as warm and solid as ever.

Gramps didn't say a word about what they'd done. When they got to the cabin, he made hot dogs on a big grill.

Cody scoffed down three, smothered with mustard, fried tomato, and onions. He burped. "That was great, thanks."

"You guys will make me old before my time." Gramps stared into the glowing coals. "It's tragic what happened to Tim Treadwell. He was a goofy type of guy, but I liked him. A local was talking stink about him at the airport, saying he asked for it."

"That's unfair!" Cody said. "All he was doing was trying to protect bears from poachers."

Gramps nodded. "Yeah. But he took his chances. Grizzlies are wild animals."

"Was it just bad luck?" Cody asked, trying to come to terms with what had happened.

"I don't know, son," Gramps scratched his salt-and-pepper beard. "If you play with fire, one day you'll get burned. Tread-well ditched the bear spray and an electric fence. Still, he managed to survive thirteen summers in bear central. Not many could do that."

"I know we should never have gone to the grizzly maze, Cody said.

His grandfather raised his eyebrows. "You've got that right. That was one of the scariest moments of my life—when the Park rangers called and told me the three of you were in the maze. I thought you were at the Best Western in Kodiak."

"I'm sorry," Samantha said, her face flushed.

"I dashed down to the park ranger's office," Gramps said. "A ranger broke it to me that Treadwell had disappeared. He said you three were in the grizzly maze and that there was a killer bear on the prowl." Gramps cleared his throat. "Yep. I nearly had a heart attack."

Cody felt his face grow hot.

"Your parents called," Gramps said. "They want you home immediately—sooner if possible." He cleared his throat. "Guess this is the last time they trust you with me."

"It never would have happened if Cody hadn't bought those tickets with his dad's credit card," Matt muttered.

Cody leaped to his feet. "Lying jerk!"

"Cool it, guys." Gramps grabbed Cody's arm. "Thank goodness you're okay."

"Sorry, Gramps," Cody said.

"I know you're sorry, son." Gramps wrapped one arm

around Cody's shoulders. "How about a four-way cuddle. Remember how we used to do this when you were little?"

"I'm not a big cuddler," Matt muttered.

"Aw! Come on, son."

Scowling, Matt joined them.

Cody hugged his grandfather and Samantha. Then he forced himself to hug Matt too, although he didn't feel like it. Matt was a jerk, but he was family.

After a moment, Matt returned his hug.

Cody stifled a surprised gasp.

Gramps brought out marshmallows, and they gathered closer to the fire to make s'mores.

"I love your place here." Cody looked up at the dark firs and the snow-covered mountains. "I want to come back to Alaska. Do you think being an Alaskan park ranger would be a good career?"

Gramps scratched his beard. "Certainly an interesting one. I admire the park rangers—they're a brave bunch."

"I could go to college in Anchorage," Cody said.

Gramps smiled. "That would be good. I'd see a lot more of you then."

Cody grinned. Despite what happened, he loved the wilderness. And he admired Tim Treadwell for trying to protect wild animals. He also admired the rangers and state troopers. They protected wild animals too. His heart stirred at the possibility of joining them one day.

He mashed a hot marshmallow and a chocolate square between two graham crackers and popped it into his mouth. "I can't believe we did that, wandered all over grizzly territory right before hibernation season."

"We had no idea what we were getting into," Samantha agreed.

"Nope. That place belongs to the bears. We were lucky, very lucky. But we did it," Cody said, looking at his cousins. "I don't know how, but we survived. The three of us. We escaped the grizzly maze!"

THE END

Turn the page for amazing facts about grizzlies and more!

10 TIPS TO SURVIVE A GRIZZLY ATTACK

1. Don't run. Stand your ground and slowly wave your arms up and down to look bigger. Pick up small children and warn them to be quiet.
2. Avoid eye contact; move away quietly, slowly and sideways so as not to trip. Do not scream—that will accelerate the situation.
3. Get to a safe place like a car or a building. Know that grizzlies can climb trees.
4. Throw a hat or your jacket to distract the bear.
5. Ask rangers about bear sightings and areas to avoid.
6. Carry bear spray and read how to use it. Keep it within reach, and practice pulling it out fast.
7. If the bear attacks, use whatever you have to hit the bear in the face or muzzle.
8. Never approach any bear, especially a mother bear with cubs.
9. If a bear attacks your tent, do not play dead. It's looking for food and sees you as prey. Keep bear spray, a flashlight, or an air horn handy—you may have only minutes to find them in the dark.
10. Never eat or keep food in your tent. Store food in bear-tight containers away from the tent. Do not leave garbage around.

DID YOU KNOW?

AMAZING GRIZZLY FACTS

Despite their ferocious reputations, up to 80% of a grizzly bear's diet consists of insects, grass, berries, roots, and broad-leaved plants. The other 20% consists of meat and fish, such as rodents, wolves, elk, moose, clams, salmon, and even the occasional whale carcass.

Grizzlies have an excellent sense of smell. They can smell an open peanut butter jar from two miles away. They can also smell clams through the sand, which helps them dig them up.

A grizzly standing on its hind legs is tall enough to look through a second-story window.

Grizzles can run at speeds of 35 miles per hour.

A grizzly is so strong that it can kill a wolf with one swipe of its massive paw.

The big hump on a grizzly's back is made of muscle, giving the bear its mighty strength. In fact, they have the strongest front limbs of any animal in the world.

Bears love honey. Their furry, thick skin protects them from bee stings when they pull apart a bee hive.

The grizzlies in Katmai National Park are among the largest bears in the world. They live longer than bears in regions where hunting is allowed and grow up to 1,400 pounds.

Grizzlies rarely kill people. About eighty percent of those attacks are by mother bears defending their cubs or bears defending their food cache. Predatory attacks are rare. However, they do happen.

Grizzly bears have been a threatened species since 1975.

The State of Alaska has around 32,000 bears and only 670,000 people. That's one bear for every 21 people!

Participate in Fat Bear Week!

Do you love bears? Participate in Katmai National Park's Fat Bear Week! It's an annual tradition. Every fall, internet users watch live bear cams and vote for their favorite fat bear.

Learn more at: https://explore.org/fat-bear-week

WHO WAS TIMOTHY TREADWELL?

Timothy Treadwell was a Californian wildlife activist with the unusual ability to communicate with the largest omnivores on the planet. Treadwell loved grizzly bears and wanted to protect them from both illegal poachers and sports hunters. He also wished to convince everyone that they're not the ferocious predators they seem.

Treadwell spent thirteen summers living closely with grizzlies in Alaska. In winter, Treadwell returned to California to campaign passionately for the bears. He wanted to be part of their lives and to educate young people about them.

He documented his experiences in writing and videos. Treadwell wrote a touching and fascinating book called *Among Grizzlies: Living with Wild Bears in Alaska*.

He also formed an educational, non-profit company called *Grizzly People*.

The last thing Treadwell would have wanted was to become known as Katmai National Park's first grizzly fatality.

Park Rangers and other bear researchers repeatedly warned Treadwell that getting close to grizzlies was dangerous. Treadwell was aware of the danger.

In interviews, he warned:

"Do not do this. Do not copy me."

He said that if a bear killed him, he didn't want the bear to be blamed:

"If they ever come to pick me up and find me dead, I hope they just bury me and don't say a word."

Treadwell had not planned to be in the park in October 2003. He tried to fly back to California but argued with the airline ticketer over the high ticket price. He decided to wait until the prices came down and returned to the park.

On October 5, he talked to a friend via satellite phone and mentioned no problems with the bears. The following day, however, a Kodiak air taxi pilot found their campsite deserted, apart from a massive bear. The pilot contacted park rangers, who quickly determined that Timothy Treadwell and Amie Huguenard had not survived.

A film, *Grizzly Man* (2005), documents Treadwell's life and was aired on the Discovery Channel. *The Grizzly Man Diaries* (2008) is an 8-episode miniseries that premiered on Animal

Planet and also documents Treadwell's work and life using interviews and historical footage.

While people disagree over whether Timothy Treadwell was right or wrong to live so close to grizzlies, his work has given us a fascinating and unique understanding of grizzlies and their habitats.

FASCINATING QUOTES

"I felt a great deal of paranoia, and rightfully so... A nearby creek was loaded with bears and trouble. The chemistry between the bears was volatile—three mean bears . . . I felt the tension growing."
Timothy Treadwell, August 21.

"But, let me tell you, ... every fish, every bear was here. We made the best friggin' choice of our lives. Once the rain settled down, boy, it was amazing out here."
Timothy Treadwell, two days before his death.

"Bears wishing to traverse the area would have had to either wade in the lake or walk right next to the tent. A person could not have designed a more dangerous location to set up a camp...His decision not to have any defensive methods or bear deterrents in the camp was directly responsible for the catastrophic event."
Larry Van Daele, Biologist.

"If it happens, it happens. God forbid, if a bear takes me, let him go."
Timothy Treadwell.

"We are deeply saddened by the loss of our friend and admired environmental warrior."
Pierre Brosnan, actor, after learning of Treadwell's death.

"At the top of the food chain, the magnificent grizzly bear has no animal to fear but the two-legged kind.

Two hundred years ago, Europeans settled in the best habitat and killed thousands of grizzly bears, which they saw as competition or a threat. Grizzly bear numbers plummeted in the lower 48 states, reduced to just 1% of their former numbers and relegated to the most remote remaining wilderness areas.

Grizzly People Pamphlet.

"I had a lot of special guests come in. Timothy was always the one they'd remember. He was always the favorite. In part, it was the bears, but it was really his personal style...He was like a little kid, almost like a jumping bean. He had so much energy. This was his passion. His love. He was so honest, and the kids identified with that.

Valerie Roach, 3rd-Grade Teacher, California

"I admired how serious Timothy's messages were. He risks his life for the bears."

Californian School Student

"Watching him perform in a classroom, you saw a magician who explained the mysteries of bears and their lives in such a way that children emerged glowing as if they too were the discoverers of wild America. Hearing him talk about his bears, by name, with their bonds of affection, quirky behavior, and playful antics, you felt that you were let in on great secrets that few receive today or have forgotten as wilderness has been paved over and subdivided."

Louisa Willcox, Director, Natural Resources Defense Council.

BIBLIOGRAPHY

Jans, Nick, *The Grizzly Maze, Timothy Treadwell's Fatal Obsession with Alaskan Bears,* Dutton, Jan 2005.

Herzog, Werner, *Grizzly Man,* documentary film, 2005

Treadwell, Timothy, *Among Grizzlies, Living with Wild Bears in Alaska,* Feb, 1999

https://www.yellowstone-bearman.com/Tim_Treadwell.html, *Night of the Grizzly,* 2005

NPS Report Treadwell Grizzly Fatality, Nov, 20, 2003, Dalrymple, Derek. Katmai Park Ranger. 2003 National Park Service Incident Report, pages 11, 12.

Ellis, Joel. Katmai National Park Ranger. 2003 Scene Investigator. 2003 Park Service Incident Report; pages 1-9

I ESCAPED
THE HAUNTED
WINCHESTER HOUSE

THE BESTSELLING KIDS SURVIVAL SERIES
ELLIE CROWE + SCOTT PETERS

CHAPTER ONE

It was almost midnight. Dark shadows filled every corner of the Winchester House Ballroom, and ghostly fog swirled.

Fifteen-year-old Jesse peered into the gloom. His blue eyes flared in shock. There, across the empty floor, a figure was materializing.

Yikes!

A tall, thin man wavered, ghost-like, fading in and out. He stared at Jesse, his hair writhing like squiggly octopus tentacles.

"I see something," Jesse whispered, trying to keep his voice steady.

At his back, his fifteen-year-old cousin, Emma, stiffened.

"What sort of thing?" she whispered.

"A weird thing. Look! Over there." Jesse pointed.

Emma's bushy hair tickled his nose as she peeked over his shoulder. "Eek, what is that?"

"Might be a spirit. I've got to get a picture."

"Take it fast and let's go," she hissed.

Jesse set the Kodak Brownie on a rickety table and opened the shutter.

"Hurry up!" Emma hissed. "It's moving this way."

A sudden shriek broke the silence. A small boy with wild, curly hair charged across the ball-room, nearly knocking over the camera.

Emma made a futile grab for her nephew. "GL!" she called after the retreating boy. "Get back here!"

Jesse groaned. "So much for my shot. I can't believe you brought him."

"GL," Emma shouted, "Where are you going?"

Jesse snatched up his camera, slung it around his neck, and raced after GL. Good old Sniffer, Jesse's black Labrador, galloped alongside, his tongue hanging out.

The house creaked and moaned.

GL reached the corridor's far end and clambered up a steep, narrow stairway. At the top, he scrambled crab-like onto a landing. Jesse grabbed the kid's ankle, stopping him dead. GL's floppy blue hat flew over the wooden railing. It spun into the pool of darkness below.

"My hat!" GL yelled.

"Shh!" Emma gasped, catching up. "Someone's coming. Hide!"

Sniffer let out a low whine.

"Good boy, it's okay," Jesse whispered.

Footsteps—shuffling footsteps—scratched along the hall-way. Slow and steady, heading in their direction.

Then, an angry moan shook the walls. A horrible shriek followed.

Eyes bugging out, Jesse stared at the space where a person should be. There was no one there!

This wasn't good. How did you run from something you couldn't see?

"Through here," he said, pointing at one of the many oak doors lining the corridor.

Emma tried the handle. "Locked."

Jesse grabbed another brass doorknob. "Locked, too."

Emma wrapped a protective arm around GL. Her pointed face was ashen with fear. "I told you this was a bad idea."

"What about this room?" Jesse reached for a third door-knob, but as he grabbed it, the knob began to rattle and turn. "That's not me doing that."

"Then who is?" Emma said.

Someone, or *something*.

Jesse snatched his hand away as though the knob was red hot.

"Don't let go, Jesse! What are you doing? They'll get out!"

She was right. Jesse grabbed the doorknob and held on for dear life. But it kept turning, spinning powerfully in his palm. His lizard brain buzzed *danger* loud and clear.

Gritting his teeth, he clung on.

CHAPTER TWO

JESSE'S HOME
SAN JOSE, CALIFORNIA
8 HOURS EARLIER

"That's not fair!" Jesse said. "I only called Pete a rotten jerk because it's true."

Dad's broad face turned an ominous shade of red.

"And you're never on my side," Jesse added.

"You'd better apologize fast, Son."

Sizzling with frustration, Jesse said, "Pete started it."

"Don't talk back."

"So, Pete's not even being punished?" Jesse stammered.

Dad said, "This is my house, and I make the rules. You're grounded. I hope you think long and hard about what you said."

"But it's Saturday night. And it was Pete's fault! Why don't you believe me? You never believe me."

Dressed in a tight, white undershirt, Pete leaned against Jesse's bedroom wall, his arms folded across his bulging chest. He flashed Jesse a shark-like grin from behind Dad's back. Nineteen years old, he always got off scot-free.

Why couldn't Dad back Jesse up just once?

Worst of all, Jesse had big plans for tonight. He and his cousin Emma were supposed to sneak into the haunted Winchester House. Looks like he'd be stuck in his room instead.

"You're never fair." Jesse stared at the floor.

"Is that what you think?" Dad said in that low voice that meant trouble. "Based on what? Why don't you give me an example?"

Jessie hated when Dad acted like he was some sort of expert interrogator, trying to trap him up, trying to find a crack in his story.

"Based on right now." At once, Jesse realized it was a dumb thing to say.

"Right, if that's how you choose to speak to me, you can spend the whole weekend in your room. And when you get out, you can apologize to Pete for calling him names and to me for lack of respect."

Jesse opened his mouth to backtrack.

Dad said, "Not another peep." He left without waiting for a reply.

Gee whiz. What a dictator.

Pete grinned like a cat with a canary. His white teeth flashed in his suntanned face. "Loser!"

"Takes one to know one."

Pete stretched, showing off his famous pitcher forearms. "Enjoy your weekend." He sauntered off.

From downstairs, Dad shouted, "And clean your room. The place looks like a pigsty."

Jesse took quick stock of his bedroom. It looked like it always did—like a bomb had blown apart his closet. Okay, Dad had him there.

Still, at least the walls looked good. He'd tacked up some great posters from the amazing 1904 St. Louis World's Fair.

He studied one of his favorites: a dripping waffle ice-cream cone. Looked yummy. Ice cream cones had been invented right at the St. Louis World's Fair. He admired his other great posters: the giant ferris wheel, dinosaur skeletons, an elephant made of almonds, the massive clown on the Temple of Mirth, the Asian dancers, the African Pygmies.

What fun it would be to ride in a hot air balloon like a photojournalist, taking pictures at the World's Fair. Photojournalists did some great stuff. When he finished college, that's what he wanted to be.

He'd planned to start his new career tonight by taking pictures inside the Winchester House, the weirdest house in America. He hoped he could even get a photo in the paper. That was off, now, though.

Frustrated, he flopped onto his bed, legs dangling. Pete never got punished. He knew how to get around Dad. Because, like Dad before him, Pete had made star pitcher on the San Jose High School's baseball team. His fastballs had hit eighty-five. And every time he scored a strike-out, Dad yelled, "Way to go, son!"

Also, Pete was a crack shot with Gramp's Winchester hunting rifle.

Dad treasured that hunting rifle because Gramps helped

design it. He'd told them a million times how famous it was—
The Gun That Won the West. Dad thought it was a supreme
honor when he allowed Pete and Jesse to take it hunting.

But Jesse wasn't a great shot. Not even a good shot.

Whenever they headed to Suisun Marsh for a day of wild-
fowl hunting, Pete brought down at least two flying geese, one
for dinner and one that Mom would preserve for later.

Every time, Dad cheered, "Well done, son! Way to go,
Pete!"

Jesse had never brought down a flying goose in his life.
Not even when great flocks filled the sky. He missed
every one.

Pete called him blind as a bat. Of course, Pete never got
into trouble for saying that.

It wasn't Jesse's fault for being nearsighted. He rubbed his
eyes, annoyed at the unfairness.

"No way am I staying in my room tonight," he muttered.
"I'm sneaking into that spooky Winchester House no matter
what. I've been planning this for weeks. I'm going to borrow
Dad's Kodak Brownie and take pictures of the weirdest stuff I
can find. I'll be the first one to take pictures in there, and no
one's going to stop me. And when I get my pictures in the
paper, even Dad and Pete will be impressed."

CHAPTER THREE

JESSE'S HOME

2 MINUTES LATER

Jesse stood staring out his bedroom window, mulling over his plans. Dark clouds massed on the horizon, and the dry trees stood like skeletons, their brittle limbs rattling in the wind.

Across the fields, he could just make out the Winchester House's gothic-looking turrets and domes.

What a weird place. Seven stories high! And tonight, all one-hundred-and-sixty rooms and miles of zig-zagging hallways were empty. Dad was the building foreman, and he said Sarah Winchester was out of town. The builders, who normally worked day-and-night around the clock building the place, had been given a break.

It was the perfect night to sneak in. Jesse could hardly wait.

Emma, on the other hand, wasn't quite so keen. Still, she'd said yes, adding that he'd need her brains in case he got into trouble. He grinned. She'd been joking, but she'd gotten them out of a few jams in the past. He tended to charge into things full-speed ahead, which didn't always end well. She, on the other hand, liked to puzzle things out first.

Anyway, as long as they weren't chased by angry spirits, they'd be fine. He didn't *actually* believe the stories— that ghosts haunted the house because they were angry at the family who invented the Winchester repeating rifles.

According to Dad, though, Sarah Winchester believed it. She thought they wanted to kill her and take their revenge on her family. That's why Mrs. Winchester kept building so many rooms, halls, and stairwells, to confuse the spirits so they couldn't find her. She even slept in a different bedroom each night to escape them!

A breeze sent a brown, leathery leaf skittering through his open window. It twirled toward his face, making him jump back. As he swatted it aside, a loud crack made his heart stutter. Was that a rifle?

No, just a branch breaking in the wind.

Something shuffled under his bed, and he turned quickly.

Sniffer, Jesse's black lab, stuck out his nose. Sniffer didn't like it when Dad yelled.

Jesse let out the breath he didn't know he'd been holding. "Hey, boy. Ready for a big adventure?"

Sniffer cocked his head.

"At the Winchester House?"

Sniffer responded with a low whine, tucking his chin between his paws. Usually, Sniffer was up for action. Tonight, he didn't seem into it.

"It'll be neat, Sniffer, I promise."

As long as they didn't get caught. Otherwise, he'd be grounded for the rest of the year.

He ran his fingers through his cropped brown hair. He'd have to wait until Mom and Dad were asleep—after eleven at least. He just hoped Emma would still be up for it. He didn't like the idea of going alone. Only one way to find out.

He tiptoed down the hall. Mom and Dad's voices echoed from the kitchen. Pete was nowhere in sight.

Jesse made a silent sprint for the small table that held the family telephone and snatched up the handset.

"Number, please," the operator said.

"One, four, two, six," Jesse said.

"Trying now."

Emma answered on the fifth ring.

Low and quick, Jesse whispered, "Change of plans. I can't get out till eleven. Let's meet at that wrought-iron front gate in front of the Winchester House. At five after."

"What?" Emma said. "I can't hear you."

Jesse winced. Next thing, Dad or Pete would come looking to see who he was talking to. He spoke slightly louder. "The Winchester House plan is on. But we're going later. Meet me at the gate at five after eleven."

"Still can't hear you," Emma said.

From her end came a noise like a siren going off. "What's that racket?"

"It's GL," Emma said. "My nephew."

"Gotcha." Checking to make sure the coast was clear, Jesse spoke louder. "Meet me at the Winchester House front gate at eleven-oh-five."

There was a rustle on the phone line. That wasn't good. Was the nosy operator listening in? Or one of the neighbors on the party line?

"Eleven? That late?" Emma said.

"Has to be. I'll explain later."

Emma was silent a moment. "I don't think we should," she said. "If our parents find out, we're dead. And what if it really is haunted? And there's a storm coming. Besides, it'll be dark in that huge, creepy place. We said we'd go before sunset."

Jesse took a deep breath. Emma was going to back out. "If we get in there, we'll be famous," he said. "Our names will go down in school history."

"How?" Emma said. "No one will believe us."

"They will. Because here's the thing. I'm borrowing Dad's Kodak Brownie camera. Come on, you have to help me. You know how bad I want to be a photographer, and this is my best chance. Please? I need your brains in case I get into trouble, remember?"

Long pause.

"Your dad will kill you for borrowing it without asking," Emma said.

True. But Jesse ignored the warning. "Wait till we show Pete the pictures. He'll be green with envy. Remember last year when Pete and his girlfriend tried to sneak into the house on Halloween? And got caught by that handyman? My brother's still never been in there."

"Yeah." Emma laughed. "For once, we'd be the top dogs. Instead of Pete always showing everyone up."

"It's the only night the place will be empty."

"I'll think about it," she said.

"I'll be waiting at five after. Please don't let me down, Emma!"

CHAPTER FOUR

Jesse's home

Jesse slid the telephone handset back into its holder.

He had to grab Dad's Kodak Brownie camera out of the living room cabinet without getting caught. He'd get the flashlight while he was at it.

Ears on high alert, he tiptoed along. Dishes clanked in the kitchen sink. The murmur of his parents' voices rose and fell.

Not far now.

The living room cabinet came into view. His bare feet moved silently across the carpet.

In a few hours, if all went according to plan, he'd be running across a different carpet in the Winchester House. The one Dad had installed in a room called the Witches Cap. That carpet was a strange shade of blue—*haint-blue,* that's what Dad called it. Even the name sounded funny. Supposedly the *haint-blue* color fooled the spirits because it looked like water and spirits were scared of water.

Or so people said.

Anyway, forget *haint-blue*, who called a room the *Witches Cap?*

He couldn't wait to see it. And get a picture of it. Especially because that's where Pete was headed last year when he'd tried to sneak inside. Double win!

A floorboard creaked.

"What do you think you're doing?" Dad's voice boomed. "What part of staying in your room don't you understand?"

Jesse jumped. Whoa. Way to look guilty.

"Just looking for a snack," he said.

"Back to your room. You already had dinner."

The telephone rang. Saved by the bell!

Dad went to answer it.

Heart slamming, Jesse darted to the cabinet and grabbed the flashlight and camera.

Crash.

Oh no!

He'd knocked over a framed family picture—a skinny Pete, seven years old, struggling to hold a chubby toddler. Jesse. Both were laughing. Both were hanging onto each other, their brown eyes so alike. When had things changed?

They didn't laugh together much now.

Quietly, Jesse set the picture back on the sideboard. Then he sprinted to his room and locked the door.

CHAPTER FIVE

JESSE'S HOME

At a quarter to eleven, Jesse pulled on a dark-blue shirt and loaded up his knapsack with the flashlight and Kodak Brownie. Then, he slid open his bedroom window.

Creeeeeeeak.

He winced and listened for Dad's footsteps.

Silence.

Quietly, he swung his legs over the sill and scrambled onto the flat roof.

"Come on, Sniffer," he whispered.

Sniffer followed, his ears quivering.

They crossed carefully to the garage roof, dropped onto a pile of wooden planking supplies, and then onto the grass.

Sniffer galloped around, racing up and down the lawn. He

thought this was some new game. At any moment, the lab would bark, and it would be all over.

"Shh, down boy. Good dog!" Jesse grabbed Sniffer's leather collar and hurried away from the farmstead.

An eerie quiet filled the country lane. In the distance, across dry, lumpy fields and leafless orchards, the Winchester House loomed against the sky.

Jesse broke into a jog with Sniffer trotting at his side.

Overhead, clouds, like dark sky-dragons, flew across the bright half-moon.

Something caught his eye. Black shapes, hundreds of them.

What the . . .

Birds, the sky teemed with them!

How weird. Birds didn't fly at night, not as far as he knew. But there they were, flocks of geese, wings flapping. Some soared high above, some barely missed his head as they swooped past.

Freaked out, he ducked.

Now, a flock of pigeons flew by, right at eye level. He dodged, throwing up his arms. Where were they going? Did they know something he didn't? Maybe they were running from the coming storm?

In that case, he'd better get a move on.

He'd barely started running when his feet slid on something wet and mushy. Catching his balance, he saw the road was crawling with earthworms. Ugh! They squished under his sneakers.

A group of rabbits hopped by.

Sniffer lunged.

"No! No chasing rabbits." Jesse pulled Sniffer back.

In the distance, coyotes howled. Long, echoing howls.

Hairs rose on Jesse's neck. Something was off. Why were the birds on the move? And the rabbits? Even the worms?

Well, he had other things to worry about. He needed to get inside the house before it started pouring and drenched Dad's precious camera.

As if on cue, thunder rumbled. He ran.

Emma, wearing a navy dress, black stockings, and boots, stood waiting for him at the Winchester House gate.

"You came!" he called, grinning.

"Yep. We have to show up your brother once in a while, right?" Her frizzy blond hair was tied with green ribbons.

A kid stepped out from behind her back, small and skinny and dressed in a sailor suit with a floppy blue cap over his long, white-blond hair.

The shrimp started doing his best to kick down the wrought-iron gate.

Jesse stifled a groan, inched up to Emma, and whispered, "Why'd you bring GL?"

"I had to," Emma said. "I'm babysitting him."

"I thought it was your sister's turn."

"He kicked her. So, she dumped him on me. I couldn't just leave him."

George, or GL—short for Greased Lightning—was a four-year-old terror.

Jesse scratched at his hair, turning it into spikes. "Yeah, but . . . we can't take him inside," he said as GL started body-slamming the gates. "You know what he's like!"

Emma crossed her arms. "You wanted me to come, I'm here."

GL abandoned the gate and hollered, "Hey Jesse! Make Sniffer do the trick. Make him do it!"

Emma rolled her green eyes. "He got into the candy. He's completely bonkers. Worse than usual."

"Make him do it!" GL shouted.

Jesse pulled his black baseball cap lower. "Sniffer will do his trick later. Promise. We have to stay quiet."

"Now!" GL shouted. "Now! Do it now!"

Sniffer's tail was down. He slunk behind Jesse. Maybe all the geese and weird animals were creeping him out. Plus, he didn't like thunder.

Jesse stroked the lab's soft dark fur. "Sniffer doesn't want to right now."

"Make him do his trick!" GL yelled.

"Shh!" Jesse said. "You can't come if you keep yelling like a baby."

"Make him do his trick," GL whispered. "Please, please, puh-lease."

"Just do it," Emma said, glancing at the road. "Someone's going to see us. If my parents find out I took GL, I'm dead."

Jesse said, "Give me one of your sneakers, GL. Quick."

GL pulled off a sneaker and handed it over.

"Hide behind that plum tree down there," Jesse said.

"Don't let Sniffer see where I go," GL said.

"I won't. I'm turning him around."

Beaming a gap-toothed smile, GL ran off along the lane.

Jesse held the sneaker under Sniffer's nose. "This shouldn't take long. Pee-ew, this sneaker stinks just like GL."

Sniffer stuck his nose into the sneaker.

"Got it? Good dog! Seek. Seek GL!"

Sniffer sniffed the air and the road with his big, wet nose, doing his super-scent-tracker thing. Within seconds, he made a beeline for the plum tree where GL was hiding.

GL ran back, giggling with delight. "Good dog, Sniffer!"

Emma beamed. "How did you train him to do that? It's amazing."

"Dogs can smell forty times better than humans," Jesse said, knowing Emma loved her facts.

"Ooh, that's neat. Forty times?"

"Yeah, but can you imagine? That means stinky stuff is forty times stinkier."

They both laughed at that.

GL yelled, "Super stinky!"

Jesse put his finger to his lips. "Come on, let's do this. Follow me."

The iron gate was fastened with a thick chain and padlock. Checking that no one was watching, Jesse slid through a narrow gap between the gate and the fence, and the others followed.

CHAPTER SIX

WINCHESTER HOUSE

11:05 PM

Jesse, Emma, and GL stood in a row, all staring up at the spooky Winchester House. It loomed over them, monstrous in the moonlight.

A lightning bolt highlighted the endless towers, turrets, and cupolas, while the dark, dark windows reflected like eyes.

Hold on, something moved in one of the windows! But the place was supposed to be empty. Jesse squinted, trying to catch sight of it again.

Wind rustled the trees. A weathervane on the top of a cupola moved. But in the window, all was still.

"What's up?" Emma asked.

"I thought I saw someone watching from up there."

Emma frowned. "A caretaker?"

"I probably imagined it."

"I don't want to go in there if there's some massive Frankenstein caretaker inside."

"Who said massive? Anyway, no one's there."

GL said, "Bats in the belfry!"

Emma rolled her eyes. "Where did you hear that expression?"

"Ghosts," GL replied, as if that made sense.

Jesse took a deep breath. "There are no ghosts."

"Are you sure about that?" Emma asked

"I don't know." He raised his camera. "Can you imagine if I got a picture of one, though? They'd print it in every paper in America."

"Haha." Emma laughed nervously. "Don't tell me that's why we're here. I thought you wanted to get pictures of the weird stairs and stuff."

Lightning flashed again. High above, the pointy Bell Tower stood out in sharp relief.

Emma pointed at it. "I wonder why Mrs. Winchester rings the bell every midnight."

Jesse started to reply but held his tongue. Better not to mention that—according to Dad—she rang it to summon the angry spirits. She'd have some kind of meeting with them to announce her building plans. Then she'd ring it again at two in the morning to send them away.

What a strange way to live.

Well, as long as they didn't ring the bell, the spirits wouldn't show up.

Except, what if he summoned them? And got a picture of it?

While terrifying, that would be something.

He shivered. Did he dare? Did he even want to see a ghost? In a way, he did because Pete would go nuts with jealousy, and Jesse could tell all the guys at school about it.

Emma probably wouldn't like it, though.

And what if Sarah Winchester was right, that the spirits were after revenge? Jesse had shot a Winchester rifle lots of time, even if he'd never taken down a bird. Dad worked on this house. And Gramps helped design the gun. Would the spirits come after him if he snuck inside? Would they attack him?

He shivered again. He wasn't sure if the shiver was excitement or fear. "Let's go before it gets too late and someone finds us gone."

A paved path wound past a fountain and around a rose garden. A sickly-sweet smell of rotting rose petals filled the air.

"Look at all these varieties," Emma said, naming off roses as they went. Sometimes she sounded like a walking encyclopedia.

They neared the front porch. Up close, the monster-sized mansion looked like some kid built it using weirded-out giant blocks.

GL squeaked and skidded to a stop. Jesse almost fell right over him.

"G-g-ghost!" GL stammered.

Jesse gulped. A white figure hovered at the massive front door. Spirits already! He froze and realized what it was.

"Statue," he said. "That's just a statue."

"Duh." GL stuck out his tongue and crossed his eyes. "I knew it."

"Did not," Jesse said.

"*You* didn't." GL giggled. "You peed your pants."

Jesse rolled his eyes. "Right, as if!" A few drops of rain spattered his face. "Let's go round the back and find a basement window," he said. "Basement windows are easiest to get through."

Emma said, "Stay close, GL, don't go running off."

Jesse helped GL through a narrow space between a brick tower and the main wall of the House. Emma and Sniffer followed.

Wind howled across the courtyard. Leafless branches clawed the sky, skeletal in the dark.

Crack!

He jumped. What was that?

Emma grabbed his arm. "Sounded like a gunshot." Wind whipped her hair. "Someone's shooting at us!" She dropped to her stomach, pulling GL down. "Hit the ground!"

Jesse crouched low. "Must be a hunter out in the fields."

Another crack. Louder than the first.

"A hunter? Not in the middle of the night," Emma said.

"Er . . . maybe not."

It sure sounded like gunshots. Dad said there were rifles in a display cabinet in the House. Could the spirits have got hold of them? Were the spirits shooting at them?

A gruesome thought arose: *Maybe they want to take over our warm, living bodies.* No—that was aliens, not ghosts. Ghosts didn't take over human bodies, did they? Or maybe they did.

Gramps once told him, *You have nothing to fear, except fear itself—if you don't mind the consequences.*

Trouble was, he hadn't worked out what that meant.

Gramps often talked in riddles and gave dire warnings. And Gramps had been around so long that he saw danger everywhere. Probably, rightly so. Maybe danger did lurk everywhere. But a kid had to take risks once in a while, or life would be totally boring!

Squinting, he scanned the back courtyard. Empty.

Another gust of cold wind.

Another loud crack.

A branch hit the ground, barely missing GL's head.

Jesse blew out a relieved laugh. "It's dead tree branches. The wind is breaking them."

"Oh, of course!" Emma said. "They're all extra dry because of the drought. Good thing this rain is coming. We need it."

"Come on, let's find that basement window."

A fat raindrop hit Jesse's nose.

"Here it comes," Emma said. "Get under the eaves. We can track along the back wall until we find a way in."

"Good idea."

Moments later, Jesse pulled aside the branches of a fig tree and saw a narrow basement window. "Jackpot!"

The shutters opened with a push.

Easy. Too easy.

Jesse frowned. It looked like someone had climbed

through here recently. Were squatters living inside? If so, he didn't want to run into them.

He wiped the thought away, squeezed inside, and dropped to the floor.

Turning, he held out his arms, "GL, you're next."

After GL, they got Sniffer safely through.

Last came Emma.

The whole group was inside. They'd done it. They were here.

CHAPTER SEVEN

WINCHESTER HOUSE

THE BASEMENT

Jesse, Emma, GL, and Sniffer stood for a long moment, frozen in silence. Jesse listened for squatters but heard nothing.

A breeze whispered, and creepy fingers brushed his face.

He reeled back.

Sniffer barked.

Only cobwebs. Get a grip!

He blinked hard, waiting for his eyes to adjust. They didn't. This place was darker than dark. Nothing was creepier than a pitch-dark basement. Except, maybe, a basement with a basement squatter. Or a spirit. Yeah, a basement with a spirit or two would be horrible. Anything could be hiding in the corners. Or under the stairs.

"Dark," GL whispered. "Dark, dark, dark!"

"Hold on," Jesse said. He dug into his pocket for the flashlight and worked to find the button. Suddenly, light blazed.

"Whoa!" Emma said. "Where did you get that?"

"Borrowed it from my dad," Jesse said. "But he doesn't know. It's a flashlight." He panned it around the room, sending light bouncing and casting shadows everywhere.

Hulking dark shapes loomed. Just furniture, he told himself. Sheet-covered furniture. Trunks and boxes, and old stuff nobody wanted. What a huge basement, filled with hidey-holes—hordes of squatters could be living down here. Yikes! The House was every bit as spooky as he'd thought it would be. Maybe even too spooky. It smelled bad—dank and musty. Like something died. Maybe the last squatter. But probably a rat.

Emma sneezed. "The dust is tickling my nose."

"Me too," GL whined. His little button nose twitched. "I want to go home."

"Let's just look around for a few minutes." Jesse placed the Kodak Brownie on a box to keep it steady, opened the shutter, and pressed the side lever. He heard the click.

"It's too dark to get a good picture," Emma said.

"I know. But maybe I'll get something. Let's go." Jesse led the way up a creaking, long stairway, only to find that it looped sideways and started going down again instead of rising to the first floor.

Jesse stood scratching his head. Without warning, GL climbed onto the wooden banister. He slid away, yelling at the top of his lungs.

There was a pause and then a wail, "I'm back in the basement! I hate the basement!"

"Well, you better get back up here," Emma yelled.

"Crazy!" Jesse grinned. "Why build a staircase that comes halfway up from the basement and goes straight down again?" He aimed the flashlight at the stairs and took another picture. His friends at school would love this weird stairway.

"Imagine building it," Emma said. "It's enough to make your head go funny."

"Maybe that's what happened to my dad. He's been super uptight since he started working here."

They waited for GL and then tramped along the strange stairs until they spotted a landing. If you climbed over the banister, you could just reach the landing.

One by one, they clambered onto it, then walked forward to see patterned windows. Moonlight filtered inside. A maze of corridors led deeper into the house to their left and right.

"What do you think, which way?" Jesse said.

"Well, if we always turn right, we can do the opposite to find our way back," Emma said.

"Smart. Except look at that corridor. It has no doors and ends at a blank wall. It's the corridor to nowhere."

Instead of laughing, Emma shivered, wrapping her arms around herself. "I wouldn't want to be lost in here."

"Check out the portraits!" The beam from Jesse's flashlight bobbed over life-sized portraits of solemn men and women.

Emma said, "Those are some fancy clothes, all velvet and satin. Look at the jewels! Emeralds. Diamonds."

"The Winchesters sure were rich," Jesse said.

"Yes, but unlucky. Sarah Winchester's husband died young. And her daughter had some strange problem and died, too."

Out of the corner of Jesse's eye, he saw something move. Whipping around, he came face-to-face with a portrait of a regal-looking woman in coronet-like braids. She stared back at him, thin lips turned down, eyes grave and disapproving.

As he began to turn away, her gaze followed.

Yikes. Did her eyes really move?

He stared at her again. Inscrutable, she stared back.

Huh. Must have been the flashlight. Don't be nuts.

"Let's get going, I'm getting the creeps," Emma said.

GL was strangely silent as they crept along.

Emma whispered, "I don't know if staying-on-the-right is working. Didn't we walk this way already?"

"I'm not sure." Jesse felt lost but didn't want to say so out loud. The House seemed designed to make you lose your way.

They crept up a steep stairway with teeny-tiny steps.

"My shoes hardly fit on these stairs," Jesse said, walking on tiptoe.

Emma said, "Imagine living in here? What if you had to go to the bathroom or wanted to get a snack from the kitchen?"

"Or answer the telephone," Jesse said.

"Imagine getting lost in your own house!" Emma said.

Bang.

His head hit the ceiling.

GL giggled, the first noise he'd made in ages. "Funny!"

"Whoa!" Rubbing his head, he looked up. "That is kind of funny. I banged my head. This staircase goes nowhere!"

Emma gave a surprised laugh. "That's so strange! Why build it?"

"I guess to fool the spirits," Jesse said.

Emma glanced around. "Spirits aren't real. But if they are, I don't want to see any. We should go."

"Soon. Let's just look around a little longer."

"Building this place must cost oodles," Emma whispered as they clambered back down and paused on a landing furnished with velvet sofas and chairs.

"Gramps says the Winchesters made a fortune like you'd never believe off those rifles," Jesse said.

"Like how much?"

"I don't know. Enough to build a million crazy rooms. Dad and his carpenters come here almost every day to build more. Extensions everywhere."

Emma said. "If I had that much money, I'd build a big game room and put a pool table in it, and we could be pool sharks!"

"I want to play sharks!" GL said. "I like swimming pools."

Jesse grinned. "Different kind of pool."

"Has your dad seen any ghosts?" Emma asked.

"No," Jesse said. "But he never comes inside the house at night."

An icy gust swept down the hallway.

Emma whirled around. "Did you feel that?"

Jesse shrugged. "Just the wind."

"What wind?" Emma said. "The windows are closed."

Bang! A door slammed shut.

Emma grabbed Jesse's arm in a crushing grip. "What made that door slam?"

"I want to go home," GL whined.

Emma said, "He's right, we should go. We did it, we got in here, now come on. Let's leave."

"What about the Witches Cap? Don't you want to see it?"

Emma shoved her hands into her frizzy hair and stared at the ceiling.

Jesse said, "Just one picture."

She groaned. Her face looked pale in the flashlight's glow. "Why is it called the Witches Cap? Are there supposed to be witches in here, too?"

"No. It's just a name."

The name of the place that the spirits supposedly come after Sarah Winchester rings the bells at midnight. But it wasn't midnight.

"What are you hiding, Jesse?" Emma said.

"I'm just thinking we should get there before . . . before the bell rings. You know?"

"Who's going to ring the bell if Sarah Winchester isn't home?"

"Excellent point."

"Let's get this over with," Emma said, marching off with GL and Sniffer in tow.

Even though Emma was stomping along, he realized that —scared or not—she'd never miss out on seeing the Witches Cap. Not if he was going there. They pretty much did everything together, even if they didn't always agree on things.

Jesse felt buzzed. There might even be wispy spirits

hovering inside. He'd be careful; he'd keep his distance. But if he captured them on film, he'd be famous.

He put his eye up to the Kodak Brownie's viewer, opened the shutter, and took another picture of the stairway. He wished cameras came equipped with lights. He'd never get a good shot in these dark rooms.

At least the moon was shining through the racing clouds. He needed to find a room with big windows letting in more moonlight.

"I'm thirsty," GL said.

"That's because you ate too much candy," Emma said.

"You're being mean," GL yelled. "I'm going to tell my mommy on you."

"Well, you *did* eat too much candy," Emma said.

"I'm going to tell my mommy you brought me here and were mean to me," GL wailed.

The noise was way too loud, making Jesse cringe and glance around.

"Oh great," Emma said. "Now GL's going to blab."

Jesse glared at GL. "Snitches get stitches and end up in ditches."

Right away, seeing GL's scared face, Jesse wished he could take it back. Snitch or not, GL looked terrified, and he was only four. Jesse recalled how Pete said mean things to him. He didn't want to be like that.

"No!" GL wailed, crossing his legs and grabbing his pants. "I need to go potty."

Jesse said, "Uh oh."

"What?" Emma said.

"Dad says there's only one working toilet. And I have no idea how to find it."

CHAPTER EIGHT

WINCHESTER HOUSE
THE BALLROOM

Jesse went to GL and said, "Don't worry, buddy, we'll figure this out." But he wasn't sure how.

Standing in the shadowy hallway, GL wailed, "I need to go potty! I need to go potty!"

Emma said, "Hundreds of rooms and only one working toilet? What a nightmare! Why?"

"The rest are fake to fool the spirits."

"Spirits need to use the toilet?" Emma said.

"All I know is that there's only one that works, and I have no clue where it is."

Emma shot GL a worried glance.

"I need to go. NOW." GL jumped up and down.

"Okay. Just hold it. We'll find the toilet." Jesse led the way back along the hallway. A steep stairway went down to a landing, and a spiraling stairway rose to a level two stories above. No toilet. He turned around.

"We can try upstairs," he said. "Maybe that's where the bedrooms and bathrooms are. The toilet must be up there."

Jesse led the way up the long, spiraling stairway. Double doors opened to a cavernous Grand Ballroom covered with carved woodwork right up to the twelve-foot-high ceiling. A gold and silver chandelier swung slowly.

Moonlight shone through stained-glass windows, highlighting the silver spiderweb patterns. That could make an interesting picture. He grabbed the Kodak Brownie from his knapsack.

"Look! There's writing on those windows over there." Emma read slowly. *"Wide unclasp the tables of their thoughts. These same thoughts people this little world.* That's a quote from Shakespeare."

"Is it?" The odd words made Jesse uneasy. This was a serious, dark place with a strange feel. "Do you think the quote is about spirits?"

Emma looked thoughtful. "I think it's two quotes from different Shakespeare plays. Maybe Sarah Winchester wanted it to be about spirits."

Sudden gloomy music filled the room.

Jesse whirled around.

GL was thumping the keys of a big pump organ.

"Hey! Stop that!" Jesse said.

"You can't make me." GL climbed up onto the organ and stood defiant, thumping the keys with his feet.

"Get off there," Jesse said. "You'll break it!"

With one final bang, GL climbed down and began jumping back and forth on the dark and light parquet squares. "I need to go potty!"

Sniffer growled. A low warning growl in the back of his throat.

Jesse started and nearly dropped the flashlight. A ghostly white fog swirled in the far-left corner of the Ballroom. A figure was materializing. Whoa! The figure was long and thin, with hair like squiggly octopus tentacles.

"There's something over there," Jesse whispered.

Emma jumped behind Jesse and peered over his shoulder. "What sort of thing?"

"A weird thing. Look!" Jesse pointed. "Might be a spirit. I've got to get a picture."

Emma clutched his arm. "Okay. But fast. Then let's get out."

Jesse set the Kodak Brownie on a table to steady the shot and opened the shutter.

"Hurry!" Emma hissed. "It moved!"

With a sudden shriek, GL charged out of the Ballroom.

Emma made a futile grab for her nephew. "GL! Hey! Get back here!"

Jesse raced after GL.

The kid was already at the far end of the corridor, scrambling up a steep, narrow stairway.

"Get back here!" Jesse yelled. He started up the stairway, with Emma and Sniffer right behind him.

At the top of the stairs, GL scrambled like a crab onto a landing. Jesse grabbed his ankle. GL's floppy blue hat flew over the wooden banister and down into the pool of darkness below.

"My hat!" GL yelled.

"I hear footsteps," Emma said. "We've got to hide."

Jesse could hear footsteps too. Shuffling footsteps, coming up the stairs. Eyes bugging, he searched for an escape. All five doors facing the landing were closed. He grabbed the closest doorknob.

"Locked," he gulped.

They tried more, but all were locked.

Jesse tried another. As he held on, the brass knob rattled and began to turn of its own accord.

Yikes!

Sniffer barked.

"Someone's t-t-turning it from the other side," Emma stammered. "Don't let them out!"

Hands shaking, Jesse clung to the doorknob. It wasn't working! How long could he keep holding it?

"I'm going to count. When I get to three, we run," he whispered. "We dive through the first open door we find and lock ourselves in."

Emma nodded and grabbed GL's hand.

"I have to go potty," GL whimpered.

"One, two, three," Jesse hissed.

Panting, they raced down a wood-paneled corridor and dived into the first open room. It was a bedroom, a very grand bedroom, with a big, four-poster bed. Long red velvet drapes framed daisy-patterned windows. Moonlight cast blue shadows everywhere.

Jesse tried to lock the door.

The keyhole was empty. He needed the key to turn the bolt!

"Find the key," he hissed. "Quick!"

Frantic, flashlight in hand, Emma pulled open the desk drawers and shuffled through the papers inside.

GL ran into a bathroom.

"See if there's a key in there," Jesse called.

"Toilet!" GL cried in delight.

Jesse was hot with fear. Surely there was a key somewhere.

From down the corridor, he heard a banging sound.

Emma cried out. "They're coming."

Someone or something was coming down the hallway, banging on doors.

Bang!

Bang!

Bang!

"W-w-what's that?" Emma stammered.

"It's not good," Jesse replied as the room grew icy cold.

"Could be the wind," said Emma in a hopeful, trembling voice.

"Dad says the house has two thousand doors." Why Jesse said it, he had no idea.

"Two thousand?" Emma said. "What does that matter now? Look at Sniffer! He's petrified."

Sniffer lay on his back, his legs in the air.

"Dogs can sense spirits," she added. "I read it in a book."

"We don't know that for certain." Jesse crouched, putting his arm around the dog.

GL lurched out of the bathroom. "It's coming to get us! It's coming!"

It was. The banging grew nearer and nearer.

The room was tombstone cold.

Something, someone, thumped on their door.

Jesse jumped. The banging went right through his body. Emma joined him, and they put their backs against the door, leaning on it to keep it shut.

Whatever this thing was, it was nuts.

And menacing.

Real menacing.

"Maybe it's the cops!" Emma whispered. "Maybe someone saw us and reported us."

"I wish," Jesse said. He'd love to see two policemen right now. But they would have said they were police.

The door shook. Cripes!

"Maybe it will go to another room," Emma whispered.

Crash!

"It's trying to break the door down," Jesse whispered.

Jesse shot a look at GL. The kid stood silhouetted in the bathroom door. He'd gone strangely silent and wore a weird, blank stare.

The banging ratcheted up to a fever pitch. The noise was deafening. Sometimes it sounded as if it was in the room next door. Then in the room across the hall. Then it was at their door again.\

"What is it?" Emma whispered. "What does it think it's doing? Is it banging with its whole body? Does it have a body?"

The hammering on their door switched to little patting sounds. Like something was feeling around the edges, looking for a way in.

The patting sounds were almost worse than the banging.

Jesse threw himself away from the door and grabbed the oak dresser. "Help me pull this. We need to block the way in!"

Together, he and Emma dragged it into place. Would it keep out whatever was trying to get in?

Bang!

Bang!

"Go away," Jesse shouted. "You can't get in."

For a moment, there was dead silence.

Then the banging returned.

"Great," Emma groaned. "Now it knows for sure that we're in here."

Pounding—furious pounding shook the whole room. The handle rattled furiously as if something meant to open it no matter what.

CHAPTER NINE

Jesse glanced at Emma and suddenly felt horrible for bringing her, GL, and Sniffer here.

Whatever was chasing him, he hated it. This was exactly how he felt when Pete had him in a headlock because he was bigger and knew how to get away with it.

They added more furniture to the dresser blocking the doorway—a heavy armchair, side tables, a wooden trunk.

He climbed atop it all and thumped on the door himself, hard. "Leave us alone! We didn't do anything to you. Leave us alone, or you'll be sorry!"

Emma stared, horrified. "Cool it, Jesse! I don't think you should threaten it."

"Listen," GL squeaked. "It's talking."

Talking? More like hissing. The eerie sounds swirled

through the keyhole. Words began to form, words that made Jesse's stomach clench.

Help me, Jesse, help me.

Emma cried, "It knows your name. How does it know your name?"

"I . . . I don't know."

"Wait, is this a trick?" Emma said in a shaky voice. She crossed her arms; the flashlight beam danced across the wall. "Are you tricking us? You better tell me right now."

"No! Why would I do that?" Jesse said.

"To scare us."

"We're best friends, Emma. I'd never trick you."

Emma shot him a skeptical look.

"I mean it." His lips felt chapped, his tongue dry. "I don't know what's going on. But I'll get us out of here. I promise."

How he had no idea. Usually, Emma was the brainy one who got them out of scrapes. But she was glaring at him like this was up to him now.

Maybe they imagined the voice. Maybe they'd been watching too many horror movies. In the movie theater, it was fun joining the audience as they shouted: *Don't go in there!*

But this wasn't fun. Not in real life.

Through the daisy-patterned windows, moonlight shone on GL's white-blond hair. Racing clouds cast ghoulish shadows. The air smelled of mothballs and fear.

He was about to say, *Let's go, I'll open the door, and we'll run,* when the voice hissed again.

Jesse . . . Jesse! Come out, come out wherever you are!

Standing next to Jesse, GL yanked on his sleeve. "It wants you."

Emma groaned. "We'll never get past it. That thing is waiting for us to open the door."

An awful realization struck. Of course, the spirits wanted Jesse. His very own gramps had helped build the famous Winchester repeating rifle. The spirit must know! It was thirsting for revenge!

And he'd brought his best friend, his dog, and GL into this mess.

Emma gripped his arm.

"Maybe if we stay in here long enough, it will leave," he said, turning to her.

Except Emma wasn't holding onto him at all. She wasn't even close. Emma was crouched way over behind the writing table with her arms around GL.

Frantic, Jesse squinted around the bedroom, searching for another door. "There's got to be another way out. Hand me the flashlight."

"No," GL said. "It wants you to stay."

"Quit it," Jesse said. "Don't say that."

"Yes. Quit it," Emma said.

GL gave a strange, maniacal grin. His little white teeth shone in the dark. "Snitches get stitches."

Jesse had never noticed GL's sharp, little incisors. Or what pale-blue eyes GL had. Lightning flashed outside, and GL's eyes seemed to glow.

"It wants you to stay," GL said in almost a man's voice. "Jesse, *JESSE!*"

"Stop that right now," Emma said, yanking him to face her. "Stop it."

GL leaped forward and sank his teeth into Emma's arm.

Emma shrieked.

With a gasp, Jesse grabbed the kid and yanked him off.

GL snarled.

Emma rubbed her arm. "You hurt me. Look! You drew blood. Why'd you do that, GL?"

"Snitches get stitches and end up in ditches." GL laughed wildly.

"What's the matter with you?" Jesse said.

Had an evil spirit taken over the poor kid? Cripes, what would GL's mother say if they took him home like this? The kid stood frozen, staring into space.

"We have to get out of here," Emma said. "He's gone crazy. Maybe he needs a doctor."

Jesse pulled up GL's eyelids, suspicious. "Maybe he's faking it?"

"We need to get him home."

There was a distant sound of cackling laughter.

Sniffer crawled under the bed.

Jesse felt panic rise. Sniffer was usually a great guard dog. He loved barking at anything threatening.

Cackling laughter swirled, echoing, bouncing. He gripped his head with both hands. It wasn't coming from the hallway. Was someone hiding in the bedroom?

"Enough!" he shouted and ran around, pulling back the long, red drapes. "Show yourself! Come out!"

Another cackle.

It was coming from the bathroom.

Emma handed him the flashlight and watched as he approached the bathroom's partially open door. Inside, thirteen narrow windows lined the wall. Each window held thirteen panels of glass.

A gurgle rose from the shower stall drain. It sounded like a shower monster itching to get out. Was that where the laughter came from?

No, impossible.

He shone the beam on the wood-paneled wall above the sink. It held thirteen round holes.

He peered into one. And whipped back as a hiss came through.

This was it! Whoa!

Wait, was this some sort of communication panel? So that people in different rooms could talk to one another? Yes, the holes were labeled, with the names of other rooms.

"Emma. Get in here. Listen to this,' he whispered. "The weird voice is coming from this hole. These are communication holes. They're marked to show which room they come from."

She inched up to him with a now silent GL in tow. "If that's true, and I believe you're right, which room is the noise coming from?"

Jesse leaned in to read the writing. "The Witches Cap."

The place where the midnight meeting of spirits took place. But no one had rung the bell. Had the spirits come anyway out of habit?

Emma pressed her ear to the hole. She leaped away as if it was burning hot. "Someone's there! I heard them talking. There's someone in the house."

CHAPTER TEN

WINCHESTER HOUSE
THE DAISY BEDROOM

The bells in the Bell Tower began to peal.

"Someone's up there ringing those," Emma whispered. "Bells can't ring themselves."

Bong . . . bong . . . bong . . .

On and on they rang. Twelve chimes in total.

"It's midnight," Jesse whispered.

The Witching Hour.

Jesse said, "Um—I probably should have told you this before, but—"

"Told me what?"

He gulped. "Sarah Winchester rings the bells at midnight to call the spirits."

"Wait, she does *what?*" Emma whisper-shouted. "And

you're only telling me this now?"

"She's not here, I figured the bells wouldn't ring, there would be no summoning."

Emma grabbed her mass of frizzy hair. "Why would she even want to summon a bunch of spirits?"

"Dad said she talks to them about the house. She uses this thing called a Ouija board."

"That's just creepy. I saw a Ouija board once, Mother wouldn't even let me touch it. It looked like a game board decorated with the alphabet, and it had a pointy arrow thing. You put your finger on the arrow and ask a question. The spirits make the arrow move, and they spell out an answer."

But Jesse was still thinking about the bells. "Sarah

Winchester must have come home early. Or maybe she never left at all."

"How can she live in an awful place like this? Maybe she knows we're here. Maybe she's the one who's been making all that noise. To scare us."

"Maybe, but I know one thing."

Emma shot him a sideways glance. "Oh yeah?"

"I'm not leaving without a picture of her using that Ouija board in the Witches Cap."

She glared at him. "Forget it, Jesse, I'm done. I came here, I'm scared out of my mind, and we're leaving."

The house had gone oddly silent. It was like it was listening.

Jesse breathed out. "Look, you take the flashlight. I'll meet you guys outside. I've just got to get a picture! Otherwise, why did I even come here?"

Emma looked skyward with a frustrated noise.

"This is important," Jesse said.

"Fine. But I'm definitely leaving. Look at GL! I need to get him away from this place."

Jesse snapped his fingers in front of GL's glassy eyes.

GL just stared.

Maybe he was in shock?

"Yeah," Jesse admitted. "You better get him home."

"Wait, how am I supposed to do that?" She pointed at the furniture they'd piled in front of the door. "Even if I could get out, I don't exactly want to meet whatever's in that hallway."

Jesse glanced around thoughtfully. "I'm pretty sure this house is loaded with secret passageways. Maybe there's another way out?"

Emma didn't bother to reply. Instead, she started running her hands over the walls. Jesse did the same. After checking the whole room, he gave up. If there were fake panels, he couldn't find them.

"Look under the carpets," he said. "Maybe there's a trap door."

Emma rolled up the Persian rug. "Nothing."

Jesse pulled open the closet. "Jackpot," he called.

Yes! In front of him, a dark, narrow passage led to a steep, rising stairwell. Emma was beside him in an instant, tugging GL along.

"But it goes up," Emma said. "We want to go down."

"You know the stairs in this place, they go all sorts of ways. Maybe this one goes up and then down on the other side."

Emma went first, dragging GL. Glad to have Sniffer by his side, Jesse grabbed his dog collar to help him up the narrow stairs. It ended at a funny, waist-high door.

Emma whispered, "I hear voices."

Jesse put his ear against the tiny door and listened. Voices came to him, low and muffled.

Emma backed away. "We better turn around."

Jesse said, "We don't know for sure that's where the voices are coming from. This is our best way out."

Slowly, he cracked open the small door. It was so low he had to stoop to see through.

The room that stretched before him seemed like a place spirits would love—huge, gloomy, and octagonal, with a high domed ceiling that looked perfect for floating in the air.

As for the carpet, he shivered. It was a watery shade of blue.

Haint-blue.

Which could only mean . . .

A thrill of terror and excitement rushed through him. "The Witches Cap," he whispered.

Emma muttered, "Oh no."

Sniffer gave a low growl.

Jesse crept forward, peering into the gloom.

Red, purple, and yellow satin cloaks hung on hooks to his right. He counted quickly. Thirteen cloaks. Thirteen hooks. Lots of things in the house seemed to come in thirteens, from the windowpanes to the wooden panels.

He'd always thought thirteen was an unlucky number.

But maybe tonight, he'd be lucky. Maybe he'd get a picture for the newspaper. Maybe they'd escape without being caught. Maybe this would be their best adventure ever, one they'd talk about for the rest of their lives.

Or maybe the opposite. That was too awful to consider.

As his eyes adjusted to the layered dark, he spied three tall, shadowy figures in the room's distant corner. He froze, but none turned around. So far, Jesse hadn't been spotted.

An oil lamp hung from the ceiling, lighting the top of their heads. The high collars of black capes hid their faces. Jesse squinted, trying to see better.

Who were they? It couldn't be Sarah Winchester, Dad said she was only around four feet tall. Cripes, who were they?

"They look like the Salem witches," Emma whispered.

Jesse put his finger to his lips. What if this was a real live witches' coven?

The figures seated themselves at the round table.

Behind him, he heard Emma's nervous breathing. He could feel GL's head wedged against the back of his knees. If either made a noise, the witches would hear for sure.

Spellbound, he watched the witchlike figures place their fingers on a wooden board.

"Ouija board," Emma whispered.

"Shh!"

He blinked to see better. What a time to be near-sighted. Was this a séance? Were they calling up spirits?

A deep voice made him jump.

"Who are you?" the voice boomed.

CHAPTER ELEVEN

WINCHESTER HOUSE
THE WITCHES CAP

"Who are you?" the voice boomed again.

Oh no. The witches had seen him! Jesse nearly stammered out a reply.

Then he realized the question was addressed to the spirits.

The arrow moved slowly across the Ouija board in the cloaked figures' hands. It paused now and then, probably stopping at the letters. The spirits were spelling out a message. An excited murmur passed between the three witches.

Emma nudged Jesse and pointed to an open, arched door. She raised her eyebrows in a question.

Jesse nodded. Could work. They had to try. While the

witches concentrated on the Ouija board, he, Emma, and GL could tiptoe across the room.

He raised one finger, motioning her to hold on a second.

Hands shaking, he steadied the Kodak Brownie on his knee and opened the shutter so light could pass through the lens. It was a long shot but the best he could do. He squinted through the mirrored viewfinder and pressed the side lever.

JESSE'S
KODAK
BROWNIE
CAMERA

The Ouija arrow kept moving. One of the witches began to read out letters:

A—V—I—C—T—I— M

A second hissed, *"A victim!"*

"Why have you come to us?" boomed the deep voice.

"W-a-i-t-i-n-g," came the hissed reply. "It says it's waiting."

"Waiting for what?"

"F-o-r-j-e-s-s-e."

Waiting for Jesse.

Emma gasped, and Jesse's heart lurched. It *did* know Jesse's name. It knew he was here!

Gulping for air, he snapped a picture. If he was going to die, maybe someone would find the film and know what happened.

Without warning, GL shoved past and bolted across the room. With a desperate look at Jesse, Emma flew after him. They disappeared through the arched door.

Jesse took another picture wildly.

Time to get out of Dodge. One witch, a tall figure with white, luminous skin, glided across the Witches Cap, claw-like hands reaching for him.

Fast as a greyhound, Jesse streaked across the Witches Cap, out the arched door, and slid down a hallway.

Sniffer was glued to his side, nails clicking on the wooden floor.

Mirrors lined the corridor. Jesse saw four reflections of himself, googly-eyed with fear, and four Sniffers. When he skidded around a corner, he spotted at least ten witches in pursuit. Cripes! How many were reflections, and how many were witches?

Round the next zigzag, he nearly slammed into a closed door. He grabbed the doorknob. Locked. He whirled to see a big oak door a few feet away. It opened into blackness.

The yawning space looked ready to swallow him whole.

A howl echoed from down the corridor. A chilling, mocking howl.

They were close. Too close.

It was a choice between the devil and the deep, blue sea.

Jesse dived inside the dark room and slammed the door.

"Emma?" he whispered. "Are you in here?"

No reply.

Another wolf-like howl. That didn't sound like witches. What was after him? How would he ever escape?

CHAPTER TWELVE

WINCHESTER HOUSE
THE HALL OF FIRES

Jesse fiddled frantically for a way to lock the door.

The howls grew to wild yelps. *Werewolves?*

Like the other door, he found a skull-shaped keyhole but no key. There wasn't time to drag the table across to barricade the door. His pursuers were too close.

He looked around wildly for a weapon. Nothing. Just some books in a bookcase. All options gone, he tensed for a fight.

Wait, he had the flashlight; he'd forgotten to give it to Emma. Body spring-loaded for action, he held it at the ready. When whatever chased him entered, he'd hit it in the eyes with the beam. That would dazzle it and give him a chance to escape.

Thumping footsteps stopped outside the door.

Jesse tensed. Ready or not, this was it.

The door swung open.

Jesse shouted, "Get away from me!"

A voice yelled, "Got you!"

What was happening? It was his brother's voice.

Pete stood there laughing so hard he couldn't catch his breath. "Hi, Jesse. What a loser! You should see your face. I bet you peed your pants."

Jesse stared, open-mouthed.

Pete's best friend, his skin covered in white greasepaint, made a chicken-wing movement with his elbows. "Chicken! *Chicken!* Squark! Squark! Squark!"

Pete's cheerleader girlfriend giggled and tossed her auburn ponytail. "Chicken! Chicken! Squark! Squark! Squark!"

Fury ripped through Jesse. Pete had totally humiliated him. He hated his brother. *Hated him!*

Pete said, "I never knew you could scream like that! You sounded like a little girl. Funniest thing I've ever seen! Right guys? Wait, is that Dad's Brownie camera? And flashlight? Haha, you are in so much trouble." Pete grinned.

Face flaming, Jesse said, "How did you know I was here?"

Pete smirked. "I heard your telephone call to Emma. What a loser! Can't even keep your voice down when you're making sneaky plans."

Pete was really enjoying this.

Pete's friend said, "What a hoot!"

"You should have seen your face," Pete's girlfriend shrieked. "You and your friends, listening to the séance. All goggle-eyed. What twerps!"

"You're all jerks." Jesse glared at Pete.

"How about when he charged across the room?" Pete howled with laughter. "I can't wait to tell my friends. And *yours.*"

"I'll kill you," Jesse yelled. "I'll kill you if you tell anyone!"

Pete snorted. "I'd like to see you try."

Rage and hurt bubbled hot in Jesse's chest. For this; for all those times Pete sat on him and farted in his face; for the wedgies—done hard and mean with Pete's buff arms, all built up from bench presses.

Why couldn't he have a nice brother? Or, even better, no brother at all. He wished he could squash Pete into a smear on the floor.

His blood pumped hard, and his breath came fast and furious.

With a crazy yell, he launched himself at Pete. His right hand, wrapped around the flashlight, connected hard with his brother's nose.

With a startled look, Pete reeled back.

Jesse reeled back, too, almost as shocked as his brother.

Blood streamed from Pete's nose. "You've done it now!"

Jesse leaped into the dark room and slammed the door. "I hate you!" he shouted. "I hate your guts!"

With a thrill of relief, his fingers found a bolt high up that he hadn't noticed earlier. He slid it fast.

"You're finished!" Pete shouted. "Open up."

"Just leave me alone."

"Fine. We'll end this when you get home."

Pete and his friends' footsteps trailed away.

Shaking from adrenaline, Jesse slumped. He was furious, but he hadn't meant to give his brother a bloody nose. Still, it served Pete right for making him feel like an idiot.

Pete would tell Dad. He'd blab to everyone in town. Jesse would be labeled a loser. The kid who believed in spirits. The kid who fell for the dumbest prank ever.

No one would be interested in Jesse's story of sneaking into the haunted House. Even his pictures would be useless—because Pete's story was better.

Outside the door, Sniffer whined. Oh no! Poor Sniffer was out there. In all the chaos, he'd failed to notice he'd left his loyal friend behind.

"I'm coming, Sniffer," he called and slid back the bolt.

He reached for the doorknob and found that, on this side, there wasn't one. Just the keyhole with no key.

He tried to pry the heavy oak door open. It wouldn't budge. He must have triggered a spring lock when he slammed it shut. And now he was stuck inside.

What was it about this place and weird doors? The House was like a fat spider crouching in a web, waiting to trap you. No wonder Sarah Winchester wasn't happy. Who would be?

His mind went to Emma and GL. He hoped they'd escaped and were on their way home.

But if not . . . He banged on the door. "Emma! *Emma!* Are you out there? I'm stuck."

Silence.

Then, grudgingly, "Pete? Pete! Let me out. I can't get out!"

He body-slammed the door. Hollered. Kicked. Pounded.

Silence.

Yeah, of course Pete wouldn't help him. He never would. What was the point of having a brother if he was always out to get you? If he was always trying to make you fail?

"Emma," he called, his voice hollow. "Can you hear me?"

Sniffer pawed at the door again. Jesse's chest squeezed. Good old Sniffer, at least he'd stand by him no matter what.

"I'm coming, Sniffer. Don't worry."

Weak moonlight colored everything grey-blue. He fumbled with the flashlight. No go. It didn't work. Pete's big nose had put an end to it. Dad would be furious.

He ran his hands over the walls feeling for light switches. Nothing.

There had to be another way out.

Along one wall, he could just see four fireplaces with stone hearths. This room must be the Hall of Fires. Dad told him Sarah Winchester would light the fires and turn on the vents until the Hall felt like a sauna.

It didn't feel like a sauna now. It felt cold as a tomb.

He opened a set of heavy drapes to let in more moonlight.

Beside a fireplace, he found a narrow door hidden in the paneling. Yes! A secret exit!

It opened . . . to a blank wall.

Well, that was no use.

A thin shadow slid across the ceiling. Something rustled. Something brushed the back of his neck.

"Pete!" he yelled. "I know you're doing this, Pete."

But how could he?

The hair on his arms rose.

Something was wrong.

Get out of here!

Above, a brass chandelier swayed. The lights flickered on, throwing everything into stark focus. Then they went out. On and off, they flickered in blinding flashes. The chandelier swung wildly. He leaped clear.

Too late.

The chandelier crashed down, side-swiping his head.

Thrown backward, Jesse reeled and hit the floor. As crystals and chunks of glass flew across the room, he gasped.

Then, he blacked out.

CHAPTER THIRTEEN

W INCHESTER H OUSE
T HE H ALL O F F IRES

Jesse came to, lying on the floor, his skull thumping with an awful headache. That chandelier had hit him good. He felt his scalp gingerly. Something sticky had dried there—blood. A hot lump stuck out like a goose egg.

I'm fine. I'm alive. That's a plus.

He forced himself to sit.

Oh wow, he felt terrible. The whole world spun. He couldn't think straight. He had to get moving, get out, escape.

He hauled himself to his feet. His head reeled.

Something touched the back of his neck. Hands. Icy hands. He whirled around. "Pete!"

The hands pushed hard. Jesse careened across the room. He stumbled against the wall. He couldn't see straight.

Swirling fog poured from all four fireplaces. It materialized into human shapes. Men. Spirits. Whoa. He rubbed his eyes. No way this could be happening. It had to be another trick.

But how could Pete pull off something like this?

The spirits flew at him, mouths opening wide.

"I know it's you, Pete!" he yelled. "Quit doing this. I hate you. You think you're so smart. You think you can make a fool of me. You think you can joke about me to everybody at school. I'll get you. I swear. I don't know how you're doing this, but you'll be sorry!"

Beads of sweat formed on his lip and forehead. His stomach lurched. He clutched at an oak table.

Five misty figures with gaunt faces shrieked, and their mouths stretched even wider. They looked hungry. They would swallow him whole.

No—no, it was a trick!

Breathing hard, Jesse rubbed his eyes.

They were still there.

Spirits!

Ghosts!

The Undead!

He stumbled away from them. Cold sweat soaked his flannel shirt. "I don't believe in you!"

One figure shot forward, materializing right before him. An angry, beak-nosed young man in military uniform.

Jesse kicked out, but his foot made no contact. Instead, it went right through. Dread filled him. "Who are you?"

Matthew. The sound drifted in the air. *Matthew Taylor.*

Matthew didn't look friendly. He looked furious. His eyes, beady above his gaping mouth, drilled into Jesse.

"What do you want, Matthew?" Jesse managed.

You know, boy. Revenge. Revenge!

The others echoed the call, shrieking and howling *Revenge!*

"For what?" Jesse said, but he knew.

I was killed by one of them Winchester rifles. On the twenty-fifth of June 1876.

Jesse's heart rate broke a personal record. "I'm sorry. I'm really sorry." He gulped. Unable to help himself, he asked, "W —who killed you?"

Soldiers. At the Battle of Little Bighorn. I was only eighteen.

The voice broke. Cripes—the spirit was really upset. And who could blame him?

"What happened?"

General Custer led the Seventh Cavalry into battle. Crazy Horse and his braves came galloping at us by the thousands. Those braves were armed with Winchester repeating rifles. We had no chance against a gun like that, one you didn't have to reload. Shot after shot, they mowed us down. We were massacred.

Wow, Matthew was talking about Custer's last stand! Jesse had learned about it in school. "Why didn't the seventh Cavalry have repeating rifles?" he asked, curious despite his terror. "How did the braves get them?"

I don't know. I just know what I saw.

"That's terrible what happened to you, all of you. But in 1876, I wasn't even born."

You're here now, Matthew hissed.

An Indian woman, her white braids swishing, flew at Jesse until her bitter, ravaged face floated inches away.

Those rifles slaughtered herds of Cheyenne buffaloes, she shrieked. *Without the buffaloes, my people starved.*

"That's awful, really, I mean it," Jesse cried and ducked as a third spirit, a haggard man in a filthy, rotting uniform, swooped from the ceiling.

I was nineteen years old, he crooned in a frightening voice. *It was the summer of 1863. The Union soldiers mocked us. Called us graybacks. Lice. They used their cursed Yankee rifle to raze us Confederates down.*

The spirit's mouth was a black hole.

Involuntarily, Jesse jumped back.

I hate you, Winchesters. All of you.

"I'm not a Winchester. I just came inside to take pictures!"

Then, he thought, except Dad works for Sarah Winchester, building stairs that go nowhere to drive the spirits crazy. And Grandpa helped build that weapon. If the spirits find that out, you're as good as dead.

You may not be a Winchester, but you're here. And you understand hatred, boy, the spirit hissed. *You understand it very well.*

"No. No, I don't. War is terrible. Hate is terrible."

I heard you shout, and I know. You hate your brother. Don't you? You hate him.

Jesse froze. "I was mad, but I don't hate him."

He'd said it, though. Right to Pete's face. And then he'd punched him with the flashlight and drew blood.

He was angry, he was hurt, but did he hate him? They were brothers. They used to be inseparable. Somehow, they'd lost their way.

And now this was happening. Had his anger made these spirits appear? Were they drawn by his black thoughts?

Suddenly, he heard a loud rumbling.

It sounded deep down, like underground thunder.

Spirits poured from all four chimneys. They swirled and screeched. The walls shuddered, and the floor shuddered.

Jesse staggered sideways.

Were they going to destroy the whole House? Bring it down, and him along with it?

CHAPTER FOURTEEN

WINCHESTER HOUSE
THE HALL OF FIRES

Jesse crawled under the massive table as the spirits flew around him in a wild frenzy.

The House shook from side to side. Furniture swayed, and walls vibrated. With an explosion of breaking glass, gilt-framed portraits crashed down.

Jesse dashed from his hiding place, ran to a narrow window, and looked out. He was at least three stories up. Too high to jump.

A man pushing a wheelbarrow staggered across the storm-whipped courtyard below.

Thank goodness. A handyman.

"Help!" Jesse shouted. "Help!"

The handyman didn't hear.

Jesse struggled to open the window, but it was sealed shut. He banged on a glass panel. "Hey!" he shouted. "Hey! You!"

The handyman disappeared. The earth just swallowed him up.

Thick ash and coal dust poured from all four fireplaces. Choking, Jesse rubbed his burning eyes. His head throbbed. He could no longer see the spirits, but his head buzzed with a sound like marching feet. It sounded like an army of spirits marching right at him.

He heard singing. Faint, but growing clearer. Men's voices, singing a marching song:

I wish I was in Dixie, hooray! Hooray!
In Dixie's Land I'll take my stand
To live and die in Dixie.
Away, away, away down south in Dixie.

The rumbling sounded like an approaching freight train. The floor moved; the walls writhed. The ceiling buckled. Whoa! A ceiling board crashed down. Plaster filled the room. Walls creaked and groaned.

All four fireplaces begin to blaze.

Within minutes the room became boiling hot. Clouds of

smoke whirled, and he couldn't make out if the spirits were there or not.

Oh man, he never, ever, should have come to this haunted house.

And what was happening to Emma and GL? Had they gotten out?

And what about Sniffer? He could no longer hear his dog. His heart squeezed in agony for his loyal friend.

He went to the door and shouted, "Run, Sniffer. Get out of here, go!"

What if the spirits went after Pete, too? Pete would be clueless about what was going on. What if big, knucklehead Pete had boasted to his girlfriend about how Gramps helped design the Winchester repeating rifle and the spirits heard him? The spirits would demolish him.

"Pete!" he yelled. "Pete! If you can hear me, get away from this house. Run for your life! Fetch Pa!"

Sweating, he dove back under the solid oak table and huddled there. Frantically, he tried to think what to do. The twisting and writhing increased. Would it never, ever stop?

"I'm sorry!" he shouted at the spirits. "I'm sorry you got hurt. But none of us did anything to you. Please, let us go."

CHAPTER FIFTEEN

Winchester House
The Hall Of Fires

For a moment, the House seemed to stagger and then right itself.

Jesse could hardly believe it. Apologizing had worked!

He crawled out from under the oak table. The awful rocking started up all over again. Ornaments fell from the mantlepieces, and books flew from the bookcases.

When the books were gone, he spotted something, a flaw in the wood paneling beside the third shelf.

Did he dare hope? Could it be . . . a secret door?

Jesse scrambled through the debris, floor surfing as he went. He ran his hands along the paneling, found a button-sized hole, and pushed. A section of shelving moved on creaking hinges.

It *was* a secret door!

He charged through.

What the . . .?

There was nothing under his feet. No floor. Nothing.

He fell.

And fell.

Down.

Down.

"Help!" he screamed.

He was falling—from three stories high. He reached out wildly. His hand connected with something. He grabbed it and held on for dear life.

It was a branch; he'd grabbed onto a branch. Jesse was hanging, swinging, from the limb of a tree.

It's not the fall that kills you, it's the sudden stop. Another of Gramp's not-so-funny sayings.

Jesse choked and began laughing, a hysterical laugh. He'd have to tell Gramps about this.

Beside him, the house still swayed. Below, the earth moved as if a monster snake crawled under it. What was going on out here?

He searched frantically for Pete, Emma, GL, and Sniffer. But there was no one in sight.

The tree branch snapped, taking him with it. He slammed down, landing on his back.

Ow, that hurt. His head hurt even more. At least Dad always said he had a thick skull. He hoped it was true. Jesse moved his fingers and wiggled his toes. Nothing broken. Not so bad.

You'll live. That's what Dad always said. No matter how bad he felt. *You'll live.*

Yeah, he'd like to see Dad handle the spirits and live!

Spots rose in front of his eyes. The grass down here was soft. He'd lie still for a while. Get his head straight.

A chunk of brick thudded to the ground beside him.

Whoa. He sat up again with a start. Adrenaline flared through him.

More bricks thudded down.

Must get away!

Wait, where was the camera? He felt around. Had he dropped it when he fell?

He struggled to his feet, staggered and reeled; the earth was still moving! A sickening sway threw him flat on his face. His outstretched hand closed on a hard, square object. The camera. At least he hadn't lost that. He looked around, trying to get his bearings.

As the ground continued to shake, a slow realization dawned.

He thought about the strange migration of birds and rabbits he'd seen on the way here. He thought about the lurching ground beneath his feet. He thought about the swaying house, the flying bricks, and it all gelled into a single word.

Earthquake.

He couldn't explain the spirits, but deep in his gut, he knew this swaying, thrashing world had nothing to do with them. The ground was shaking because he was in the middle of a massive earthquake!

He stood unsteadily. The sky was growing light.

In the distance, across the brittle orchards and dead strawberry fields, great, gray clouds of dust shot into the air with a massive explosion. Flames whooshed outward, setting the land on fire.

Through his haze of confusion, something told him he had to record this. He balanced the Brownie on a large stone and, winding the knob to advance the frame, he took a picture.

Faintly, but clearly, he heard cries. That sobered him up.

"Emma, GL! Sniffer! Pete!"

What was he doing, standing safely out here? Pete could take care of himself, but Jesse's friends? Emma hadn't even wanted to come here.

He staggered around the perimeter of the house, trying to see into the dark windows.

"Emma!" he shouted. "Sniffer! Come on, boy, where are you? Sniffer! GL?"

In reply came the screams of hundreds of people—but not from the house. They came from the massive building across the fields. They came from The Great Asylum.

Then he saw them, small shadowy figures coming across the fields. Heading toward him, running pell-mell in their dash to escape the Asylum. Some of them were dangerous.

He had to find Emma and the others and get them safely away.

Panting, he stumbled down a path and found himself lost between tall cornstalks. He turned in circles and realized he was inside last year's Hallowe'en corn maze. He loved mazes, but he wasn't good at them. Last Hallowe'en, it had taken him a whole morning to get out of one filled with mirrors and loud buzzers.

Something rustled.

He heard a faint voice. "Jesse?"

Relief filled him. "Emma!"

Jesse pushed through the corn stalks to find his cousin standing there with her big green eyes locked onto his. She looked as frightened as a deer. And why shouldn't she? He probably looked the same.

"Emma!" Jesse whispered. "Where's GL? And Sniffer?"

CHAPTER SIXTEEN

Emma looked ill as she stood staring at him in the corn maze. "I don't know."

Jesse's heart stuttered. He grabbed Emma's arm. "You don't know where GL is? But you were together, I thought—"

"One minute we were running along those corridors, then we got to the basement, and this massive crack opened in the floor. Right at my feet. I nearly fell in, and when I turned around, I saw GL darting back up the stairs. I screamed for him to come back, but he got to the top and disappeared. Before I could go after him, the stairs crashed down. I climbed out the basement window and have been trying to find another way in to get to him. Oh Jesse, what a nightmare. Poor GL!"

"This is my fault. Why did I ever think this was a good idea?" Jesse said. "Did you see Sniffer?"

Tears filled Emma's eyes. "No. Jesse, I was responsible for GL. And I don't even know where the little guy is."

Footsteps crunched on the gravel path.

"Someone's there," Emma whispered. "Maybe it's GL!"

"Stop, wait. I saw people escaping from the Asylum. They might be dangerous."

Despite his throbbing head, Jesse's mind was growing clearer. The fog that had gripped his brain since the chandelier hit him was beginning to lift. He said, "I got us into this, I'll check who's out there."

Commando-style, he crept forward.

Sure enough, it wasn't GL. Or Pete, for that matter.

Instead, a greasy-haired man staggered along the corn maze path wearing a long nightgown and carrying an odd assortment of items: an alarm clock, a trumpet, dress shoes, and suspenders.

The man spoke to himself, crying: "Will he never come? Will he never come with the combination? Oh, why doesn't he come?"

Two men in mud-stained clothing followed on his heels. One yelled, a furious yell. The men were nose-to-nose, like feral dogs.

"You took it," a man with a white Santa Claus beard shouted. "You took it and it's mine. Give it back!"

"No! Never. It's mine now." The second man held a brick above his head with his skinny, tattoo-covered arms. "Come and get it. I dare you."

"I want it!" Santa Claus man howled. "I love it. I love it more than anything."

The tattooed man screeched with laughter. "It's mine. I stole it."

"Give it to me. I love it. Give it to me!"

"No! You can't make me. What are you going to do?"

"I'll bend you till you break."

Yikes! Jesse ducked out of view.

Not fast enough, for a stick flew, arrow-like, nicking his shirtsleeve. Had he been spotted? He sprang to his feet like a stunt man in a Wild West Show and ran back to Emma.

"Quick, they're coming! Run!"

To the north, a great plume of smoke grew blacker.

"Look at the sky," Emma gasped. "Something terrible is happening way over there."

"Oh my gosh. I think San Francisco is on fire!"

"Sure looks like it," Emma said.

Jesse broke through the corn maze wall and found himself back at the Winchester House. A strange yellow light glowed through the windows. Was a fire starting in there, too? The house tilted. The whole building was askew. Hands shaking, barely aware of what he was doing, he raised the camera and snapped a picture. Through the viewfinder, he spotted movement in a window.

His heart clenched. "Someone's in there."

Emma said, "GL? Is it GL?"

"No, too tall. But . . ."

Pete.

Pete, the brother who'd tormented him? Who'd made a fool out of him? Maybe. But he was also the brother he'd looked up to when he was small. And that brother was trapped in a crumbling building.

The Bell Tower leaned, bending at an impossible angle. The bell clanged out an urgent tempo. With a shriek of twisting wood and bricks, the top three stories of the house toppled. Debris slammed down.

Jesse stared aghast. Four stories of the house remained. But how much longer would they stay standing? GL and Sniffer might be in there. Maybe Pete, too. He had to get back in and find them.

A man in a flannel shirt and white trousers, covered from head to toe in ash, ran across the debris-strewn grounds.

"Help!" the man shouted. "We need help at the Asylum. Everything's gone. The walls. The ceiling. The roof. Patients are escaping. We need help!"

"We can't." Jesse was sprinting, heading toward the house. "We have to find a little boy. He's only four."

The man grabbed Jesse's arm, stopping him in his tracks.

The man's blue eyes gleamed. "I saw a little boy. He looked about four. I saw him back there in the fields."

A wave of relief shot through Jesse. "A little boy? Wearing a blue and white sailor suit?"

"Yes!" The man nodded. "That's the one. I saw him."

"Thank goodness," Jesse said. "Quick! Where did you see him?"

"Too late." The man dropped Jesse's arm. "He was eaten by wolves in the strawberry field."

CHAPTER SEVENTEEN

WINCHESTER HOUSE
THE HOUSE GROUNDS

Emma stuttered. "GL was eaten by w-w-wolves?"

Jesse stared, speechless, then dropped to his knees. No. *No!*

More patients staggered across the Winchester House grounds, jumping over downed willow branches. The earth rippled as if some mammoth monster was crawling underneath.

"It's the Kraken," said the man in white. "It lives under California. It's breaking loose tonight."

Jesse's eyes swiveled to him. "The Kraken?"

"Oh yes. The Kraken, boy! Soon, you'll see it. We're doomed. We're all doomed. If the wolves don't get us, the Kraken surely will."

Hands dropping, Jesse got to his feet. "You didn't see a boy, did you? You're lying."

The man laughed. "Choose your poison. Wolf or Kraken?"

"Something's wrong with him," Emma whispered in Jesse's ear.

Jesse agreed. "He's a patient. I bet he didn't see GL at all. I bet GL is still trapped in the house. And Sniffer. If he was out here, Sniffer would have found us. I know he would. I know my dog. Sniffer must be in the house."

"We have to call the police," Emma said.

"We have to go back in before the whole thing comes down," Jesse said. "I'm going to climb up that tree."

Emma shook her head. "We need to find the police."

"Wait, there's that handyman again!" Jesse cried as a dark-haired man rushed around the corner, pushing a wheelbarrow.

"Handyman?" Emma echoed, "Where? I don't see anyone."

"He went that way. He can help, he'll have shovels to dig through the rubble. Come on." Jesse darted after the man.

Emma followed.

"Sir!" he shouted. "We need help! There are people trapped in the house!"

The handyman ignored them.

"Sir!" Jesse ran after him. "Wait!"

"We need your help!" Emma screamed.

"I'm Clyde," the man said, his voice oddly faint. "I'm the handyman."

"That's why we need your help," Jesse called.

Clyde swerved down a side path, shoving the wheelbarrow through mud and ash. He disappeared around a corner.

The friends ran after him.

The handyman had vanished into thin air.

"Where did he go?" Emma said.

"I don't know."

"Are you sure you saw someone?"

"Yes," Jesse said, his head aching.

"Jesse, what if he was . . . a ghost?"

Instead of answering, he said, "We have to find GL and Sniffer."

They stared at one another. Jesse's thoughts raced.

Do you run away from danger, or do you run toward it? Gramps once told him it took real courage to run toward danger.

Out loud, Jesse said, "We have to get back into that house."

She set her jaw. "No. We have to get the police. This is too big for us! What can we do? The police will have tools, they'll know what to do."

Jesse swallowed hard. "But what if it's too late? I have to try, Emma. This is my fault, don't you see that? I can't leave them in there. You go. Run, find help. Your dad and my dad. Tell them to call the police."

Emma nodded. "All right." She grabbed his arm. "Please be careful."

Then she turned and sprinted away.

Jesse took a deep breath. *Ready or not, here I go.*

The Winchester House loomed above him.

Waiting.

Waiting to swallow him up.

CHAPTER EIGHTEEN

WINCHESTER HOUSE
THE HOUSE GROUNDS

Jesse studied the house, searching for a way in. The quickest way would be the fake doorway he fell through.

He caught hold of a swaying branch and swung himself up into the tree. Soon, he reached the top limbs, but the fake doorway was still too far away. Inching carefully along a thin branch, he got closer to the wall. Then he pushed off with his feet and caught hold of the drainpipe. Risky move—the drainpipe was wet. He should have thought of that.

His hands slipped.

Clinging on for dear life, he managed to find a foothold. With a thrill of success, he shimmied upward until he was close to the fake door. With a leap, he flung himself inside, landing face down on the floor.

Puffing, he jumped up. He was back in the Hall of Fires.

Now, though, all was relatively silent. As he stared around, it seemed like the ghosts had been a dream, an awful dream. Maybe it had been. Maybe he'd dreamed it all after the chandelier hit him in the head.

He didn't plan to stay in the Hall of Fires to find out.

The door into the hallway was still locked. He returned to the fake one he'd just climbed through and peered out. The drainpipe continued up past the balcony to the floor above.

Right. Time to start climbing.

He pulled himself, spider-fashion, up the slippery, wet drainpipe. With all his strength, he hauled himself up and over the balcony railing.

Inside the room, dawn light streaked across oak cabinets filled with Winchester repeating rifles, shiny and well-polished. This had to be the Rifle Room. A portrait hung on the wall. A man, a woman, and a baby. The woman was small; she reached just below the man's shoulder. That had to be Sarah Winchester with her husband and child. She wore a gentle expression as she looked at her baby.

Jesse had a sudden longing for his solid, reliable dog.

"Sniffer!" He shouted as loud as he could. "Sniffer. I need you, Sniff. Come on, boy. Where are you, Sniffer?"

From way down the corridor, he heard a woof. His heart leaped. A black shape flew through the open hallway door and into the Rifle Room.

"Sniffer! Good dog, Sniffer. Good dog!" Jesse flung his arms around his dog's neck.

Sniffer was covered with brick dust. But underneath, he had that warm doggy smell. Jesse buried his nose in it. "I love you, Sniffer, you're the best dog ever. Oh, Sniffer. Thank goodness you're not hurt."

Sniffer's tail wagged wildly. He held something in his mouth. Something small and blue. A floppy blue hat. GL's hat.

Jesse grabbed it and held it under Sniffer's nose.

"Fetch GL," he muttered, his voice low and urgent. "Sniffer. Fetch! Fetch! Fetch GL."

Sniffer's dark, doggy eyes lit up—like nothing was so bad that a good game of seek and find wouldn't fix it. He took a deep sniff of the hat, and with an excited bark, he took off.

Jesse followed, almost tripping over Sniffer as he ran in circles around the hallway. Down a corridor, Sniffer charged. He scrambled up a stairway with tiny stairs to a landing. With an eager look back at Jesse, he bolted down a zig-zagging corridor and into a kitchen, a vast room lined with carved wooden cabinets and a big oak table.

He came to a halt, barking with excitement.

A high voice rang out. "Sniffer. Sniffer. Is that you, Sniffer? I want to go home."

"GL?" Jesse shouted.

GL crawled out from under the kitchen table. He buried his head in Sniffer's fur.

The house shuddered again. Yikes! Aftershocks? Another earthquake?

GL shrieked.

Jesse grabbed his hand. "GL! Sniffer found you! Good dog, Sniffer! Come on, we're getting out of this place."

A faint, deep voice rang out. "Help. Help!"

CHAPTER NINETEEN

Pete. That sounded like Pete.

"Pete?" Jesse yelled.

"Jesse! Help!"

"Where are you? Pete! Where are you?"

"Help!"

Jesse tensed, and his heart rocketed. His brother sounded frantic.

"Sniffer, find Pete," he said. "Fetch!" He didn't know what else to do. This wasn't a real game of fetch. He had nothing for Sniffer to smell. Could Sniffer find Pete?

Sniffer flashed Jesse an excited doggy look and took off again. With his hand tight around GI's wrist, Jesse followed. As they re-entered the Rifle Room, he saw Pete hanging from the outdoor balcony's railing, trying to climb inside. But something was wrong.

Jesse gaped. What on earth was Pete doing out there?

"Pete!" he yelled.

"This thing's breaking up," Pete shouted. "Help!"

The railing lurched backward, out into space, as Pete thrashed, clinging on for dear life.

"Pete!" Jesse shouted.

A nervous glance showed the problem. The balcony Jesse had climbed onto had pulled away from the house, and the twelve-inch gap at the glass door reminded him how high they were. Pete was about to go plummeting four stories to the ground.

Pete's face was ashen. "Help! My leg, it's stuck."

"Stay still," Jesse shouted.

Jesse dropped onto his stomach. He inched toward the opening grabbed for his brother's hand but couldn't reach it.

If he crawled much farther, his weight could make things worse.

"I can't get my leg out," Pete cried.

The balcony creaked. Swayed.

Jesse tried to ignore the warning sounds and snaked forward. He stretched and locked his hand around Pete's wrist. Chest heaving, he tugged with all his might.

Pete groaned. "It's not working, my leg's trapped. You can't pull me off." He yanked his leg without success. "Just get back, or we're both goners."

The brothers stared into each other's eyes.

"I'm gonna get you off there," Jesse said.

There was a loud crack. Yikes! Iron screws popped. The railing swung into space. Any minute, the whole balcony was going to collapse.

With a desperate surge of strength, Jesse pulled again. Pete, his face red with effort, yanked up his trapped leg and thrust his body forward. They both collapsed through the door and landed in a heap in the Rifle Room.

For a moment, they both lay panting. Then Jesse inched back, tugging Pete's sweaty hand. Inch by inch, they crawled further inside.

"What were you doing out there?" Jesse puffed.

"I came back for you," Pete growled. "This place was falling to pieces, you nincompoop. I came back for you." Pete glared at Jesse. "I didn't want to lose my kid brother. I didn't expect to be nearly killed."

Jesse could hardly believe it.

Pete cleared his throat. "Thanks for having my back."

"I didn't want to lose you either," Jesse said.

A wail came from behind a rifle cabinet.

Pete started. "Who's that?"

"It's GL, we need to get him out of here. Sniffer's here, too." Jesse said. "What about your friends? Are they safe?"

"Yeah. They're long gone. I ran back to the House when the earthquake started. I saw it swaying." Pete glared at him. "Let's get out of here."

A fresh scream rang out. It wasn't GL, and it wasn't Pete or Jesse.

"What's that?" Pete said. "Who else is here?"

"It's probably the spirits," Jesse said.

"Hah!" Pete gave a dry laugh. "Give up on the spirit idea. That was us. There are no spirits."

"I should take you to the Hall of Fires and leave you stuck in there," Jesse said.

The scream came again. "Help me! Help me!"

Pete's eyes widened. "That sounds like a woman."

CHAPTER TWENTY

The scream came again. "Help! Help me! I'm trapped in the Daisy Bedroom. Help!"

"I've been in the Daisy Bedroom," Jesse said. "I think I can find it."

He grabbed GI's hand. The three, followed by Sniffer, charged down the corridor, sliding in brick dust. Rubble blocked the door to the Daisy Bedroom.

From inside, someone shouted, "Help me! My house is crashing down."

"It's Sarah Winchester," Jesse said. "We have to get her out."

"We can't dig through that," Pete said. "We don't even have shovels. We've got to get help."

Jesse nodded. "We can't get to you, Mrs. Winchester," he shouted. "We'll go for help."

"Fetch the police," Sarah Winchester shouted. "I'm trapped! Fetch the police."

SARAH WINCHESTER

"We will." Pete frowned at the winding corridors ahead of them. "Follow me, kiddo."

But it seemed to Jesse that Pete didn't know the way. Jesse looked into Sniffer's bright, doggy eyes. "Home, Sniffer. Home!"

Pete scoffed. "I'm not going to follow a dog. You've got to be kidding."

"Sniffer is smart," GL yelled. "Sniffer knows a lot."

Sniffer led the way downstairs and along zig-zag corridors to the basement. They reached the window and scrambled outside.

"Wow, I'm glad to be out of there!" Jesse said.

"Cripes. Look at the smoke! San Jose is on fire," Pete said. "This must be the biggest earthquake ever."

Jesse stared at the orange sky. "We've got to tell the police about Sarah Winchester."

"Where's Emma?" GL yelled.

"Yes. Where's Emma?" Pete said. "You better not have left our cousin behind."

"Of course, I didn't. She went to get help," Jesse said. "We didn't know where you or GL were. Emma went to get our dads."

"Oh. Well, we've got to get home," Pete said. "Let's go via the city center. We have more chance of finding a policeman there."

Jesse crouched in front of GL. "Come on, GL. I'll give you a ride."

Smoke hung in the air. Although it was morning, the sky was as dark as twilight. With GL on his back, clinging to his neck, Jesse hurried across mud-covered fields and orchards.

They reached First Street. Every building over two stories high had fallen down. Even his school was a flattened mess of rocks and rubble. This was worse than he'd thought. He prayed his parents were alright.

Panting, he rushed down Second Street, jumping over the wild tangle of wires snaking across the road. Telegraph poles had snapped like matches, and the cables shot blue sparks.

His heart thumped fast at the thought of his parents and what might be happening at home. They should have gone there first!

"I don't see any police," Jesse gasped. "We have to get to Mom and Dad."

"Agreed," Pete said, picking up the pace.

In the country lane leading to their house, Jesse saw a horse-drawn fire cart coming to a halt.

He raced to it. Two grim-faced firemen sprayed water at burning cottages. Jesse felt numb. Was his house burning too? He prayed his parents hadn't been hurt.

One of his neighbors stood outside, watching the chaos and holding her cat.

"Mrs. Brennan," he cried. "Have you seen my mom and dad?"

The neighbor shook her head.

Pete ran up to the fire cart. "Officer, we need help."

"Move back, son. Stay away from the horses," the officer shouted.

The two horses reared and tossed their manes.

"Officer," Jesse called. "We passed the Winchester House and heard Mrs. Winchester screaming for help. She's trapped in her Daisy Bedroom."

The gray-haired fireman sighed. "We'll send someone to check that out."

"Winchester House is blocked with rubble, sir," Pete said.

"You'll need crowbars," Jesse said. "And shovels."

"That bad, huh?" The fireman wiped sweat from his face.

320

At that moment, two familiar figures came running down the road: Dad and Emma. Jesse breathed out with relief.

"Boys!" Jesse's dad shouted. "We've been looking all over for you. We were so worried."

Emma grabbed hold of GL. She gave Jesse a wan smile.

"Dad, we're fine," Jesse said, his heart swelling as his dad caught him and Pete in a hug. "What about Mom?"

"She's fine, too. She'll be glad to see you're safe."

Jesse said, "Mrs. Winchester is trapped in her bedroom. The Bell Tower collapsed. Winchester House is crumbling down."

Dad gasped. "The Bell Tower collapsed? Oh, my heavens!"

The fireman said, "Don't you worry, we're on our way. We'll get her out."

Pete and Dad ran alongside the fire cart. "We'll help."

Watching them, Jesse felt an unexpected surge of pride. What a great picture—he couldn't miss this moment. He pulled the Brownie from his knapsack and took a picture of the firemen, the fire cart, his dad, and Pete.

Then he took a picture of Emma holding GL. "Are you alright, Em?"

"Yes. Thank heavens you saved little GL."

GL, his face red from crying, had one arm around Emma and the other around Sniffer's neck. "Sniffer saved me. Sniffer is my best friend forever."

"You can come and play fetch with him anytime," Jesse said.

"You, me, and Sniffer can be best friends." GL gave a trembling smile. "Because you saved me too."

"That was really brave, what you did, Jesse," Emma said. "You're a good friend. The best."

He didn't know what to say to that. Embarrassed, he said, "I'm just glad you're not mad."

"I never said that," Emma replied, but she was grinning.

"There's just one more thing I have to do." Jesse ran to catch up to his dad and Pete. When they reached the Winchester House, the lower rooms were burning. While Pete grabbed a shovel, Dad helped the fireman unwind the second hose.

"Dad," Jesse said, "I'll do this."

For a moment, his dad looked confused, then he handed over the hose. "Okay, son! Keep it up."

Jesse turned the fire hose on full blast. Whoa. It looked good to see the water dousing the flames.

He made sure to keep the water away from Dad's Kodak Brownie camera hidden in his knapsack. Thank goodness he hadn't lost that. If he had some good pictures, he'd send them to the San Jose News. He'd sign them *Jesse Johnson, Photojournalist.*

His mind lit up as he planned it.

CHAPTER TWENTY-ONE

"Jesse! Hey, Jesse, come here."

Jesse ran into the living room. Dad held up the *San Jose Mercury* Sunday newspaper. Jesse's picture of the Bell Tower tilting and about to crumble to the ground was front-page news. What a picture! The dawn highlighted the side of the Bell Tower, just as he'd hoped it would. Perfect!

Page two showed the thick clouds of smoke from The Great Asylum, backed by the glow of the San Francisco fires.

Page three showed the burning buildings, the firemen, and Pete and Dad as they took turns spraying the fires.

"You got a good picture of Pete and me." Dad grinned. "Look at me spraying that hose!"

A short article told how Jesse, Pete, and Emma were

passing by the Winchester House, saw the Bell Tower crash down, and called the firemen who saved Sarah Winchester.

The pictures and article were attributed to *Jesse Johnson, Photojournalist.*

Jesse grinned, hardly able to believe he'd made the front page.

"Did you really take these pictures?" Dad said. "Did you write the article?"

Jesse nodded. "Yes, Dad."

With a bemused smile, Dad shook his head. "I don't know what you were up to over there, but well done, son. These pictures are good. Way to go, I'm proud of you, Jesse."

The praise felt so good. Coming from Dad, the praise meant more than anything in the whole world.

Then, Dad said, "You know what a good photojournalist needs?"

Jesse shook his head. "No, Sir." Was he going to get another lecture now?

Dad grinned. "He needs his own Kodak Brownie camera. Seems like you know how to handle it. It's all yours."

"Wow!" Jesse took the camera and wrapped both hands around it. He swallowed hard. "Thanks. This is great, Dad. Thank you."

Emma showed up that afternoon. They hadn't had a chance to tell their friends the whole story. He could hardly wait.

"Are you going to tell them about the scary spirits you saw?" Emma asked.

"Pete says I only saw them because the chandelier hit my head."

"Well . . . it does make for a good story." She grinned at him.

Was Pete right, or had Jesse really seen the spirits? Had he spoken to them? It sure felt like it.

Sarah Winchester thought spirits visited the House. She talked to them every night. What a strange place.

He heaved a huge sigh of relief.

Sniffer nudged Jesse's leg, and he stroked the dog's head. Sniffer had been there—had he seen the spirits, too? Jesse would never know.

Out loud, he said, "You're right. It does make for a good story. But I sure am glad we're out of there."

"Me, too," Emma said. "Wild horses couldn't drag me back there again."

Jesse said, "I have a feeling we're going to be talking about what happened for the rest of our lives. It was touch and go there for a while. But one thing I can say for sure is—we did it. You and me. We went there, we got the pictures to prove it, and we escaped the haunted Winchester House!"

Turn the page for fascinating facts
about the Winchester Mystery House!

10 Fast Facts About The Winchester House

1. Has 160 rooms, 40 bedrooms, 6 kitchens, 52 skylights, 4 elevators, 47 fireplaces, 13 bathrooms, and only one working toilet.
2. A door opens to a 15-foot drop into the garden
3. Another door will drop you 8 feet into a kitchen sink.
4. Staircases circle back or lead to the ceiling.
5. Secret passages are found inside cupboards and under trapdoors.
6. A cabinet door opens to 30 more rooms.
7. There are 13 ceiling panels in the entrance hall, and 13 ceiling panels in the greenhouse. Some closets have 13 hooks, and the 13th bathroom has 13 windows.
8. Time Magazine ranked the Winchester House one of the most haunted places in the world, alongside the Amityville House and the Tower of London.
9. Located in San Jose, California, the house with all its oddities and mysteries is open to the public. It's especially popular at Halloween.
10. A designated California historical landmark, the Winchester House is listed on the National Register of Historic Places.

Did you know?
READ ON FOR MORE FASCINATING FACTS!

~

Who was Sarah Winchester?

Sarah Winchester is said to have been a child prodigy, very talented, and beautiful. She married the wealthy gun tycoon William Winchester. When her husband died, she inherited his fortune. It included:

- $20 million in cash (worth around $550 million in 2020)
- Ownership of half of the Winchester Repeating Arms Company, so she earned more money every time a rifle was sold.

Why did she build such a strange house?

No one really knows why she built the vast, strange mansion. However, theories abound.

According to popular legend, Sarah Winchester believed she was cursed by the spirits of those killed by the Winchester rifle. She felt that the only way to protect herself was to continually build more rooms in her San Jose home.

Legend also says that Sarah Winchester was overcome with grief at the death of her husband and daughter. She feared vengeful spirits had killed them.

How long did it take to build the house?

Building continued day and night for 38 years until Sarah Winchester's death in 1922. The odd features of the house may be the result of her attempts to confuse and evade the angry spirits.

Before the 1906 earthquake, the house stood seven stories high. Several floors were toppled during the disaster and were never rebuilt.

DID SARAH WINCHESTER HOLD NIGHTLY SÉANCES?

A popular myth claims that she held a nightly séance ritual. However, this has never been proven. She was said to have been a reclusive person, and her staff reported she was a kind and generous employer.

~

THE SPIRITS OF THE WINCHESTER HOUSE

Does the Winchester House deserve its haunted reputation? Are the spirits real? Read on and decide for yourself . . . We've collected 7 spooky facts for you to ponder!

1. Visitors and staff report seeing shadowy shapes resembling people coming around corners and at windows.
2. Footsteps are heard going up stairs when no one is there.
3. Some visitors feel taps on their shoulders, hear sighs and voices, see chandeliers sway, and feel changes in temperature.
4. In 2021 a chandelier swayed continuously for no reason.
5. Many tour guides avoid the corridors of the third floor because of ghostly voices and footsteps.

6. A small entity in dark clothing, thought to be Sarah Winchester, has been heard sighing in the Daisy Bedroom and seen coming down the hallway.
7. The most frequent apparition is Clyde, the handyman, who is seen repairing the fireplace, or pushing a wheelbarrow along a hallway and in the basement.

～

10 FAST FACTS ABOUT THE 1906 SAN FRANCISCO EARTHQUAKE

Although our story is a fictional tale, it takes place during the actual historical, 1906 San Francisco earthquake. This massive earthquake was one of the largest disasters of its time. Read on to learn all about it.

1. On April 18, 1906, one of the deadliest earthquakes in U.S. history shook San Francisco, California.
2. The earthquake, 7.8 on the Richter scale, killed more than 3,000 people and destroyed 80% of San Francisco.
3. Between 227,000 and 300,000 people were left homeless, forcing them to camp in makeshift tents for years after.
4. The Army, attempting to stop the rapidly spreading fires, destroyed whole city blocks with dynamite.
5. The earthquake caused extensive damage to the surrounding countryside and to San Jose.
6. In San Jose, all brick or stone buildings over 2 stories high were destroyed.

7. San Jose's 3-story high school collapsed.
8. Sarah Winchester was trapped in the Daisy Bedroom and had to be dug out.
9. The Great Asylum for the Insane, about 5 miles from San Jose, collapsed and buried more than 100 patients and medical staff.
10. Witnesses claimed that animals behaved strangely anywhere from weeks to seconds before the earthquake struck.

BIBLIOGRAPHY

Winchester Mystery House, *A Moving Day*, https://www. winchestermysteryhouse.com/a-moving-day, access date 8.2021

Russell, Herbert D., *Lest we Forget. The Complete Story of the San Francisco Horror*, 1906, https://www.mariposaresearch.net/ santaclararesearch/06sanjose.html access date 9.2021

MIT, Edu, *Winchester House*, http://web.mit.edu/allanmc/ www/winchesterhouse.pdf access date 8.2021

Winchester Mystery House, *A Haunted History*, https:// www.winchestermysteryhouse.com/sarahs-story, access date 8.2021

Wikipedia, *Agnews Developmental Center*, https://en.wiki pedia.org/wiki/Agnews_Developmental_Center access date 9.2021

THANK YOU

We hope you enjoyed this book, Dear Reader!
We're always hard at work crafting stories with you
*   in mind.*
Please consider giving this book some stars using
*   Amazon's star feature. Your feedback means the*
*   world to us!*

- Ellie Crowe and Scott Peters

I Escaped North Korea!

I Escaped The California Camp Fire

I Escaped The World's Deadliest Shark Attack

I Escaped Amazon River Pirates

I Escaped The Donner Party

I Escaped The Salem Witch Trials

I Escaped Pirates In The Caribbean

I Escaped The Tower of London

I Escaped Egypt's Deadliest Train Disaster

I Escaped The Haunted Winchester House

I Escaped The Gold Rush Fever

I Escaped The Prison Island

I Escaped The Grizzly Maze

I Escaped The Saltwater Crocodile

I Escaped WWII Pearl Harbor

More great adventures coming soon!

JOIN THE I ESCAPED CLUB

Get a free pack of mazes and word finds to print and play!

https://www.subscribepage.com/escapedclub

Made in the USA
Monee, IL
03 October 2024

67114024R00186